In the Blink of an Eye

A Young Adult Novel

A BADGER BLISS BOOK

By

Karen D. Badger

DEDICATION

I dedicate this book to all of the innocent lives that have been lost due to senseless gun violence and the lack of government action to enact sensible gun control legislation. A child should never fear going to school. A grandmother should never fear going to church. No one should ever fear going to the movies…to the mall…to a night club…to a rock concert. No one should fear stepping outside their home.

We must take our country back from those who value money above life.

We need to make the world safe again…especially for the children.

The madness must stop.

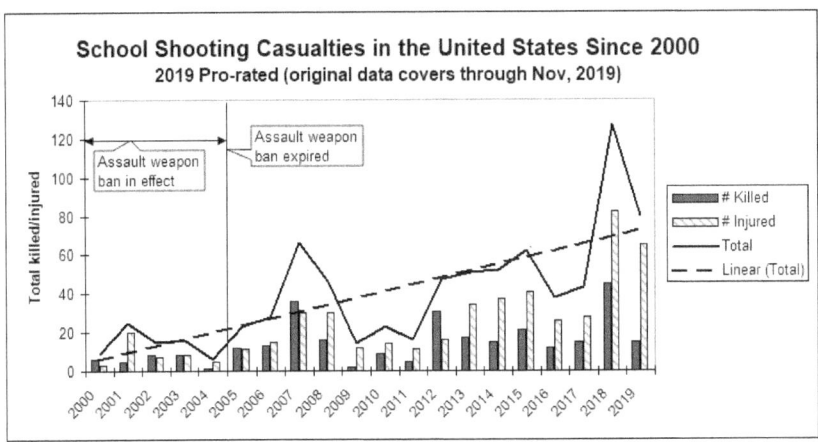

Dotted line represents trend since 2000. Despite the saw-tooth nature of the total casualty line, the linear trend is increasing at an alarming rate.

Source:
https://en.m.wikipedia.org/wiki/List_of_shootings_in_the_United_States?fbclid=IwAR2xGr4C1C
UTs7bFTj-xb_bT12mvgDOLh8NLUqLv9Jp9WkZphQ91TeBDsKc

ALSO WRITTEN BY KAREN D. BADGER AND
AVAILABLE FROM BADGER BLISS BOOKS:

ON A WING AND A PRAYER
YESTERDAY ONCE MORE
THE BLUE FEATHER
ALL MY TOMORROWS
1140 RUE ROYALE
OVER THE CRESCENT MOON
IN THE BLINK OF AN EYE (Young Adult Novel)

The Billie/Cat Commitment Series:
  IN A FAMILY WAY
  UNCHAINED MEMORIES
  HAPPY CAMPERS
  COLLECTIVE IDENTITY
  SWEET ANGEL
  RELATIVE-LY SPEAKING
  TAILSPIN
  FLASHPOINT

www.badgerblissbooks.com

In the Blink of an Eye

A Young Adult Novel

A BADGER BLISS BOOK

By

Karen D. Badger

This is a work of fiction. All characters, locales, and events are either products of the author's imagination or are used fictitiously.

IN THE BLINK OF AN EYE – A Young Adult Novel

Cover image: Karen D. Badger
Cover design by Karen D. Badger & Barb Sawyer

A Badger Bliss Book
Published by Badger Bliss Books
Georgia, VT 05468

www.badgerblissbooks.com

Print book ISBN 13: 978-1-945761-28-7
Ebook ISBN 13: 978-1-945761-29-4

First Edition, December, 2019

Printed in the United States of America and in the United Kingdom

ACKNOWLEDGMENTS

In every book I write, I thank those who worked to find my typos and fix my literary errors. A mere thank you is not enough to acknowledge the contribution of these wonderful women.

My literary squad includes: Ellie Atherton (my 85-year-old mom and number one fan), Kacie Chagnon, 'Chief Eagle Eye' Carol Poynor, Donna Brown, Aretta Saunders, and last but not least, Barb Sawyer, AKA, 'Bliss' (my better half and keeper of my *aumakua* soul). A special thank you to Nat Burns (amazing editor and sister from another mother), who worked tirelessly to make this story the best that it could be.

A special shout-out to Barb Clanton who provided me with invaluable advice and wisdom on how far to push the young adult envelope. It is amazing to have a community of other talented authors as resources.

An honorable mention to my friend, Barb Shiffler, who shared with me, her experiences and feelings about school lockdown drills from a teacher's perspective.

Finally, I want to thank my squad of 'professional consultants', grandchildren, Kyren Badger (age 14), Ariana Badger (age 13), Ellie Badger (age 11) and Hannah Chagnon (age 10), who provided a wealth of information and firsthand experience on lock-down drills, and of the impact on them physically and emotionally. I love you, my sweet babies.

Teen-speak words used in this book

The English language is incredibly versatile and each generation adapts their own way of expressing their ideas and emotions. For the young adults reading this novel, I anticipate you'll have no problem understanding the dialect and syntax native to your age group, and I sincerely hope I didn't represent it too poorly. For readers of other demographics, I have included a short list of young adult slang that I used in this story that may help you better understand the unique language of today's brilliant young people.

Adulting – To grow up and act responsible

Bruh – A casual nickname for 'Bro (similar to the use of dude)

Can't even – Describes someone/something you can't handle

Cray (or cray-cray) – Crazy

Crush on – Like (as in…has a crush on)

Dank – Really cool

Extra – Over the top, dramatic behavior

Fam – A group of friends who feels more like family

Flexing – Showing off

Ghosted – Suddenly ending all contact with a person romantically

High-key – Straight up truth

Low key – Low intensity / slight / kind of

Salty – Acting upset or bitter

Savage – Petty

Shook – Confused or in utter disbelief

Squad – A group of friends

Thirsty – Horny

Trill – True and real

Wrecked – Out of control, feeling intensely emotional

Guns don't kill people – people kill people! Well, No shit!

We need mandatory safety courses for people – not guns!

We need more thorough background checks for people – not guns!

We need stricter negligence penalties imposed on people – not guns!

If you're stupid enough to think activists are pissed at guns and not at people…you're too stupid to own one!

--Author Unknown--

Chapter 1

Beep, beep, beep…

"Noooo!" Fifteen-year-old Tara Charland hit the snooze button on her alarm clock and snuggled back under the covers. Moments later, the offending sound returned.

Tara cried out and then turned her alarm off and slammed her head back into the pillow. She stared at the ceiling. "I hate mornings," she said.

Tara thought about the day that lay before her– the first day of her sophomore year. She was not looking forward to attending classes in a wheelchair. That was gonna suck—big time! But at least she would be able to spend more time with Kelly since they were in a few classes together.

"Tara! Are you awake?"

Tara's attention was drawn to her mother, who knocked on the door and poked her head into the room.

"Yes, Mom. I'm awake." Tara struggled to drag herself into a seated position.

Billie pushed the door open and crossed the room. She sat on the edge of Tara's bed. "Big day today."

"I guess," Tara whined. "It's just school."

"Look, sweetie, I know this won't be easy—especially since you're starting school a couple of weeks late. You shouldn't be behind though, thanks to the tutor you've had for the past two weeks."

Tara lowered her chin to her chest. "I know, but I'm gonna look like a freak in this chair."

Billie laughed. "I thought you liked being unique."

Tara couldn't stop the grin from forming on her face. "I do, but I could think of better ways than being stuck in a dorky wheelchair."

1

"It won't be forever. Your doctor said you should be able to use crutches in the next month or so."

"I can't wait!"

Billie tucked a strand of hair behind Tara's ear. "Mama sent me to help you get into the shower."

"I can bathe myself, Mom," Tara said.

Billie chuckled. "Yes, you can. I'm here to help with the transfer into and out of the shower."

"Yeah, but you still need to see me naked."

"It wouldn't be the first time I've seen you, naked, Tare. Besides, we're both girls. Imagine if you were being raised by two dads instead of two moms."

"Ugh! Okay, let's get this done."

Tara maneuvered her legs to the side of the bed and carefully placed her feet on the floor. She shifted her weight to her good leg and accepted Billie's help to stand, pivot, and lower herself into the nearby wheelchair.

"Let's roll!" Tara said.

Billie stood behind the wheelchair and pushed her daughter across the hall into the bathroom where she helped her to disrobe and position herself onto the seat inside the walk-in shower. "There you go. Give a shout when you're finished. I'm going to get your brother and sister up and then help Mama make breakfast." Billie closed the door behind her.

Tara sat for several long moments under the warm spray of water and thought about the events of six weeks ago that had landed her in a wheelchair.

While on a camping trip to Yellowstone National Park, she and her family had been caught in a wildfire. When the fires began, her brother, Seth, and mother, Cat, were hiking, while she, and her other mother, Billie, were enjoying a kayak ride. The only person safe from the fires was her younger sister, Skylar, who was attending a junior ranger program that day.

Tara remembered vividly how she and her mom had flipped their kayak and hidden under it to save them from the fire raging overhead. And how, drifting too close to a waterfall, they had no time to react, and were soon sucked over the falls and onto to the rocks below.

2

So much was a blank after that…until she woke up in the hospital with a fractured leg, internal bleeding and a head injury. Her doctors told her that she was a miracle child—that she should have died. She stayed in the hospital for a month and was confined to home for another month before she was released to go to school.

She wasn't the only one in the family injured during the wildfires. Her mother, Cat, had been be trapped by a falling branch, and had also suffered a broken leg and shattered foot. Despite their injuries, Tara was thankful they all survived.

As much as Tara dreaded attending school in a wheelchair, she was going out of her mind being confined at home. Sure, her friends, Karissa and Kelly came to visit, but it wasn't the same as going to the movies or to the mall. She especially missed the alone time that she craved with Kelly. The wheelchair forced her to stay in the downstairs guest room, with her family a few feet away in the living room. The privacy her second-story bedroom once provided was non-existent.

Tara thought about Kelly and a warm rush spread through her abdomen. She'd met Kelly, who was her age, through mutual friends after she moved into the neighborhood about six months earlier. Kelly's father was serving in the Marine Corps and his career moved them around the country every few years. They immediately hit it off. There was something about Kelly that touched Tara's soul. Tara also found Kelly's short cropped blond hair and boyish style very attractive. Kelly was very gallant, and she had a way of making Tara feel special.

The night before she left for the Yellowstone vacation, Tara had kissed Kelly for the first time. It felt like her insides melted when their lips touched. After a month in the hospital, she couldn't control the tears that flowed down her face the first time she saw Kelly again…or how it felt when Kelly kissed the tears from her cheeks.

She found it hard to breathe when Kelly was around. When they were alone together, there was an awkward tension between them. Tara struggled to understand it. When Kelly was near, all she wanted to do was touch her…even if it meant merely holding hands. Neither of them had taken what they felt further than that first kiss. Tara often felt like she would explode because of the tension between them. It wasn't as strong when Karissa was with them…but it was always there.

Karissa Swenson was Tara's best friend and was a mini-me duplicate of her mother, Jen, with curly blonde hair and a dimpled chin. Their families had become close more than ten years earlier when Tara and her family moved into the neighborhood. In the beginning the neighborhood wasn't very accepting of her non-traditional family and it took a devastating fire at Karissa's house, and Billie saving Karissa's dad and brother, for the neighborhood to come around and accept them. Since then, Karissa's brother, Steve, and Tara's brother, Seth, had also become best friends, and Karissa's mom and dad considered her two moms to be family.

Tara couldn't imagine anything coming between her and Karissa, although Karissa was a little jealous of Kelly originally. All of that had smoothed out when Tara and her family returned home after their disastrous vacation at Yellowstone. Since that time, Tara, Karissa and Kelly were inseparable.

Tara was snapped out of her reverie by a soft knock on the bathroom door.

"Tara, how's that shower coming?" Billie asked.

Tara grabbed the shampoo and quickly lathered her short, strawberry-blond hair. "Almost finished, Mom," she lied.

"Okay, sweetie. Let me know when you need help."

"I will."

***

Tara wheeled herself into the kitchen just as Billie placed a large plate of sausage and pancakes on the table. "Smells great!" she said.

"I hope you're hungry. Mama insisted on standing at the stove with her crutches to cook, despite my protests. I told her I would do the cooking," Billie said.

Tara's eyes opened wide. "*You* cook? Seriously, Mom?"

Tara's ten-year-old sister, Skylar, entered the kitchen. "Did someone just say Mommy cooked breakfast?" she asked, a look of trepidation on her face.

Tara laughed. "She's got *your* number!" Tara said to Billie.

Billie grasped her chest. "I'm wounded! I thought you were on *my* side, Sky."

"Not when it comes to cooking, Mommy," Skylar replied, quite seriously.

Cat removed the used pod from the coffee machine. "Okay, you two. That's enough torture for Mom. Take a seat and dig in. Billie, could you please carry our coffee cups to the table for me?"

"Sure thing." Billie grabbed the two cups of coffee and followed Cat as she hobbled toward the table on her crutches. She placed the coffee cups on the table and kissed her red-headed wife's cheek. She poured glasses of juice for the kids, returned the juice to the refrigerator and turned to look at her family. "So, where is that son of ours?" she asked.

"Right here, Mom." A deep male voice sounded from the kitchen doorway.

"Good morning, Seth," Billie said to the tall, blond, seventeen-year-old. "I hope you're hungry."

"Famished!" Seth took a seat at the table and grabbed his plate. He filled it and addressed his sister. "Are you looking forward to school today, Tare?"

"I'm looking forward to getting out of the house, but I'm not crazy about being stuck in this chair at school."

"Just think about all the attention you'll get, not to mention the special privileges," Seth pointed out.

"What do you mean?"

"Well, you'll get to go to the head of the lunch line, and you'll get out of doing gym."

Tara raised her eyebrows. "Wow! You're right! Maybe this won't be so bad!"

"And you don't have to ride the bus, since you're riding with me."

Tara put her fork down beside her empty plate. "Ah, is it okay if Kelly and Karissa catch a ride with us, too?" she asked.

Seth frowned. "We're gonna have a full car. Steve's also riding with us. The back seat will be pretty crowded, but I think we'll all fit if I can get your chair into the trunk."

"Thanks, bro." Tara pushed herself away from the table. "I'll call Kelly and Karissa and tell them to be ready."

Cat watched her daughter wheel herself into the living room and turned to address her son. "You're a good brother, Seth. She loves you very much, you know. It warms my heart to see the bond between you two."

Seth grinned. "I know. She'd do the same for me."

"That, she would," Cat replied. "That, she would."

Chapter 2

Steve held the arms of Tara's chair while Seth helped her out of the front seat of the car and into her wheelchair. He pushed her onto the sidewalk in front of the high school and handed control of the chair to Kelly.

"Thanks, guys," Tara said.

"No problem. I need to park the car. I'll meet you right here around three-fifteen, okay?" Seth replied.

"Three-fifteen. Got it."

"I'll go with you, dude," Steve offered.

Seth nodded. "Okay, climb in. Have a great day, Tare."

Tara, Kelly and Karissa watched the boys drive away and then headed toward to entrance to the school.

"I need to go to the office before homeroom," Tara said. "I think I can take it from here."

"I don't mind pushing you," Kelly said.

"Yes, but you need to get to your homeroom. I don't want you to get into trouble." Tara saw the look of concern on Kelly's face. "Look, Kel, I'm a big girl. I can wheel myself around. I do it at home all the time. Karissa, you need to get to your homeroom too."

Kelly and Karissa exchanged expressions of doubt.

"Jeesh, you two! I'm not an invalid, you know!" Tara insisted.

"Yeah—you kind of are," Kelly pointed out.

Tara grabbed the wheels on her chair and spun herself around. "No—I'm not!"

Karissa handed Tara's backpack to her. "Okay. If you say so."

"I do. We're all in the same first period class. I'll see you both there."

Tara watched her friends walk away and then wheeled herself toward the main office. Just as she reached the door, it swung open and a young man exited. As soon as he saw her, he stood to the side and held the door open for her. Tara smiled brightly.

"Thank you!"

The young man smiled back. "Any time. It looks like you did a number on yourself there," he said.

"This is what happens when you go over waterfall without a barrel!" Tara chuckled at her own joke.

The young man frowned. Clearly he didn't understand what Tara was talking about.

"It's a long story. Thanks again for holding the door."

"You're welcome." He extended his hand to Tara. "My name is Ryan. Ryan Porter. I'm new here. We moved into the area this summer from Syracuse."

Tara took his hand. "I'm Tara."

Ryan smiled once more. "Maybe I'll see you in the halls. Gotta get to homeroom!"

"Later!" Tara replied.

Tara wheeled herself to the main desk and handed a release from her doctor to the receptionist. While she waited patiently for the receptionist to read it, Tara noticed a woman standing nearby who appeared to be absorbed in reading the bulletin board.

The receptionist looked over her glasses at Tara. "It looks like you've been through quite an ordeal, Miss Charland." She looked at the letter again. "It says here your only restrictions will be physical education. We'll have to add a study hall to your schedule during the PE time slot."

"Excuse me."

Tara's attention was drawn to the woman who had been reading the bulletin board as she inserted herself into the conversation.

"Excuse me. I couldn't help but overhear." The woman extended her hand to Tara. "I'm Ms. Warner. I'm the new phys ed teacher. I can see why you are on physical restrictions, but instead of adding a study hall, I'd like to propose an alternative that may still help you earn your PE credit."

The receptionist raised her eyebrows as Tara tilted her head to one side. "I'm listening."

"What PE class are you signed up for?" Ms. Warner asked.

"I'm not sure."

"Volleyball," the receptionist offered.

Mrs. Warner clapped her hands. "Perfect! How much do you know about volleyball, Miss…,"

"Charland. Tara Charland." Tara offered her hand to the gym teacher.

"Nice to meet you, Tara. So, how much do you know about volleyball?"

"I've played before, and I know the rules, if that's what you're asking."

"That's a start. Because of your injury, you can't physically participate in the class, but you can still learn the basics and you can assist with strategy and coaching…that is, if it's something you'd be interested in doing."

"Are you sure I can get credit for the class?" Tara asked.

"I'll clear it with the principal, but I think so. What do you say?"

"I'm in!"

***

Kelly carried Tara's lunch tray to the table and moved a chair so that Tara could maneuver her wheelchair up to the table. She sat across from Tara.

"How's it going so far?" Kelly asked.

"It's going okay, except I really feel like a freak in this chair," Tara replied.

Kelly reached for Tara's hand. "You're not a freak, Tara."

Tara squeezed Kelly's hand. "I know. It's just that I look pretty conspicuous with my leg sticking straight out."

"You did some severe damage, Tara. The last thing you need is for that leg to heal wrong. You need to do what your doc says. I, for one, am looking forward to taking you to the spring dance."

Tara could feel her face turn red. "You want to take me to the dance?"

"You're damned right I do."

"Aren't you worried about what the other kids will say?"

"Worry about what? That I asked the most amazing girl at school to go with me? They snooze...they lose!"

"You're making be blush!"

Kelly lifted Tara's chin with her fingertips. "And you are very pretty in pink."

Tara couldn't look away. Her face was burning up and the fire in her abdomen was nearly as hot.

"Hey, guys! Sorry I'm late!"

The moment was broken by Karissa as she sat beside Kelly. "I had the hardest time getting away from Robert."

Tara regained control of herself in time to respond. "Robert?"

"Yeah. Robert Johnson. It seems he's taken a liking to me. God help me!"

"Jesus! That dude gives me the creeps. Isn't he a senior?" Tara asked.

"Exactly. He's like nineteen or something, and he's greasy. I mean, you can smell him from a mile away."

"Have you thought about telling Steve? He probably knows him. Maybe he can back him off," Tara suggested.

"Maybe. How are things going for you so far today?"

"I was just telling Kelly that I feel like a freak in this chair. It's hard to get around in the halls when they're crowded between classes. Oh...and I forgot to tell you, Kelly, when I went to the office this morning, the new PE teacher was there and instead of canceling my gym class, she asked me to help her coach."

Kelly's head snapped up. "Seriously? What class is it?"

"Volleyball. She thinks she can talk the principal into giving me full credit for the class if I help her with coaching and the matches."

"Wait! I'm in a volleyball class this afternoon," Karissa said. "What time?"

"It's the last session of the day at two o'clock."

"Yes. I'm in that class. Cool! I'll meet you at the end of your previous class and help you through the halls to the gym."

"That would be great. Thanks, 'Rissa."

***

Tara sat next to Kelly in their social studies class immediately after lunch. Halfway through the class, Tara dropped her pen to the floor between their desks. Kelly immediately picked it up and handed it back to her. Tara slipped her a note in the transfer. Kelly narrowed her eyes at Tara and immediately turned her attention back to the teacher in front of the class. When she felt it was safe to do so, the opened the note.

This is lame! I am so far behind in this class. It looks like they are farther along than my tutor thought. Help!

Kelly folded the note and slipped it into her pocket. She spared a glance at Tara and nodded her head.

Tara mouthed the words *thank you* and returned to taking notes.

Karissa met Tara in the hall after her class and immediately took control of Tara's wheelchair.

"Excuse me...excuse me. Coming through!" Karissa repeated as she pushed Tara through the halls toward the gym. Kelly followed close behind.

When they arrived at the gym, Tara noticed that Kelly was still with them. "Kel, don't you have a math class to get to?" Tara asked.

"Yes, but I want to get a look at the new gym teacher," Kelly replied.

"Why on earth do you care what she looks like?" Karissa asked.

"Give me a minute and I'll tell you." Kelly entered the gym ahead of Tara and Karissa. Ms. Warner was in the middle of the room, setting up the net. "Hmm. I thought so," Kelly mumbled to herself.

"I'll be right back. I need to change into my gym clothes," Karissa said.

Tara reached for Kelly's arm. "Kel, what is it?"

Kelly turned toward Tara so that her back was to Ms. Warner. "She's gay."

"What?" Tara said louder than she intended.

Tara's outburst drew the attention of Ms. Warner. "Tara! I'm glad you're early." Ms. Warner approached them. "Who's your friend?"

"This is Kelly," Tara said.

Kelly offered her hand to the teacher.

"Nice to meet you, Kelly."

"Likewise." Kelly looked at Tara. "I gotta get to math class. I'll meet you out front after class?"

"I'll be there," Tara replied.

Tara and Ms. Warner watched Kelly leave.

"She seems like a nice girl," Ms. Warner said.

Tara replied while continuing to watch Kelly walk away. "Yes. She is very special to me."

Ms. Warner smiled. "I understand. So, are you ready to get to work?"

Tara looked at her teacher. "Does that mean the principal agreed to your plan?"

"One hundred percent. You'll get full credit for the class."

"Awesome! Okay, coach—put me to work!"

***

"That was an awesome dinner, Mrs. Charland. Thank you very much."

"You're welcome, Kelly. Actually, Cat deserves the credit. All I did was carry things to the table for her. Surely you've heard about my cooking skills?" Billie said while trying to keep the grin from her face.

"I'm sure you're a fine cook," Kelly replied, despite the fact that Tara was giving her the slit-throat sign.

"I saw that, Tara," Billie teased.

"Sorry, Mom, but yes, we *have* all suffered through—er, I mean, experienced your cooking skills."

"Very funny, Tara. Don't you girls have homework to do?" Billie suggested.

"Yes we do." Tara pushed herself away from the table. "Are you ready, Kelly?"

"Right after I help your mom with the dishes," Kelly said.

"No need. I'll take care of it, but thank you for offering," Billie said. "You two go do your homework."

Kelly jumped to her feet and grabbed the handles of Tara's wheelchair. "Let me do that for you." She pushed Tara toward the living room. "Thank you again for dinner," she called over her shoulder.

Cat and Billie watched the girls disappear into the living room.

"I like her," Cat said. "She's a very polite young lady."

"Suffered through my cooking?" Billie replied. She looked at Skylar and Seth who were both still seated at the table.

"I plead the fifth!" Seth said.

***

"Close the door," Tara said once she and Kelly were inside her room.

Kelly closed the door and leaned against it. She watched Tara move her chair close to the bed and lower the support that kept her injured leg extended. "What are you doing?"

"I've got to get out of this chair."

Kelly moved toward the bed. "Let me help you. Tell me what to do."

Tara reached her arms forward. "I need to stand on my good leg and swing around to sit on the bed. Put your arms around me and lift."

"Okay." Kelly straddled Tara's legs. She leaned forward and slipped her arms under Tara's and around her back in a hug-like gesture.

"All right, now you lift, and I will shift my weight to my good leg. That's it. Keep going."

Kelly pulled upward with all her might until she had Tara balanced on her strong leg. She continued to hold her close. They were nearly the same height, and stood nose to nose. Their gazes met and neither was willing to look away.

"Ah...I have to turn a little so I can sit on the bed. You'll need to slowly lower me because I have to keep my injured leg straight with no weight on it," Tara finally said.

Kelly froze. "What if I hurt you, Tara?"

"I trust you, Kel. You can do this."

Kelly nodded. "Here goes nothing." She slowly lowered Tara to the bed until she no longer had to support her weight. Finally, she released Tara and took a step back.

"See? Easy peasy," Tara said. "Now we need to lift my leg onto the bed so I sit against the headboard."

Kelly stepped back and put her hands on her hips. "You're quite bossy, do you know that?"

Tara threw a pillow at her. "Are you going to help me or not?"

"You know I'd walk on glass for you. So how do we do this?"

"We need to get the injured leg on the bed so I can use my arms and good leg to scoot back. I'll lay back. All you need to do is lift the leg and swing it onto the bed. Trust me...it sounds harder than it is."

"Okay. I'll apologize now in case I hurt you."

"You won't hurt me. Now lift!"

Moments later, Tara was completely on the bed and sitting against the headboard. "There! We did it. Now grab the tablets and join me." Tara patted the bed beside her.

For the next hour and a half, Tara and Kelly worked to bring Tara up to speed in social studies. When they were finished, Tara shut off her device and threw it to the foot of the bed.

"Done!" She picked up Kelly's hand and squeezed it. "Thanks, Kel."

Kelly entwined their fingers. "You're welcome."

Their eyes met and held for what felt like an eternity to Tara. She simply couldn't look away. Before she knew it, Kelly leaned in and their lips met in a tender kiss. A slight tremor passed through her abdomen as the kiss deepened. When it ended, her heart beat so strongly that she was sure Kelly could see it through her shirt. She rested her forehead against Kelly's.

"Wow. I have never felt this way before," Tara confessed. "It's kind of exciting and scary at the same time."

"Me too," Kelly admitted. "Is this what love feels like, Tara?"

"I don't know." Tara pulled back and looked at Kelly. "Are you trying to say you love me?"

"I know I feel things for you I've never felt for anyone else...not that I've ever had a girlfriend before...but this feels very different from the love I know I feel for my family. It almost feels like a *need*," Kelly explained.

"I know what you mean. I feel the same way."

"So does this mean we are girlfriends? I mean…will you go out with me?" Kelly asked.

Tara grinned. "I thought you'd never ask! Of course I'll be your girlfriend. Now, will you please kiss me again?"

In the Blink of an Eye

Chapter 3

Cat closed the dishwasher and wiped her hands on a towel just as the kitchen door swung open. Her best friend, Jen, walked in, followed by her daughter, Karissa.

"Hey, neighbor!" Jen crossed the kitchen and hugged Cat.

"Good morning, Jen. Good morning, Karissa. Tara is just about ready if you want to go speed her along." Cat looked around. "Where's Steve?"

"He's outside with Seth, waiting for the girls," Jen replied. "I really appreciate Billie dropping me off at the school on her way to her law office. Hopefully, my car will be ready at the end of the day. It's rough when Fred is out of town, otherwise, I would ask him to take me."

"No problem, Jen. If it wasn't for Seth having a full car, he could have dropped you off since the middle school is just across the parking lot from the high school."

Jen crossed her arms and laughed. "Well, I'd rather not be stuck in a car with a bunch of teenagers anyway! Where is that gorgeous wife of yours this morning?"

"Right here!"

Jen and Cat swung around to see Billie standing in the doorway to the kitchen.

"I'm running just a little late this morning. Give me a sec to grab a coffee and I'll be good to go," Billie said.

Billie set up her coffee to brew and then kissed Cat tenderly. "Good morning, Kitten. How are you feeling today?"

"Not too bad, but I'm anxious to be off these crutches. I see the physical therapist today. Hopefully, I'll be in a walking cast soon," Cat replied.

"At least you're still able to drive," Jen pointed out. "Imagine if it had been your right foot that was injured."

"You are right about that, my friend. I'm thankful for small favors. As bad as this break was, it could have been worse.

Look at Tara, for instance. It'll be a while before she's healed enough to even be on crutches," Cat replied.

"Speaking of Tara, where is she?" Billie asked. "If the kids don't get moving soon, they'll be late for school."

***

Karissa pushed Tara's door open and stepped inside. "Hey, Tare."

"Hey, 'Rissa! I'm glad you're here…just in time to help me into my chair," Tara replied.

Karissa helped to lift Tara from the bed and slowly pivoted her around so she could sit in her chair. "Not that I mind doing this, but how do you get in and out of this thing when I'm not around?"

"My mom usually helps…and last night, Kelly was here to study and she helped me. Oh! Speaking of Kelly, she asked me to be her girlfriend."

Karissa's eyes flew open. "Seriously? That's awesome, Tare! Did she kiss you?"

Tara could feel the heat rise into her cheeks, and she struggled to keep the grin from her face.

"Judging by the blush, I'm guessing that she did!" Karissa teased.

Tara looked directly into her friend's face. "I've never felt this way about anyone before, 'Rissa. I mean…you're my best friend, and I love you to the moon and back, but this is a different feeling. Know what I mean?"

"Actually, I do. There's this boy at school that I really like, and he makes me feel all warm inside."

"Really? Who?"

"His name is Ryan Porter."

Tara's brow creased. "Ryan Porter. Where have I heard that name before?"

"He has dark hair, and he's really, really cute," Karissa said.

"Does he know how you feel about him?"

"Are you kidding? I don't have the nerve to even talk to him!"

"Well, I guess we'll have to fix that!" Tara said.

18

"Oh, no you don't!" Karissa warned. "You need to stay out of it, Tara. Got it?"

Tara smiled slyly. "I got it...for now anyway."

The girls' attention was drawn the door as a soft knock sounded. The door opened, and Billie peeked in. "You two need to get going or you'll be late for school. I think your brother is getting impatient waiting for you."

"We're coming, Mom. 'Rissa, do you mind grabbing my backpack?"

***

Seth settled Tara into her chair and then walked around to the driver's side of the car.

"Thanks, Seth. Sorry I was so slow this morning. I promise not to be late meeting you here after school," Tara said.

Seth leaned his forearms on top the car. "I hope so, Tara. I have to work after school today and I can't be late."

"No problem." Tara, Kelly and Karissa watched Seth and Steve drive toward the student parking lot.

"You've got a pretty cool brother," Kelly said.

"Yes, I do. No one would ever guess that we're only step siblings," Tara replied.

"Yeah. I've known your family for what...eleven years now...and sometimes I forget you are not related by blood," Karissa added.

Karissa grabbed Tara's backpack and Kelly stood behind her wheelchair, ready to push her into the building. "Well, sometimes the best families are formed by choice instead of blood," Kelly said.

"What's your first class today, Tara?" Karissa asked.

"It's the Tuesday-Thursday schedule... so my first class is English."

"That's on the second floor. We need to head to the elevator," Karissa pointed out.

"All right. Let's do it," Kelly responded.

Kelly pushed Tara's wheelchair forward and as they approached the front doors of the school, Karissa suddenly stopped short. Kelly and Tara looked back. "What the...? Karissa, what's up?" Tara asked.

Karissa quickly rejoined her friends and whispered in Tara's ear. Tara's head snapped back. She looked toward the door and back at Karissa. "That's him?"

"Yes! What do I do? What do I do?" Karissa turned her back to the doors.

"What's going on?" Kelly asked.

Tara looked over her shoulder at Kelly. "See that guy over there by the doors?"

"Yeah. What about him?" Kelly replied.

"'Rissa likes him."

"Tare! Not so loud!" Karissa whined. "He'll hear you."

Tara looked toward the young man once more. "Wait! Ryan Porter, right? I met him yesterday morning. He held the door to the main office open for me. I think he said something about being new here."

"He is definitely new here. I don't remember seeing him last year," Karissa said. "I haven't been able to stop thinking about him."

"Wow. You've got it bad," Kelly said. "You haven't even talked to him and you're all gaga about him?"

"No...I completely forget how to talk when I'm around him. He's in two of my classes. Don't you think he's cute?" Karissa asked.

Tara tilted her head to the side and studied Ryan more closely. He was maybe five foot nine, slim and had dark brown hair. Tara admitted to herself that he was pretty good looking. "I agree that he's cute...and I know that he's polite."

"He's okay for a guy," Kelly added. "So, why don't you talk to him?"

"Are you crazy?" Karissa exclaimed.

Kelly laughed. "I think talking is a requirement if you want to get to know him better."

"I...I just don't know what to say."

Tara took Karissa's hand. "We'll have to work on that. Right now, we need to get to class. Onward, James!" Tara called back to Kelly.

Kelly pushed the chair forward and as they neared the doors, Ryan rushed forward and opened it for them, and while doing so, he made eye contact with Tara. "I guess I've found my new job...being your doorman!" he joked.

"You're hired!" Tara replied. "Thanks, Ryan."

"You remembered my name," Ryan said.

"Of course." Tara paused and then made a quick decision. "Ryan, this is Kelly," she looked back at Kelly, "And this is Karissa."

Ryan extended his hand to both girls. "Hey!"

Kelly shook his hand firmly, and Karissa was barely able to look at him as she meekly shook his hand and said hello.

"I'd love to stay and talk, but we all need to get to class. Thanks again for holding the door, Ryan," Tara said.

The three friends entered the lobby of the school and headed toward the elevator. Tara noted that Karissa kept looking at her hand. "Are you all right, 'Rissa?"

Karissa looked at her right hand again and then back at Tara. "I will never wash this hand again," she said.

"Oh, jeez," Kelly said.

The elevator doors opened, and Kelly pushed Tara inside. Karissa took one step to join them when they heard her name being called.

"Karissa! Karissa—wait!"

Karissa turned around sharply and saw Robert Johnson heading their way. "Quick, push the button!" she exclaimed.

The doors closed just before he reached them.

Karissa backed up against one of the elevator walls. "What am I going to do? I can't spend the whole school year running away from him."

"You need to grow a set of balls, Karissa," Kelly said.

"Seriously?" Karissa exclaimed.

"Seriously," Kelly replied. "Look...you're afraid to talk to Ryan, and you're afraid to tell Robert you're not interested. If you continue to let fear paralyze you, you'll never get anywhere."

"Kelly is right, Karissa," Tara said.

In the Blink of an Eye

Chapter 4

"Come on people! You'll lose every match we play if you can't keep the ball in-bounds." Tara wheeled her chair up and down courtside watching for the mistakes her teammates were making. "Jess, that was the fourth hit on your side. No more than three hits allowed!"

Jess stopped and put her hands on her hips. "You get out here and play if you're so good!" she yelled to Tara.

"I wish I could, Jess," Tara replied.

"Okay, take a break! Practice resumes in ten." Ms. Warner approached Tara while the team filed off the court to retrieve their water bottles. "Tara, you're doing a good job coaching, but you might want to lighten up a bit. It's obvious that you know the game really well, but most of them are still learning."

"I hate to lose, Ms. Warner," Tara said in her own defense.

"I understand that, but this is a gym class—not the Olympics."

Tara raised her arms up. "Okay. Okay, I get it!"

"Look, I have an idea. Why don't you put together some notes about the rules of the game that you can pass out to everyone? If you want, you can even write up a multiple-choice quiz they can take after they've had time to learn the rules."

"You want me to give them a quiz?"

"Yes. Of course, it wouldn't count against their grades since this class is more about participation than becoming a proficient volleyball player, but it might give them some incentive to develop their skills."

Tara nodded. "I can do that."

"Good. We'll resume practice in a few minutes."

Tara watched her coach walk away while Karissa approached her from the opposite direction.

"You need to chill, girlfriend," Karissa said. "I'm hearing a lot of trash being talked about you by our teammates. Seriously, Tare. This is just a gym class."

"I know. I know. Sheesh, being a teacher is harder than it looks."

"That's what my mom says. But then, she teaches in the middle school," Karissa said. "They can be brats sometimes."

"It wasn't so long ago that *we* were those brats, 'Rissa."

***

"Can I have seconds, Mama?" Skylar asked.

"I'll get it," Billie said. She rose from the table and took her younger daughter's plate. She addressed the rest of the table. "Anyone else want more dinner?"

"I'll definitely have seconds, but I can get it myself, Mom," Seth said.

"Tara, how about you?" Billie asked.

Tara pushed the chicken around on her plate. "Nah. I'm good."

Billie filled Skylar's plate and placed it in front of her and returned to her seat at the table.

"Thanks, Mommy."

"You're welcome, sweet pea. So, how was school today?" Billie asked.

"We had a drill," Skylar said.

"A drill? Like a fire drill?" Cat asked.

"No. We had to hide in the closet."

Cat's gaze captured Billie's. Concern was clearly communicated through her eyes.

"Why's that?" Billie asked.

"To practice hiding if someone shoots a gun at school."

Cat closed her eyes and sat back in her seat.

"We had that same drill in the first week of school," Seth added. "They call them ALICE drills. It stands for Alert, Lockdown, Inform, Counter, Evacuate. You lucked out by missing it, Tare."

"An active shooter drill would have been *lots* of fun in this chair," Tara said sarcastically. "I'm glad I missed it."

Billie leaned forward. "Just what happens during one of these drills?" she asked.

"We have to lock the door and pull down the shade on the window," Skylar said. "And we have to be really quiet."

"And they make us hide in the closet, or in the safe room in the back of the class," Tara added.

"Safe room?" Cat asked.

"Some of the classrooms have small storage rooms in the back. My homeroom teacher calls them safe rooms because they have extra locks on the inside of the door," Tara explained.

Cat reached for Billie's hand. She seemed to be struggling to hold back tears.

"We have to barricade the door with chairs and other furniture," Seth said. "And the teachers tell us to grab something to defend ourselves with or to throw at the shooter, and to huddle together out of the line of sight of the door if there isn't a closet or safe room to hide in."

"Are you serious? You have to huddle together?" Billie asked.

"Yeah. Go figure. I think that just gives the shooter a bigger target," Seth explained. "I tell you what…if the shooter is inside the school, I'm climbing out a window and running as far and fast as I can."

"The last time I did a drill, the teachers said our first reaction should be to hide, but it is up to us if we want to fight the shooter," Tara said.

"Wait a minute," Cat said. "They said you could actually fight the shooter?"

"Yes. I mean, if someone can sneak up behind him…"

Cat grabbed Tara's arm. "Under no condition do you engage the shooter. Do you understand, Tara?" she said angrily.

Tara pulled her arm away. "Whoa, Ma. Chill out!"

"Okay, maybe we should change the subject," Billie said.

***

After dinner, the children retired to their rooms to do homework while Billie cleared the dinner dishes away and loaded the dishwasher. Cat paced back and forth across the kitchen on her crutches.

Finally, the repeated clicking of crutches wore out Billie's tolerance. She loaded the last dish into the dishwasher, and turned to face Cat. She leaned against the countertop and folded her arms across her chest. "Cat, you knew they were having these drills. They've been having them since kindergarten."

Cat stopped pacing and leaned on her crutches in front of Billie. "Knowing they're having the drills and hearing them talk about them are two different things—especially when these shootings are happening more frequently in this country. I had all I could do to hold back the tears. What has this world come to? Our school systems are intentionally preparing our children for the possibility they'll be shot and killed in their classrooms!"

Billie wrapped her arms around Cat. "I know, love. Hearing them talk about it was like a punch in the gut for me, too. I hope to God they'll never be subjected to the horror of an active shooter, but I'd rather they be prepared to deal with it."

"Hiding in a closet is not dealing with it, Billie. Fighting a shooter off with a pair of scissors is useless," Cat said.

"True, but if it makes them feel safer, I'm all for it. Remember our parents talking about hiding under their desks in the event a nuclear bomb fell on them? As adults, we understand that a measly desk provides absolutely no protection against a nuclear bomb, but what was important back then, is that our parents *thought* it did. They felt safe under those desks…just like our kids feel secure huddled in safe rooms."

Cat broke free of Billie's embrace and pulled away. "I know you're right, but it makes me so angry that our kids have to be subjected to this."

Billie held Cat by the shoulders. "It makes me angry too, but unfortunately, this is the world we are living in right now. Look, I'm going to check in on Tara. She seemed a little distracted at dinner."

"Maybe I should go with you."

"Actually, you need to elevate your leg. Let's get you settled into the recliner in the living room. I'll make you a nice cup of tea, and then I'll go talk to Tara, okay?"

***

"Tara, honey. Can I come in?"

Tara's attention was drawn away from her homework to the bedroom door when she heard the light knock. "Sure, Mom."

Billie closed the door behind her and crossed the room to where Tara had wheeled her chair up to the desk. She pulled a chair next to her daughter and sat down.

"Wow. I will never get used to you and your brother not having textbooks. Everything is done on your tablets. I'd be lost if I had to go back to high school today. What about kids who are not computer-savvy?"

Tara raised her eyebrows at her mother. "Seriously, Mom? What kid *isn't* computer-savvy these days?"

Billie tilted her head back and laughed. "Yeah...I guess you're right. Nowadays, even two-year-olds are proficient with electronics."

"Mom, why are you really here? I suspect this is not about my homework."

"Busted. Okay. I thought you were a bit distracted at dinner and I'm wondering if you're okay."

"You noticed, huh?"

"Yes, I did. So spill it."

Tara sighed. "I kind of screwed up during gym class today."

"How so?"

"Well, you know that I'm kind of co-teaching volleyball with the new gym teacher, who, by the way, Kelly thinks is gay."

"Really? How does Kelly know she's gay?"

"She said something about her gaydar going off around her. Kelly might be right. Ms. Warner is kind of butch."

"Butch like Kelly?" Billie grinned.

"Exactly. I mean, she has a boy-cut do and she dresses pretty much like a guy...and she *is* a gym teacher."

"I see. So does Ms. Warner's sexuality have anything to do with your screw-up in gym today?" Billie asked.

"No. You see, she asked me to watch the practice from the sidelines and to note errors the team made. What I didn't understand is that she wanted me to *take* notes about the errors.

Instead, I pointed out the mistakes they made to them...while they made them."

"Ouch!" Billie exclaimed. "I bet that went over like a fart in church!"

Tara laughed. "You have the weirdest sayings, Mom!"

"You can blame that one on my mother."

"Anyway, yeah—they were not very happy with me. Even Karissa told me to chill."

"Were you right?"

"I was. They were definitely making mistakes, but I guess I could have handled it better."

"So how do you propose to fix it?"

"Ms. Warner asked me to put notes together for the team to study, and then to quiz them."

"That sounds like a good approach...but I'm sensing there is something else bothering you."

"Yeah. I don't know how to apologize to the team. To be honest, I wish I didn't have to. I mean, I was right. I just didn't say it very nicely."

Billie sat back in her chair. "Ah. I see what you mean. You know, I have a saying on the wall in my office that says, *Lord, please make my words sweet and tender today, for tomorrow, I may have to eat them.* Learning how to say things diplomatically is a learned skill, sweetheart. I recommend that you just be honest with them...and don't forget to say the words, 'I'm sorry',"

Tara nodded. "Thanks, Mom." Her gaze fell to the hands clasped in her lap.

Billie tilted her head. "Is there something else you want to say, love?" she asked.

Tara continued to look at her hands while a smile spread across her face.

"What's that smile for?" Billie asked.

Tara peeked up at Billie. "Kelly asked me to be her girlfriend last night."

"And you said..."

"Yes! I said, yes," Tara replied.

"Wow. That's a big deal, Tare. Do you want to talk about it?"

"Sure. Maybe we could sit on my bed and talk, but could you help me get ready for bed first?"

"You got it, kiddo."

A few moments later, a pajama-clad Tara sat beside Billie and leaned her head on her mother's shoulder.

"So, how do you feel about things with Kelly?" Billie asked.

"She makes me feel things I've never felt before," Tara replied.

"Like what?"

"Like, all hot inside. Like, confused and butterflyish."

"Butterflyish?"

"Yeah. Like there's a butterfly inside my chest trying to get out."

"You mean, your heart flutters?"

"Exactly. I mean, it doesn't hurt or anything. It's just a weird feeling. Kelly says she feels the same way."

"Are there times it's stronger than others?" Billie asked.

"When she kisses me."

Billie's eyebrows rose. "So, she's kissed you, then."

"Yes. I mean, I kissed her the night before we went to Yellowstone—and it was weird—but she kissed me last night and the butterfly in my chest went crazy. It was almost scary."

"I think the word you want is intense."

"Yes! That's it. It was intense. Is that normal?"

"Very normal. Technically, what you're feeling is desire."

Tara sat up, startled, and looked at her mother. "You mean, like, sexual desire?"

"That's exactly what I mean."

"Mom! That's gross! Like, I don't think I'm ready for that."

"It's not gross, Tare. It's pretty normal, actually. It means you are attracted to her."

"But, what if I'm not ready?"

"If Kelly really cares for you, she'll understand. She's may not be ready either." Billie reached for Tara's hand. "Look, Tare, the first time you commit yourself physically to a relationship, you need to know without a shred of doubt that it's the right thing to do and that you care enough for the other person for a first-time encounter…and you need to be sure the other person cares as much about you as you do them."

"I've heard that some guys tell girls they love them just to have sex, and after, they move on to the next girl. Kelly isn't like that."

"I suspect you're right about that. But you need to understand you only get one first time. You need to be sure before you take that step. Do you understand what I'm trying to say?"

Tara nodded. She looked sideways at her mother and grinned.

Billie bumped shoulders with her. "Okay...what are you thinking?"

"Do you get butterflies with Mama? I mean, you've been together for a long time. Does it ever wear off?"

Billie chuckled. "If you really, really love someone, and know you will love them forever, it doesn't actually wear off. Sometimes it's not as strong as others, but the love-butterfly is always there."

Tara's eyes opened wide. "Does that mean I love Kelly?"

Billie touched the end of Tara's nose. "Only you can answer that question, Tare. Right now, I think it means you are attracted to her physically. Ask yourself if you would feel the same way about her if she looked differently than she does...or if she was differently-abled."

"What do you mean?"

"Mama asked me once if I would still love her and still be attracted to her if she became paralyzed and was in a wheelchair."

"Would you?"

"Absolutely. She is my heart, regardless of her physical abilities. That, sweetheart, is love."

"So love is being attracted to someone's heart, not just their body?"

"Love is being attracted to someone's heart strongly enough that you can't imagine living your life without them." Billie paused while Tara absorbed that information. "I recommend you and Kelly take things slowly. Get to know one another better before you cross the first-time line. Both of you need to be sure. There's no second chance."

Tara leaned her head on Billie's shoulder again and yawned.

"All right, rug rat. Time for bed." Billie climbed off the bed. "Scoot down and I'll tuck you in."

"I'm not a little girl anymore, Mom," Tara said.

Billie kissed her on the forehead. "You'll always be my little girl, Tare. Sweet dreams, love."

***

"Cat, sweetheart, wake up."

"Huh?" Cat opened her eyes and looked at Billie. "What time is it?"

"It's nearly ten. You fell asleep in the recliner. You must be exhausted."

"Are the kids…?"

"They're all tucked in. Sky is fast asleep and Seth and Tara just hit the sheets. Now it's time to get you to bed."

"Is Tara okay?"

"She's fine. I was right—she was a little preoccupied at dinner. It turns out she put her foot into her mouth during gym class and now has to figure out how to apologize. Oh, and she and Kelly are now officially a couple. We had a long talk about her feelings."

Cat cupped the side of Billie's face with her palm. "Where did our little girl go?"

"Tell me about it!"

"Thank you for being there for her. I should be jealous that she finds it easier to talk to you, but I am truly thankful she feels comfortable enough to open up with you."

"I love her like she came from me, Cat…her and Sky both. Thank you for bringing them into my life."

"You're welcome, love. You know I feel the same about Seth. Now, how about giving me a hand out of this chair and up the stairs to bed?"

Chapter 5

When Tara arrived at school the next morning, she went to the office and scheduled a meeting with Ms. Warner during her study hall period. She went to the business center and printed out copies of the volleyball rules she had found online the night before…one for each player on the team as well as one for herself and for Ms. Warner. After securing the copies inside her backpack, she wheeled herself into the hall and toward her homeroom class. She ran into Kelly halfway down the hall.

"Hey, Tare. Did you make your copies?" Kelly grabbed the handles of Tara's wheelchair.

"Yep…and I'm on Ms. Warner's calendar during study hall."

Kelly narrowed her eyes. "Why do you need to meet with Ms. Warner?"

"I want to review the handouts with her, and I need to talk to her about something before tomorrow's gym class."

Kelly fell silent, long enough for Tara to look over her shoulder. "You're quiet all of the sudden," Tara said.

"I just don't understand why you need to talk to Ms. Warner. You don't have a crush on her, do you?"

Tara grabbed the wheels of her chair and brought them both to a halt. "Whoa. Where did that come from?"

Kelly pushed Tara's chair out of the stream of students heading to their next classes, and parked it near the stairway. She shoved her hands into her pockets and walked a few feet away.

Tara leaned forward in her chair. "Kelly?"

Kelly turned to face her. "So, what is it?" she asked.

"What is what?"

"Do you have a crush on her or not?"

"*You* are my girlfriend. And besides, she's got to be at least ten years older than me," Tara said in her own defense.

"Well, you seem to be really interested in her."

"I am helping her teach the volleyball class. It's a way for me to get my gym credit while stuck in this chair. Kelly, what are you so worried about?"

Kelly took three steps and stopped directly in front of Tara. She leaned forward. "I am *not* worried."

"Yes, you are. Look at how you're acting."

Kelly stood straight up and leaned her head back to look at the ceiling. She sighed and looked at Tara once more. "I don't want to lose you."

A euphoric feeling filled Tara's chest and she tried hard to keep the grin from her face. "You are not going to lose me, Kelly. Ms. Warner is just my teacher…that's all."

Kelly looked directly into Tara's eyes. "Promise?"

Tara reached her hand forward. "Pinky-swear promise," Tara replied.

Kelly locked pinky fingers with Tara and blinked rapidly, unsuccessfully trying to hide the tears that had formed in the corners of her eyes.

Tara pulled Kelly closer. "Are you crying?"

Kelly wiped her eyes with the back of her free hand. "Shut up." She freed her pinky from Tara's grasp and once again directed the wheelchair toward Tara's next class.

***

"Tara! Come in. I was surprised to see your name on my calendar. What can I do for you?"

Tara wheeled herself toward Ms. Warner's desk. "Thanks for seeing me. I printed out the rules for the team and I wanted your approval before I hand them out in our next class." Tara handed the package to her teacher and waited patiently while Ms. Warner reviewed them.

"This looks great, Tara. Thanks for doing this."

"Good." Tara sat there, studying her hands, as an awkward silence ensued.

Ms. Warner leaned forward. "Is there something else, Tara?"

"Actually, yes. I want to apologize for being such a jerk yesterday. Sometimes I get a little carried away. My moms get on me about it all the time."

"Your moms? As in two?" Ms. Warner asked.

Tara nodded. "I just can't help myself. I hate to lose."

"That's understandable. I've been a jerk myself once or twice...for pretty much the same reason...and my girlfriend gets on me about it as well, especially when I beat her in a board game. Believe me—I understand."

Tara grinned. "I have an older brother, and before he got bigger than me, I used to be able to take him down. Not so much anymore."

"Seth, right? Your brother is Seth Charland?"

"That's him. We're actually step-siblings, but he feels like a real brother to me. Anyway, I wanted to apologize, and I feel like I should also apologize to the team."

"That would be an awesome gesture, Tara."

"I'm kind of nervous about it, but my mom told me to just be myself and to be sure to say I'm sorry."

"That sounds like good advice. I'm sure your classmates will appreciate it."

Tara pushed herself away from the desk. "Okay. I guess I should go back to study hall. Thanks, Ms. Warner. I'll see you later."

"Let me get the door for you." Ms. Warner walked across the room and held the door open for Tara to pass through.

"Thanks again!" Tara called as she wheeled herself down the hall.

***

Karissa met Tara outside the cafeteria at lunch time and carried her plate for her through the lunch line and to the table. "I will say, it's nice to cut the line," Karissa said.

"I'm glad *something* good is coming from this stupid chair," Tara replied.

"I see a table there—near the windows," Karissa pointed out. "Lead the way!"

Tara maneuvered her chair up to the lunch table and locked the wheels. Karissa put her tray down in front of her. "Thanks, 'Rissa."

Karissa sat opposite Tara. "Where's Kelly?"

"That's a good question. Oh, there she is." Tara waved until she caught Kelly's attention.

Kelly acknowledged her and then veered toward the lunch line. Moments later, she joined her friends at the table and sat beside Tara. She reached under the table and squeezed Tara's leg. Tara grinned without looking at her.

"Hey, Kel," Karissa said.

"Hey, Karissa." Kelly turned her attention to Tara. "How was your meeting with Ms. Warner?"

"It was good," Tara said. "I think I'm all set for my next gym class."

"That's good."

"Oh, my God!" Karissa groaned. "Here he comes."

Kelly looked over her shoulder and saw Robert walking toward them. She quickly looked back at Karissa. "Balls, Karissa. Grow a pair—fast!"

Robert stopped at the end of the table and looked directly at Karissa. "Ladies. Mind if I join you?"

Karissa looked him straight in the eyes. "I'm sorry, Robert, but we're kind of having a private discussion here. You know...girl issues."

Robert physically took two steps backward. "Ah...ah...maybe another time then." He quickly turned and scurried away.

Kelly held her palm out to Karissa. "High-five, girlfriend! Quick thinking. Nothing scares a guy more than women talking about their periods!"

"Are you two going to the pep rally on Friday?" Karissa asked.

"What time on Friday?" Tara said.

"Around six o'clock at the football field. The first football game of the year is on Friday night. The rally is just before the game," Karissa replied.

"I suppose I should go," Tara said. "Especially since Seth is playing. I'm sure my moms will go too."

"Stevie is playing too," Karissa said.

Tara raised her eyebrows. "Don't let him catch you calling him Stevie. You know how sensitive he is about that."

"Steve...Stevie...whatever!" Karissa exclaimed.

"Do you think I can catch a ride with you, Tara?" Kelly asked.

"I think so. I'll ask my moms."

Tara glanced at the time on her phone. "Crap. I gotta get to my next class soon."

"I'm in that class too!" Kelly quickly ate the rest of her lunch and carried all three of their trays to the dish room while Karissa pushed Tara into the hall outside the cafeteria to wait for her. Karissa pushed her to the hallway intersection near the main lobby and handed control of Tara's wheelchair to Kelly.

"She's all yours," Karissa said. "My next class is in the opposite direction from you two. I'll see you in the gym for volleyball, Tara."

***

Kelly passed a note to Tara in the middle of their social studies class after lunch. Tara did her best to nonchalantly open it flat inside her notebook so as to not attract the attention of the teacher.

Wanna make out with me under the bleachers at the pep rally on Friday?

Tara snapped her notebook closed so quickly, it drew the attention of the whole class...including the teacher. All she could do was slink down into her seat while her face turned fifty shades of red.

Kelly had all she could do not to burst out laughing and had to cover her mouth to stifle the guffaw that threatened to escape.

"Would you like to share what's so funny with the rest of the class, Miss Barkum?" the teacher asked.

"No. No, ma'am," Kelly replied. "My apologies, ma'am."

Tara glared at Kelly as soon as the teacher returned her attention to the board.

Kelly wiggled her eyebrows up and down.

Tara lowered her face into her hands and avoided looking at Kelly for the rest of the class.

***

Kelly pushed Tara toward the gym after social studies class.

"Thanks a lot, Kelly. You almost got us both in trouble!" Tara whined.

"You should have seen your face!"

"I think my face could be seen a mile away it was so red! Don't ever do that again!"

"At least tell me what you thought about my suggestion," Kelly demanded.

"Don't you think it might be suspicious if we both disappeared during the pep rally?"

"Even for a little while?"

"Well, I suppose we could fake going to the ladies' room together. Girls do that all the time."

"Perfect! It's a date. Okay, here we are at the gym."

"Hold on. I'll get the door!"

Tara and Kelly both turned around to see Karissa running toward them. She grabbed the handle and opened the door to allow Kelly to push Tara through it.

Once inside, Kelly squeezed Tara's shoulder. "I gotta get to my math class. I'll see you after school."

"I'm going to get into my gym clothes, Tara. Be right back!" Karissa left Tara by the bleachers and ran to the locker room.

Tara pulled her handouts from her backpack and scanned through the top copy. She was nervous about facing the team and wished more than anything that she could just avoid it altogether.

The students filed into the gym and headed to the locker room. Within ten minutes, they were back on court and warming up in pairs by keeping the ball airborne back and forth between them.

During the warm-up, Ms. Warner sat on the bleachers next to where Tara had parked her wheelchair. "Nervous?" she asked.

"Terrified is more like it," Tara admitted.

Ms. Warner stood and placed her hand on Tara's shoulder. "It will be fine. Just remember your mom's advice."

Tara nodded and swallowed hard.

Ms. Warner clapped her hands. "Okay troops, let's gather on the bleachers for a moment. Tara has something to say to the team."

The students dutifully sat in the bleachers and waited for Tara to speak. Tara wheeled her chair in front of the bleachers and made eye contact each one of them.

Karissa frowned and silently stared at her with questioning eyes.

Tara nodded and addressed the group. "I'm sorry. I was too hard on you on Monday. I expected you to be experts before you even had a chance to learn the rules. I know I was a jerk. I'm asking you to give me another chance."

Tara folded her hands in her lap and sat quietly. For several long minutes, nothing happened. Then, one girl rose to her feet and approached Tara. She offered her hand for a fist-bump. Tara complied. One by one, the rest of the team followed suit. Karissa intentionally went last. Instead of fist-bumping, she hugged Tara. "You did good, girlfriend," she whispered and joined her teammates on the practice floor.

Tara spent the next hour encouraging her classmates, cheering their successes and consoling their mistakes while assuring them that practice makes perfect. At the end of class, she gathered them onto the bleachers once more and handed out the rule sheets.

"You guys were awesome! I wish I wasn't stuck in this chair. I'd give anything to be on the court with you. Study these rules and in a few weeks, we'll hand out a quiz." The mere mention of a quiz resulted in a round of groans.

"Don't worry," she assured them. "It's a practice quiz and it won't count against your grade. It's just to see where we need more practice. No sweat!"

Tara collected multiple high-fives as her classmates left for the locker room. Soon, she found herself alone in the gym with Ms. Warner.

Ms. Warner approached Tara and squatted down in front of her. She reached for Tara's hands. "You have a way with people, Tara. Have you thought about teaching?" Ms. Warner asked.

"I was actually thinking about being a doctor, like my mom. Maybe a pediatrician. I kind of like kids."

"That's also a good profession. In any case, you did a good job with them this afternoon." Ms. Warner released her hands and stood. "See you on Friday?"

"Absolutely."

Ms. Warner walked away while Tara remained where she was and thought about how well the class went.

"Hi, there, Kelly. You'd be proud of your girl today."

Tara's turned her head sharply at the sound of Ms. Warner's voice and realized she was talking to Kelly, who stood just inside the gym door. She watched as Ms. Warner left the gym and Kelly walked toward her.

Kelly stopped directly in front of Tara. "That was pretty cozy."

Tara frowned. "What do you mean?"

"Does she hold all the students' hands?"

"She was just letting me know how well practice went— that's all."

"Did you tell her about us?" Kelly asked.

"No, I didn't. Why?"

"She called you my girl."

"Well, I *am* your girl."

"Are you sure about that, Tara?"

"Look, Kelly. Being your girlfriend doesn't mean that you own me. I'm allowed to talk to other people. Either you're gonna trust me, or you're not. What's it gonna be?"

Before Kelly could speak, the door to the locker room opened and Karissa stepped through. She walked across the gym to join Tara and Kelly.

"Great practice, Tara," Karissa said. "I think everyone is chill with you now. No more trash talk in the locker room." She stopped in front of them and looked back and forth. "Trouble in paradise?" she asked.

"I'll meet you out front." Kelly turned on her heel and left the gym.

"What's wrong with her?" Karissa asked.

***

Tara retreated to her bedroom after dinner and sent a text to Kelly. *Call me. We need to talk.*

A moment later, her phone rang. Kelly's name appeared on the screen.

"Are you done being angry about nothing?" Tara asked.

"Do you always answer your phone like that?" Kelly said.

"I want to know what your problem is."

"I thought about what you said in the gym...about trusting you."

"And...?"

"And I was wrong. You're right. I don't own you."

"Then why are you so jealous? I haven't done anything wrong, Kelly. We've only been going out for what...less than a week, and already, you've accused me of cheating on you, twice!"

"I'm sorry, Tara. I don't want to lose you."

"Then you really need to lighten up. Jesus, Kelly. Ms. Warner is my *teacher*. She's done nothing to make me feel uncomfortable. It would be pretty stupid of her to hit on a student – don't you think?"

"I believe you. I'm sorry, Tara. I'll try to do better. Will you forgive me?"

"Actions speak louder than words, Kelly."

"I understand."

"Oh, you were right about Ms. Warner, by the way. She's gay, and she has a girlfriend. You wanna know why she called me your girl? Because like you, she must have pretty good gaydar. You are really butch, and I'm far from a lipstick myself. It doesn't take a rocket scientist to figure us out."

"So I was right about her," Kelly said.

"I think so, but before you get any ideas in your head, being gay doesn't make her a predator. You should know that."

"I know."

"I think you should get to know Ms. Warner. Maybe you'd feel better about her if you did."

"Maybe I should."

"Are we okay?" Tara asked.

"I want us to be," Kelly replied.

"We start over tomorrow…okay?"

"Okay. Sweet dreams, Tara."

"You too, Kel. I'll see you in the morning."

Chapter 6

"Okay, everyone. Meet us back at the car a half-hour after the game ends, okay?" Cat said.

"All right, Ma," Tara replied.

"Sky and Missy—be sure to stay together. Mom and I will be in the stands with blankets and hot chocolate if you get cold," Cat added.

"Okay, Mama," Skylar said. She took Missy's hand and ran across the parking lot toward the football field.

"Do you want help carrying the blankets and cooler to the stands, Mrs. Charland?" Kelly asked Billie.

"I think we've got it, Kelly, but thanks for asking. You girls go on and have a good time. We'll see you after the game."

Billie watched Tara, Karissa and Kelly walk away from them. "It's a good thing we have a seven-passenger van. How is it we've become the neighborhood taxi service?"

Cat chuckled. "At least we know where our kids are. And besides, Jen and Fred should be here as soon as Fred gets out of work. They can share the load on the way home."

Billie wrapped her arm around Cat as they walked toward the stands. "True enough. Hey, wanna make out with me under the bleachers?"

Cat hip-checked her tall, dark-haired wife. "You're such a guy sometimes!"

***

"This wheelchair is a real pain in the you-know-what!" Tara complained. "We can't even sit in the stands."

"It's okay, Tara. We don't mind standing down here by the fence with you. Do we Karissa?" Kelly said.

"No. I don't mind at all," Karissa agreed.

"After the pep rally is done, we can walk around. We don't really need to watch the game if we don't want to," Kelly said.

"I should probably watch at least *some* of the game. Seth is playing in it, after all. And Steve is too, Karissa," Tara pointed out.

Karissa shrugged. "I suppose."

The football team filed onto the field for warm-up stretches and an impromptu practice scrimmage.

"Hey, isn't that Ryan out there? I didn't know he was on the team," Tara said.

Karissa's attention was immediately piqued. "Where?"

Tara pointed. "There. Number thirty-eight."

"I see him. Oh, wow! He's really cute in that uniform. You're right, Tare. Maybe we *should* watch the game."

"It looks like your other boyfriend is on the team too, Karissa," Kelly said.

"My other boyfriend?"

"Yeah—Robert. Number sixteen."

"Oh, please!" Karissa exclaimed.

"Have you talked to Steve about him yet?" Tara asked.

"No. He hasn't really done anything scary, Tare."

"You mean, he hasn't done anything scary—yet," Tara replied.

"Like I said, Karissa, you need to grow a pair. Just tell him you're not interested in him," Kelly suggested.

"That's easier said than done, Kelly," Karissa said.

All three girls were startled when a football struck the chain-link fence directly in front of them.

"Jesus Christ!" Tara exclaimed.

"Sorry about that, Tara," Ryan said when he collected the ball from the ground. "That one got by me."

"That scared the daylights out of me, Ryan!" Tara said. "Do you remember Kelly and Karissa?"

Ryan looked at the other two girls. "Sure I do. How are you guys doing?"

"Considering we're not guys, we're doing great," Kelly said.

Karissa elbowed Kelly in the side.

"Hey! What was that for?" Kelly complained.

"Well, I've got to get back. Maybe I'll see you after the game." Ryan tossed the ball into the air, caught it, and then ran back to the field.

"You weren't very nice to him," Karissa said once Ryan was out of earshot.

"Didn't you see him flirting with Tara?" Kelly asked.

"He was not!" Tara exclaimed.

"Yeah—he was not," Karissa agreed.

"If you say so," Kelly said.

"Hello girls!"

All three turned around to see who was calling to them.

"Ms. Warner! I didn't know you were coming to the game," Tara said.

"I try to make as many of the school's sporting events as I can. Oh, let me introduce you to my partner, Mariana. Mariana, this is Tara, Kelly and Karissa."

Mariana extended her hand to each girl. "It's so nice to meet you," she said with a light Mexican accent. "I've heard a lot of about you from Patty."

The girls frowned.

"That would be me," Ms. Warner said.

"So your name is Patty," Tara said.

"Yes...but it's Ms. Warner to you when we're at school."

"Got it," Tara said.

Kelly possessively put her hand on Tara's shoulder and squeezed.

Tara froze at the contact.

"We're going to find seats in the bleachers. Would you girls like to join us?" Ms. Warner asked.

"It's kind of hard to climb stairs in this thing, Ms. Warner," Tara said sarcastically.

"You're right, but there is a handicapped section with a ramp so you can at least be up on the bottom riser."

"You're right. I forgot about that," Tara said.

"Okay. I hope you enjoy the game."

As soon as Ms. Warner walked away, Tara removed Kelly's hand from her shoulder and glared up at her.

"What?" Kelly asked.

"I'm not your property, Kel," Tara said.

"I was just touching your shoulder!" Kelly said.

"No, you were showing possession. I thought we talked about this."

Kelly raised her hands up. "Okay. No touching in public. I get it."

"You know that's not what this is about."

Karissa looked back and forth between her friends. "Wait a minute. Are you saying Kelly is jealous of Ms. Warner?"

Tara crossed her arms. "I'll let Kelly answer that one."

"I wouldn't call it jealousy," Kelly said.

"What *would* you call it?" Tara asked.

"Didn't she just introduce us to her girlfriend?" Karissa said.

"Actually, she said her *partner*. That's even more significant than girlfriend," Tara pointed out.

"Why don't we just drop it?" Kelly said.

"I vote we find seats in the handicapped section," Karissa suggested.

"All right. Let's go," Tara replied.

***

"That was an awesome game!" Karissa exclaimed. "Did you see Ryan score the winning touchdown?"

"It takes more than one player to win a game, Karissa. He was just flexing," Kelly said.

"He was not just flexing. He's a good ball player. Besides, it's exciting when someone you like scores. I'm glad we came."

"I think the whole team was great," Tara added. "I was actually surprised at how well Robert did. I didn't peg him as being a jock."

"Robert is okay," Karissa said.

"Are you changing your mind about him?" Kelly asked.

"Heck to the no!" Karissa replied. "Like I said before, he's kind of greasy. I don't think he's a bad guy, but I definitely don't want to date him."

"Here, let me push." Kelly took charge of Tara's wheelchair and pushed her across the grass toward the parking lot.

Kelly leaned forward and whispered in Tara's ear as she pushed, "Are you still mad at me?"

Tara shrugged without looking back at Kelly.

Kelly frowned and spared a glance at Karissa.

A look of sympathy crossed Karissa's face.

Kelly pushed Tara's chair the rest of the way to the car, in silence. "Here we are."

"Perfect timing," Cat said as she and Billie walked up behind the girls, followed by Jen and Fred. "Great game, huh?"

"It's always a good game when your team wins," Kelly replied.

"I thought Seth and Steve did a fantastic job. I guess our drills in the back yard helped," Fred said, fatherly pride clearly on his face.

"You're riding home with us, Karissa," Jen said.

"Okay. Let me help Tara get into the van and I'll be right there," Karissa replied.

"We're parked a few rows away. I'll turn my flashers on so you'll be able to find us," Fred said.

"Okay, Dad." Karissa turned so only Tara and Kelly could see her face and rolled her eyes. Both girls responded with attempts to hide a chuckle.

With Kelly on one side and Karissa on the other, they lifted Tara from her chair and helped her into the van, and Kelly pushed the chair to the back of the van. Karissa followed her.

"Call me when you get home, Kelly," Karissa said.

Kelly frowned. "Why?"

"I have some friendly advice for you…about Tara."

Kelly nodded and folded the chair. She hefted it into the back of the van and walked around to the other side to climb into the seat beside Tara.

"You two made it just under the wire!" Billie watched Skylar and Missy run across the parking lot toward them.

"Sorry, Mommy!" Skylar said. She and Missy made short work of climbing into the far back seat.

Soon they were on their way. By the time they made it out of the crowded parking lot and headed home, it was after eight o'clock. For the entire ride, Skylar and Missy dominated the conversation with talk of school, friends and the boys they crushed on.

Kelly spent the ride home worrying that her relationship with Tara would be short-lived and wondering what she could do to fix it.

***

"Hey, Karissa. This is Kelly."

"Hi, Kelly. Are you home?"

"Yeah."

"I'm surprised you called so soon. I expected you'd hang out with Tara until curfew."

"Her moms dropped me off on their way home. Tara didn't even ask me to come over. I'm afraid I'm about to be ghosted."

"I'm not sure it's that bad, Kelly. Tara's just a little upset about you going all extra on her."

"I did not overreact, Karissa. Tell me you didn't see Ryan flirting with her."

"No, I didn't."

"Then why did he basically talk only to her?"

"Because he knows her better than he does us. That's why."

"I don't know, Karissa. She's taken my head off a couple of times in just the past two days."

"She doesn't like how jealous you are."

"I'm not jealous."

"Yes, you are. Look, Kel, I know what jealousy looks like. When you first came in the picture, I was jealous of *you*."

"You were jealous of me?"

"Yes. Tara and I have been friends for more than ten years, and then you came along and she didn't have as much time for me. You bet I was jealous."

"So, how did you get over it?"

"Tara made me realize that our friendship was not dependent on other people, and that no matter what, we would always have a special bond."

"So she basically told you to chill."

"Yes, and just like me, *you* need to be more low-key. She's right, Kelly—you don't own her."

"So, what am I doing wrong?"

"How much time have you spent at Tara's house?"

"I've been there a few times. Why?"

"Have you ever watched her moms?"

"Her moms are dank. I like them a lot."

"Yes, they are, but have you ever really *watched* them?" Karissa asked.

"What exactly are you saying, Karissa?"

"Kel, Tara's moms are her role models. Their relationship is trill. They trust each other without question, and they are independent. They don't own each other."

"Not everyone's relationship is like them you know. My mom pretty much lets my dad make most of the decisions."

"And that might work fine for them, but not for everyone."

"So what's that got to do with me and Tara?"

"Think about it, Kelly. Like I said, her moms' relationship is what Tara knows…and it's what she expects all relationships to be like."

"Are you saying they are never jealous of each other?"

"I am saying they're pretty good at adulting. They *trust* each other."

"So, I need to give Tara space and trust her."

"Exactly."

Chapter 7

"Hello?"

"Hi, Kel. 'Rissa and I are going to hang out today. Do you want to come over?" Tara asked.

"Nah. I think I'm gonna chill out today," Kelly replied

"Are you sure?"

"Yes. I hope you have a good time with Karissa."

"Okay. If you say so. I guess I'll talk to you later, then. Bye." Tara listened for silence on the other end of the line and then looked at her phone.

"Is she coming?" Karissa asked.

"No. She said she's going to chill out today. That's kind of odd," Tara replied.

"Maybe she's giving you some space," Karissa suggested. "You were kind of clear with her at the football game last night about how possessive she is."

"Yeah, but I didn't expect her to pull away like that."

"You can't have it both ways, Tare."

"Yes, I can, 'Rissa. I don't need time away from her. All I want is for her to trust me."

"So you're not looking for space?"

"No. I kind of like that she wants to spend time with me, but I don't like her trying to control who I'm friends with, or who talks to me."

"Adult relationships are so complicated."

"Yeah—especially when you're not an adult yet."

"So, what do you want to do today?" Karissa asked.

"We should probably get our homework done," Tara suggested.

"Ugh! I hate homework on the weekends."

"Me too, but if we put it off, we'll have to cram it all in on Sunday. Do you have a lot of homework to do?"

"Just the work we got on Friday."

"Me, too. My moms kind of make me do my homework after school every day. As much as I hate it, it means I only have one day of homework to do on the weekend."

"Mine, too. I think our moms plan that together."

"I think you're right. Oh, well, why don't we just do it and get it done?" Tara said.

Karissa sighed. "All right. I'll run home to get my homework. I'll be back in a few minutes."

"Okay. I'll make us a snack while you're gone."

Tara and Karissa entered the kitchen just as Cat poured herself a cup of coffee. She leaned her backside against the countertop and lifted her coffee. Her crutches were propped up against the cabinet beside her.

"Hey, girls. Any big plans for today?" Cat asked.

"Homework." Tara groaned.

Cat smiled broadly. "Wow! I'm impressed."

"We want to get it out of the way. I'm heading home to get my backpack," Karissa said.

"Okay. Oh, 'Rissa, tell your mom to give me a call when she gets a chance. I want to know if she'd like to go shopping today."

"I will!"

Cat turned to Tara. "No Kelly today?"

"I called her, but she wanted to stay home," Tara replied.

Cat frowned. "Is everything okay with you two?"

Tara closed the refrigerator door and faced Cat. "I'm not sure. I think she's mad at me."

"Whatever for?"

"She's kind of being jealous and I called her on it."

"Who is she jealous of?"

"Of this new boy at school named Ryan. Oh, and she's jealous of my gym teacher too."

"Your gym teacher?"

"Yeah. Her name is Ms. Warner, and she's gay."

"How do you know she's gay?"

"She and her partner were at the football game last night and she introduced us to her. Her name is Mariana."

"So…why do you think Kelly is jealous of her?"

Tara ran her hand through her hair. "I don't know, Mama. Ms. Warner doesn't treat me any different than anyone else in the class. Kelly is just jealous of everyone. She got all possessive of me last night at the game and I told her to chill."

"I guess that explains why Kelly didn't resist being dropped off at home instead of coming home with us after the game."

"I guess so." Tara fell silent for a few seconds before addressing her mother again. "Mama, have you or Mom ever been jealous of each other?"

"How about we sit at the table so we can talk for a bit?" Walking with just one crutch, Cat carefully carried her coffee to the table and sat. She sipped her coffee and placed her cup on the table in front of her. "Have Mom and I ever been jealous of one another? Yes, we have. A couple of times, actually."

"Did you have good reasons to be jealous?" Tara asked.

"That is a good question, sweetheart. Jealousy is rooted in fear—fear that you're going to lose something you value. Sometimes that fear is based on fact, and sometimes it isn't. When it's not based on fact, it usually comes from a misunderstanding, or misinformation. With Mom and me, those times we were jealous were based on misunderstandings."

"Kelly's jealousy is not based on fact. She has no reason to be jealous of Ryan or Ms. Warner. It makes me mad that she doesn't trust me."

"That's a hard one. Trust is something that has to be earned...and it is nearly impossible to replace once it is lost."

"But I haven't given her a reason to mistrust me, Mama."

"Maybe something in her past has made her extra cautious."

"But she said I was her first girlfriend."

Cat reached for Tara's hands. "Sweetie, didn't you tell me once that Kelly and her family have moved every few years because of her dad's military career?"

"Yeah."

"Well, maybe...just maybe, because her family has had to move so often, she's anticipating losing you in the near future, and she's holding on to you tighter than she might otherwise."

"Do you think so?" Tara asked softly.

"Maybe."

Tara stared at the hands entwined with her mother's. She looked into her mother's eyes through a misty veil of tears. "I haven't thought about her leaving because of her father's job. Do you really think that will happen?"

Cat squeezed Tara's hands. "Her dad is probably in the middle of his career, so there is a real possibility that they'll move again."

"Maybe I've been too hard on her about trusting me."

"Sweetie, I don't think Kelly's jealousy is because she doesn't trust you. I think it is purely about her losing you...and in her case, losing you for a reason beyond both of your controls."

Tara tried to force a grin. "Maybe I should give her a break on this one?"

Cat nodded and smiled back. "Maybe you should. Unless of course, it becomes unmanageable."

"What do you mean?"

"I mean, you don't want to give total control to Kelly either. You need your independence and your identity."

"How would I lose my identity?" Tara asked.

"If in any relationship, your friends identify you only in terms of your partner—that is losing your identity. You no longer exist to them as Tara, but instead you are Tara and Kelly. That, my love, is losing your autonomy. Does that make sense?"

"I think so. Man, relationships are complicated," Tara complained.

"Yes, they are. But when you find the right one, they are worth the work."

"Like you and Mom?"

"Yes. Like Mom and me."

"I'm back!" Karissa said as she let herself into the kitchen, followed closely by her mother, Jen.

"I heard a rumor that someone wants to go shopping today!" Jen said.

"That would be me!" Cat replied. "Billie has a date with Sky today, and besides, she'd be happy to be off the hook for shopping."

Tara pushed herself away from the table. "Come on, 'Rissa. Let's get this homework done, then maybe *we* can do something fun as well."

Tara and Karissa headed toward the doorway to the living room when Tara stopped short and wheeled back to Cat. She hugged her firmly and kissed her cheek. "Thanks, Mama," she said before she joined her friend once more.

Cat's eyes watered and she looked at Jen.

"What was that all about?" Jen asked.

"Our girls are becoming young women, Jen. Hold on to your seat!"

***

"Done!" Tara shut her tablet off and shoved it into her backpack.

"Me, too!" Karissa said. "It's only two o'clock. What do we do now?"

"We could watch a movie, or play a game," Tara suggested.

"Or we could call Kelly. You know you want to."

"Am I that transparent?" Tara asked.

"Like glass. Hey! Maybe we can do a sleepover?" Karissa suggested.

Tara perked up. "I like that idea. I have to ask my mom if it's okay. I'll be right back." With Karissa's help, Tara climbed off her bed, transferred herself to her wheelchair and went in search of Billie. She returned to her room five minutes later. "My mom isn't here. I forgot she planned to take Skylar and Missy to play miniature golf today. I'll have to call Mama."

Tara dialed Cat's number. "Hi, Ma. Is it okay if 'Rissa stays over tonight? We might call Kelly too."

"It's okay with me. Hold on while I ask Jen," Cat replied. A few seconds later, Cat returned. "It's a go with Jen. Make sure Kelly clears it with her parents."

"I will, Mama. Thanks." Tara turned to Karissa. "Our moms are okay with it. Now, for Kelly." Tara dialed Kelly's number. It rang several times before going to voicemail. "Hi, Kel. This is Tara. 'Rissa and I were thinking about a sleepover at my house tonight. I'd love to have you come too. Call me back!"

***

Kelly sat on her bed as she watched a video on her laptop. A sudden vibration on the side of her leg drew her attention. She reached into her pocket and extracted her phone and saw Tara's name displayed on the screen. She froze, uncertain whether she wanted to answer it. After several rings, her phone went to voicemail.

Kelly stared at the screen on her phone until her usual screensaver appeared. Her heart beat wildly in her chest as she thought about the message that waited for her from Tara. Her biggest fear was that the message contained bad news...that Tara had grown tired of her jealousy and had left a Dear John message. She summoned her courage and opened the voicemail.

Hi, Kel. This is Tara. 'Rissa and I were thinking about a sleepover at my house tonight. I'd love to have you come too. Call me back!

Kelly's heart soared. *She'd love to have me come too? Maybe she isn't mad at me anymore.*

Kelly held her phone in front of her and realized her hand was shaking. She pressed the phone close to her chest and breathed deeply. *Get a grip, Kel. You don't want to sound like an idiot when you call her back.*

She dialed Tara's number and waited. It was answered on the first ring.

"Kelly! Thanks for calling me back," she heard Tara say.

"Hey, Tare."

"'Rissa and I are talking sleepover. Wanna come?"

"Sure! I'll have to ask my parents. Can you hang on a minute?"

"I'll be waiting."

Kelly put the phone on her bed and went in search of her parents. She found her mother ironing in front of the television in the living room.

"Mom, can I do a sleepover with Tara and Karissa tonight at Tara's house?"

"You should ask your father, dear," Mrs. Barkum said.

"Where is he?"

"He's volunteering at the Marine Corps recruiting station today."

"How am I supposed to ask him when he doesn't like taking phone calls at work?"

"I guess you'll have to wait for him to get home, then."

"Mom, why can't you give me permission?"

"You know your father likes to be in charge, dear."

Kelly felt anger rise in her chest and almost conceded defeat when she suddenly realized what Karissa meant when she said Tara's moms were independent. She turned back to her mother. "Mom, do you ever get tired of Dad making all the decisions for this family? You have no problem doing it when he's deployed. Do you have *any* rights in this marriage when he's home?"

Mrs. Barkum's head snapped up and she looked directly at her daughter. For several long moments, Kelly watched a play of emotions cross her mother's face. First shock, followed by confusion, and finally by determination. "You have my permission, Kelly. Have a good time with your friends."

Kelly kissed her mother on the cheek. "Thanks, Mom." She ran back to her room to tell Tara the good news. "Tare, I talked with my mom, and yes, I'll be over soon. I just need to pack a bag."

***

"She's coming," Tara said to Karissa.

"Awesome! When she gets here, I'll run home to get a change of clothes. That will give you a chance to get all kissy-face with her without me in the room."

Tara punched Karissa in the arm. "'Rissa!"

Karissa rubbed her arm. "Tell me you don't think that's a good idea!"

"I didn't say it wasn't a good idea! It's just embarrassing to hear you say it."

"I've got your number, girlfriend."

Tara opened her arms to her friend. Karissa bent down and hugged her in her wheelchair. "Don't ever change, 'Rissa. I love you just the way you are."

"The feeling is moo-chal, darlin'," Karissa said.

Ten minutes later, the doorbell rang.

"That's my cue to leave," Karissa said.

Tara wheeled herself across the living room behind Karissa and stopped just short of the front door. Karissa opened the door and threw her arms around Kelly.

"Hey, Kel! I'm going to run home for a change of clothes. I'll be back in a few."

Karissa was gone before Kelly could say anything. Instead, she closed the door and dropped her backpack on the floor. She shoved her hands deep into her pockets and faced Tara.

"Hey, Tara," she said awkwardly.

Tara purposely captured Kelly's gaze and reached out her hand. Kelly crossed the room in three steps and dropped to one knee beside Tara's wheelchair.

"I'm sorry, Kel," Tara said.

Kelly frowned. "For what?

"For judging you. For being angry with you."

"No, you had a right to be angry. I was jealous. I...I just don't want to lose you, Tare."

Tara captured Kelly's face between her palms. "I'm not going anywhere, Kelly."

"I want to kiss you so badly right now," Kelly said.

"We are the only ones here right now...thanks to Karissa," Tara said.

"Remind me to thank her when she gets back," Kelly replied.

"So what are you waiting for?"

Tara pulled Kelly's face toward her and their lips met, tentatively at first, but with growing passion as the kiss deepened.

Tara felt a fire in her abdomen that both thrilled and terrified her, followed by a pulsing sensation deep within her core that left her breathless. When the kiss ended, she touched her forehead to Kelly's.

"You make me feel things I have never felt before, Kel. My body feels like it's on fire. I want more, but it scares me too."

Kelly pulled back and looked directly into Tara's eyes. "I am so damned thirsty for you, but I would never force you into anything you didn't want, Tara. I feel it too, and yes—it makes me cray-cray as well. You can trust me, Tara."

"I know I can. I feel safe with you, Kel. I trust you…and you can trust me too."

Kelly grinned. "Why do I get the feeling you mean that in more than one way?"

"I was hoping you'd catch that."

Their attention was drawn to the front door as it swung open. "I'm back!" Karissa announced.

Kelly rose to her feet, crossed the room and took Karissa's face between her hands. She planted a big kiss, directly on her lips and abruptly stepped back.

Karissa stumbled back a step. "Wow! What was *that* for?"

"For giving me a few moments alone with my girl. You're a good friend, 'Rissa," Kelly said.

Karissa pushed Kelly back with a hand on her shoulder. "It's about time you called me by my nickname! And…you're welcome. So, let's get this party started!"

***

Cat and Billie cuddled on the couch watching a movie in the quiet house. The only light came from the television screen.

"Those girls were pretty wound up tonight," Billie said.

"Yes, they were. It reminds me of when I was a kid. My sisters and I, and our friends, would have slumber parties well into the night. We danced around in our panties and T-shirts, gossiped, played games and ate ourselves silly. Now I know how my parents must have felt. I mean, I could have gone to bed hours ago, but I don't think I would have slept until they settled down for the night. Surely you must have done the same as a kid," Cat said.

"Actually, no. I was an only child, and my parents were older than those of my peers. No slumber parties for me. It sounds like fun, though."

Cat turned around to look at her wife. "You seriously didn't have any slumber parties as a kid?"

"No, I didn't."

"That's sad."

"You don't miss what you don't know, I guess."

"I suppose." Cat yawned.

"Time for bed," Billie announced.

"Not until Seth gets home," Cat said.

As if on cue, the sound of a door opening could be heard from the kitchen.

"Seth?" Cat called out.

Seth peeked his head into the living room. "You two are still up? It's after midnight."

"Your sister had a slumber party tonight. Mother Hen here wouldn't go to bed until they settled down," Billie said.

"Did you have a good time with Steve?" Cat asked.

"Sure did! He got a dank new video game. It took some doing, but we beat it tonight." Seth kissed both his mothers on the cheek. "I gotta work tomorrow, so I'm hitting the sheets."

"Good night, love," Cat said.

"Night, Seth," echoed Billie.

Cat reached for her crutches and rose to her feet. She nodded toward the stairs. "All right, we can go to bed now."

Before going upstairs, they went to Tara's room. Slowly, they opened the door and looked in. The nightstand light was on, and all three girls were sound asleep in Tara's queen-sized bed. Tara and Karissa were facing one another; their heads nearly touching at their foreheads, and Kelly was spooned behind Tara, with her arm draped across Tara's waist. All three wore boxer shorts and T-shirts, askew in various positions around their bodies. Empty potato chip bags and soda cans littered the floor beside the bed.

Billie moved slowly across the room and turned out the light and made her way back to the door where Cat waited. They closed the door behind them. Cat looked up at Billie. "They look so cute and innocent when they're asleep."

"So that's what a slumber party looks like, huh?" Billie asked.

"Pretty much."

Billie took Cat into her arms. "I bet you were just as cute in your panties and T-shirt, sleeping all tangled up with your girlfriends."

"Right now, I'm looking forward to sleeping all tangled up with you."

Billie released Cat from her embrace and motioned toward the stairs to the second floor. "Lead the way, girlfriend!"

Chapter 8

Tara sat in her first period class on Monday and felt the hair stand up on the back of her neck. Someone was watching her. She glanced over her shoulder and noticed that Ryan sat in the next row, diagonally behind her. When their eyes met, he smiled. She awkwardly smiled back and returned her attention to what the teacher was saying. She tried to ignore her intuition for the rest of the class, but the nagging feeling of being watched persisted.

After class, Tara wheeled herself into the hallway and struggled to move her wheelchair into the stream of students heading for their second-period classes.

"Let me help."

Tara looked over her shoulder and saw Ryan behind her. "Thanks, Ryan," she said.

"Where's your next class," he asked.

"Science wing. Chemistry class. Room 101."

"First floor—got it!" Ryan maneuvered her through the throng of students until they reached the elevator. He pushed the button and grinned down at her while they waited for the doors to open. Finally, they were inside the elevator and the doors closed without admitting any other students.

Tara didn't know why, but she felt the awkwardness return. She looked up at him. "Thanks for the help, Ryan."

"Any time." A few seconds passed in silence before Ryan spoke again. "Sorry I missed you after the game on Friday. I got hung up in the locker room with the guys. Kind of a post-game victory celebration. You know?"

"No problem. My parents were in a hurry to get home anyway."

"Our next game is this Saturday. Are you going?"

"Probably. My brother plays, so I'm sure we'll go."

"Charland. Your brother is Seth, right?"

"Yes." The elevator door opened. "Here we are," Tara said.

Ryan pushed her out of the elevator. "Science wing. Room 101?" he confirmed.

"Yep!"

They arrived at Tara's chemistry class a few minutes later.

"I can take it from here, Ryan. Thanks again for the help," Tara said.

"No problem. Gotta bounce or I'll be late for my own class. See you later?" Ryan asked.

"On the flip side!" Tara replied. She watched him walk away. *He seems like a nice guy. Now I've just got to figure out how to get him interested in 'Rissa.*

***

Tara sat across from Kelly in the lunchroom. She reached across the table and squeezed Kelly's hand. "Before 'Rissa gets here, we need to think about how to get Ryan interested in her."

"What?" Kelly replied. "Don't you think 'Rissa should get her own boyfriends?"

"The problem is…she won't. She's too shy."

"So how do you propose we help her?"

"I don't know. I was hoping you'd have some ideas."

Kelly raised her eyebrows. "Are you forgetting I'm gay? I don't have a clue about how to attract guys."

"It can't be much different than attracting girls. How did you get me?"

"Really, Tara? You were there when it happened."

"Yeah, but, I mean…did you have a plan?"

"Jeez, Tara. This is embarrassing to talk about."

"Not a lot happens by accident, Kel. When did you realize you liked me?"

"I realized it the first time I saw you. You and 'Rissa walked by my house when we were moving. I thought 'Rissa was your girlfriend."

"Why would you think that?"

"Because you were holding hands."

"I've been friends with her since I was four. She's my best friend. We hold hands all the time."

"Well, I didn't know that in the beginning. Anyway, I knew I liked you that first time I saw you."

"So, how did you decide to talk to me?"

"I was scared, but I didn't think you had noticed me, so I had to take the first step."

Tara smirked. "I don't think 'Rissa is as brave as you."

"I think you're right."

"That's why we need to help her," Tara said.

"I'm not so sure that's a good idea."

"How else will Ryan notice her?"

Kelly's attention was caught by a movement from across the room. She looked up to see Karissa waving at them. "Shh…here she comes."

"Hey, peeps!" Karissa said. She placed her tray on the table beside Kelly and sat down.

"Hey, 'Rissa," Kelly and Tara said at the same time.

"Guess what?" Karissa said; excitement filling her voice. "Ryan said hi to me when he passed me in the hall."

"Really?" Tara said. "That's awesome!"

"It was more than awesome. It was majorly high-key!"

Kelly leaned forward. "It'll be all for nothing if you don't take it a step further, 'Rissa."

"What do you mean?" Karissa asked.

"I mean, the next time you see him in the hall, it's *your* turn to say hi," Kelly explained.

Karissa sat back in her seat. Her eyes grew wide. "I…I don't know if I can."

"Bruh!" Tara said. "Kelly is right. If you don't show some interest in return, he'll just think you're stuck up or something."

"But I'm afraid. What if I flub it?"

"Balls, 'Rissa," Kelly said.

"I know…I know!" Karissa replied.

***

After social studies class that afternoon, Kelly made her usual hand-off of Tara to Karissa in the lobby of the school so that Karissa could escort her to their volleyball class. As Karissa wheeled Tara down the hall, they almost ran directly into Ryan who stepped into the hall from a classroom. He had to quickly jump out of the way to avoid being run over by Tara's wheelchair.

"Oh, my God!" Karissa exclaimed. "I'm so sorry!"

Ryan quickly regained his composure. "No problem. It was my fault. I should've looked before I walked into traffic. My driver's ed teacher would have flunked me if I had done that in a car!"

"Well, I should be more careful too," Karissa said.

"No worries. I'm glad no one got hurt. I can imagine a collision wouldn't have felt very good on Tara's leg either."

"You got that right!" Tara said.

"Sorry again," Karissa said.

Ryan put his hand on Karissa's arm. "Don't worry about it. My fault. I'll be more careful next time." He looked at the clock on the wall. "Time for my next class. I'll see you guys later."

Karissa turned to watch Ryan walk away. Her heart beat wildly in her chest. "Wow! That was close," she said.

"That was awesome," Tara added. "See—that wasn't so hard."

Karissa continued to push Tara toward the gym. "What wasn't so hard?"

"You broke the ice with him. It won't be so hard to talk to him next time you see him."

Karissa grinned. "You're right!"

***

Ryan peeked his head into the gym at the end of Tara and Karissa's volleyball class. Tara was alone in the gym, as the rest of the class had gone to change out of their gym clothes. Ryan pushed the door completely open and walked in,

"Hey, Ryan!" Tara said.

"Hi, Tara. I'm glad I caught you."

"What's up?" Tara asked.

"We talked about the football game on Saturday. I was wondering if you're up to going to a post-game get-together after."

Tara paused for a moment. "I'm not sure if the girls have plans yet. I'll check with them and get back to you."

Ryan frowned. "Do you spend *all* your free time with them?" he asked.

"Pretty much. They're my fam—you know—my squad. Don't you have close friends like that?" she asked.

"Not really. Not yet, anyway. I haven't been here long enough to have friends that close."

"'Rissa and I have been friends since we were four years old. Kelly came on the scene less than a year ago, but we immediately clicked. We spend as much time as we can together, 'cause you never know when something will separate us. Know what I mean?"

"I *do* know what you mean. I had to leave my best friend behind when we moved here from Syracuse last summer. It was hard."

"Why did you move? Did your dad get a new job or something?"

"No. He didn't get a new job. He still has his old job and he commutes back and forth on the weekends."

"So…why did you move to Albany?" Tara asked.

"We kind of had to move. The neighborhood we were living in didn't really want our kind around. They didn't agree much with our beliefs."

"What kind of beliefs?"

Ryan shook his head. "It's not important. It's all in the past now."

"I can't believe you had to leave town because of beliefs. What on earth could be so bad to make you have to move?"

"Just beliefs. That's all. It wasn't too bad until I got into trouble at school."

"What kind of trouble?"

"I got into a couple of fights. I mean, a person has a right to defend their beliefs, right?"

"Absolutely, as long as they don't hurt others in the process. We don't all have to believe the same thing, you know," Tara stated.

Ryan shrugged. "I guess you're right. So…do you think you might be free on Saturday after the game?"

"I'll check with the girls and let you know."

Ryan shoved his hands into his pockets. "Okay. I guess I'll head home. I have lots of homework to do, and my mom will send out a search party if I'm late."

Tara laughed. "Parents!" she exclaimed. "Mine are kind of overprotective, too. I'll see you tomorrow."

Tara watched Ryan leave, and as he pulled the door to the gym open, to his surprise, Kelly was on the other side.

"Ah! You scared me, Ryan!" Kelly exclaimed.

"Sorry about that," Ryan said. A big smiled graced his features. "Tara's waiting for you. Maybe I'll see you after the game on Saturday."

Kelly hid her confusion behind a smile. "Maybe," she said. She watched him leave the gym and turned to Tara. "What was *that* all about?"

"He wants us to go to some post-game party with him on Saturday."

"Did you tell him we'd go?"

"No. I said I would check with you and Karissa to see if we had any plans."

"And *do* we have any plans?" Kelly asked.

"I don't know yet. I'm not even sure my moms would let me go to a party with a senior. If Seth and Steve go, maybe. Oh, and I need to feel 'Rissa out to see if she'd even be willing."

"She'd be willing, all right. If Ryan is there, she'll want to be there too."

"You might be right, Kel. Speaking of 'Rissa, here she comes."

Tara and Kelly looked across the gym and watched Karissa saunter toward them from the direction of the locker room.

"All set?" Karissa asked.

"Yes, as soon as I make a run to my locker to pick up my homework," Tara said. "I'll be right back."

"I'll go with you, Tare. I need to get my homework, too," Kelly offered.

"I'll wait out front for you. Seth and Steve should be pulling around in a minute or two," Karissa said.

Karissa went outside and waited at the curb with her back to the school. Suddenly, she felt a tap on her shoulder. She swung around quickly and saw Robert Johnson standing close behind her. "Jeez, Robert—you scared me!" she exclaimed.

Robert turned fifty shades of red and nearly fell over himself with apologies. "I'm sorry, Karissa. I didn't mean to scare you. I just saw you standing here alone and thought you might like some company."

"I'm just waiting for Tara and Kelly to get their homework. Our brothers should be here in a few minutes to pick us up," she explained. She looked around nervously, hoping Ryan wouldn't see her talking to Robert.

"I'll be quick. Some of the guys are organizing a party for after the football game on Saturday and I was wondering if you would like to go," he said hopefully.

Karissa's first instinct was to vehemently say no, but instead her curiosity was piqued. "Who'll be there?" she asked.

"I'm not sure yet. The guys are still organizing it. So far, it's me and Luke, James, Brian, Jeff, Tim and Ryan. It's supposed to be at Luke's house. His parents are going out of town on Friday and won't be home until Sunday. Maybe even your brother and Seth might come."

The only name Karissa heard was 'Ryan'.

"Really?" Karissa asked. "It sounds like fun. I'll check with Kelly and Tara to see if we have any plans yet."

Robert smiled broadly. "Cool! I'll catch up with you tomorrow." Robert walked toward the parking lot and stopped halfway to wave back at Karissa. Karissa waved just as Tara and Kelly exited the school.

Tara looked across the parking lot. "Was that Robert?" she asked.

"Yes. He stopped to see if we wanted to go to a party on Saturday after the football game," Karissa explained.

"And what did you tell him?" Kelly said.

"I told him that I would check with you two to see if we had any plans."

"You *do* realize you just agreed to be his date…right?" Tara pointed out.

Karissa looked as though she had been slapped. "No, I didn't!" she insisted.

"Ah…yeah, you did," Kelly agreed.

Chapter 9

The three friends settled into Tara's bedroom after school to do homework. Kelly and Karissa lay on their stomachs across Tara's bed, while Tara sat in her wheelchair beside them.

"So Luke's parents aren't going to be home?" Tara asked.

"That's what Robert said," Karissa replied.

"I'm not so sure it's a good idea to hang out with senior boys without their parents there," Tara pointed out.

"I agree with Tara. I'm sure if my dad found out he wouldn't let me go," Kelly added.

"What if Seth and Steve were there?" Karissa suggested.

"I'm not sure my moms would let Seth go either," Tara said. "I'll bet there will be booze."

"No duh! Of course there'll be booze there," Kelly added.

"I wonder why Ryan didn't mention to me that it would be unsupervised." Tara said.

"You *knew* about this before I told you?" Karissa asked. "*Ryan* told you?"

"Yes. He came to the gym while you were getting changed and invited us to go." Tara didn't mention that the original invitation was only for her, and that she had included Karissa and Kelly on their behalves.

Karissa sulked.

"While I was talking to him about the party, he mentioned that his family moved to Albany from Syracuse because of some trouble he got into at school," Tara said.

"What kind of trouble?" Kelly asked.

"Something about his beliefs."

"His beliefs? What does *that* mean?" Karissa said.

"I have no idea."

"Maybe his family belongs to some cult or something," Kelly suggested.

"I don't know, but whatever it is, it was bad enough to make them move. I told him he was free to believe anything he wanted as long as it didn't hurt anyone else."

"So, are we going to this party or not?" Karissa asked.

"I'll talk to Seth about it when he gets home from work, but with no parents there...and if there's booze, I don't think we should go unless he and Steve go too," Tara said.

Kelly nodded. "I agree."

***

As soon as Tara knew Seth was out of work, she sent him a text asking him to seek her out when he got home so they could talk about Saturday.

Seth was home just before dinner. Instead of going directly upstairs to shower, he bee lined to Tara's room and knocked on the door.

Seth peeked in when she responded. "I got your text," he said.

"Seth! You're home. Come in. Shut the door."

Seth came in and sat on the edge of Tara's bed. "So, what's up about the game on Saturday?" he asked.

"Well...it's not really about the game. It's about the party after the game."

Seth stood up. "You are *not* going to that party, Tara."

"Why not?"

"Because there won't be any adults there...and there will probably be alcohol and maybe even drugs."

"Are you going?"

"I don't know yet."

"Mom and Mama wouldn't want you there either without supervision."

"I know that, Tara. I don't really want to go, but I haven't come up with a reason yet that won't make me look like a mama's boy."

"What about Steve?"

"Steve doesn't want to go either."

"Well, 'Rissa wants to go. She wants to go really bad."

"Why would 'Rissa want to go?"

"Because she has a big crush on Ryan Porter, and he's going."

"Really? He's kind of odd."

"What do you mean by that?" Tara asked.

"He's really quiet…and he hasn't made many friends—even on the football team. Besides, how does she even know Ryan is going to the party?"

"Because he asked *me* to go with him, and I told 'Rissa he asked all of us to go," Tara confessed.

"He asked *you* to go with him…but it's 'Rissa that has the crush on him?"

"Cray-cray, I know," Tara replied.

"How does Kelly feel about Ryan asking you to go with him?"

"She doesn't know he asked only me. I made it sound like he asked all three of us."

"You're playing with fire, Tare. If she finds out you lied to her, she won't be happy."

"I know—especially when she's already jealous of Ryan."

Seth frowned. "Has he been harassing you? If he has, I'll…"

"He hasn't been harassing me, Seth. Actually, he's been really polite. I just feel really bad for 'Rissa."

Seth paced across the room. "How did you get yourself mixed up in a mess like this, Tara?"

"I don't know. Look…I don't really want to go to this party either. Maybe together we can think up a way to get us both out of it without looking like weenies."

"I'll talk to Steve tomorrow. Something tells me that this party is bad news."

Tara opened her arms to her brother, who promptly hugged her. "Thanks, bro."

Seth released her and stood up. "For what?"

"For being my brother…and for loving me, no matter how much of a pain I am."

"You wouldn't do any less for me, Sis. I need to get washed up before dinner. I'll see you in a few."

Tara watched Seth leave her room, and then promptly picked up her phone. She dialed Kelly's number. "Hey, Kel. I just talked to Seth about the party on Saturday night. He said that we shouldn't go. He thinks there will be alcohol and maybe even drugs there."

"Is he going?" Kelly asked.

"He doesn't want to."

"Maybe you and 'Rissa and I can plan to do something with Seth and Steve so they have an excuse not to," Kelly suggested.

"That's a good idea."

Tara fell silent for a few moments.

"Tare? Are you still there?"

"Yeah, I'm here. Kel, I have something to tell you."

Tara heard a pause on the other end of the line.

"Kelly?"

"I'm here. What is it you have to tell me?"

"I kind of stretched the truth about Ryan asking us to the party on Saturday."

"What do you mean?"

"Well, he kind of asked only me and I included you and 'Rissa when I answered him."

"And if me and 'Rissa didn't object, would you have agreed to go without us?" she asked.

"No! No—I wouldn't. I thought he would change his mind when he found out he had to be with all three of us. You were right, Kel. He's been flirting with me. He's not interested in 'Rissa at all."

"Why didn't you just tell him no?" Kelly demanded.

"I don't know, Kel. I just didn't know what to do."

"I'll tell you the same thing I told 'Rissa. Balls! Grow some balls!"

***

The three girls sat in the lunchroom the next day. Karissa leaned defiantly toward her friends. "Well, I'm going anyway," she said.

"'Rissa, you can't!" Tara said.

"Yes, I can…and I will," Karissa insisted.

"We can't let you do that, 'Rissa. It won't be safe," Kelly pointed out.

Karissa looked pointedly at Kelly. "You can't *let* me do that? Since when did you become my mom?"

Kelly raised her hands. "I'm done here," she said. She rose to her feet and picked up her tray. "If you won't listen to reason, I guess there's no point in arguing."

Tara and Karissa watched Kelly walk toward the dish room with her tray.

"Aren't you going to run after her?" Karissa asked sarcastically.

"'Rissa, she cares about you. Don't be angry with her," Tara said.

"If she cared, she would want me to have a boyfriend."

"So you think going to a party with drugs and alcohol will get you a boyfriend?" Tara said.

"Well, I'm not going to get one by just hanging out with you two!"

Tara sat back, stunned. It felt as though Karissa had just slapped her across the face. She didn't know what to say, so she just sat there, dumbfounded.

"I'm going to the party if you like it or not," Karissa declared as she stood and walked away from the table with her tray.

***

Tara didn't see Karissa for the rest of the day, until they were forced to meet on the sidewalk in front of the school where they waited for Seth to pick them up. Tara heard Karissa's voice before she saw her.

"I'll see you at school, tomorrow, Robert."

Tara swung her chair around and saw Karissa and Robert walking toward them. Karissa was smiling brightly at Robert.

"Later, Karissa," Robert said. They parted ways and he walked toward the parking lot.

Tara watched as he practically skipped away. "You shouldn't be playing with him like that," she said to Karissa.

"What do you mean? I'm not playing with him." Karissa was indignant.

"You're leading him on, 'Rissa."

"I am not."

"Yes, you are. He's your ticket to the party on Saturday."

"You're just jealous," Karissa said.

Tara so wanted to tell her that Ryan's original invitation was only for her, but she couldn't bring herself to hurt her friend. "Are you forgetting I have a girlfriend?" Tara said instead.

As if on cue, Kelly exited the school and jogged toward them. "Hey, Tara...'Rissa," she said. Kelly put her hand on Tara's shoulder and squeezed.

"Hi, Kel," Tara responded.

Kelly looked at Karissa. "Are you still mad at me?" she asked.

Karissa just turned her back on Kelly.

"I'll take that as a yes," Kelly said.

Seth pulled his car to the curb in front of where the girls stood. Steve was in the passenger seat. Steve promptly jumped out and helped Tara settle into the seat he had just vacated while the other two girls climbed into the back. Soon, they were on their way home.

***

Steve, call me.

Tara text her best friend's brother.

Why?

It's about 'Rissa. Urgent!

Tara's phone rang. "Steve?"

"Yeah. What's up with 'Rissa?" Steve asked.

"She's about to do something dangerous and I was hoping you could stop her. I really don't want to get our parents involved, but I will if I have to."

"What's that little dweeb up to now?"

"I don't know if Seth told you, but she plans to go to the party after the football game on Saturday."

"Like hell she is!" Steve exclaimed.

Tara could feel Steve's anger on the phone. "That's what I told her, but she really likes Ryan Porter and he's going to be there."

"Well, I'll set the record straight with her as soon as I hang up with you. That party is no place for someone 'Rissa's age to be."

"Yeah. Seth told me there will be booze and drugs there."

"And no parents. I won't let her go, Tara."

"I was hoping you'd say that, but I was thinking that maybe we could all do something else on Friday night. You know—like maybe go to the arcade together or something like that?"

Steve paused before answering. "You know, that might work. Seth and I don't really want to go to the party anyway. That might be our excuse. I'll talk to Seth about it."

"Thanks, Steve. Oh, and don't let 'Rissa know I talked to you. She's kind of mad at me and I don't want to make it worse."

"Got it."

***

Karissa scowled at Tara the next morning when she got into the car. Tara's heart sank and she realized Steve's discussion with Karissa the night before might not have gone well.

The ride to school that morning was quiet, but tense. Seth dropped the girls off at the curb in front of the school and drove away. As soon as Karissa's feet hit the sidewalk, she walked away, without even a notice of her two friends.

Kelly walked up behind Tara and took control of her wheelchair. "What's up with her? She's really salty this morning," Kelly said.

"I talked to Steve last night about the party after the football game. He said he wouldn't let her go. I'm guessing it didn't go too great," Tara said.

"Ouch! I can see why she's mad."

Tara looked up at Kelly. "Kel...I couldn't just stand by and let her go to that party. What if something happened to her?" Tara defended her interference.

"Chill, Tare. I didn't say you did anything wrong. I'm just sayin' I see why she's upset."

Tara looked toward the door Karissa had disappeared through moments earlier. "I kind of feel bad about going behind her back, but I was worried about her."

"I'm worried too, Tare. I hope she doesn't break our squad up over this."

Chapter 10

Tara and Kelly cheered Steve on as he ran the ball in for a touchdown.

"That was awesome!" Tara yelled.

"That's my boy!" Fred said.

The final buzzer sounded. "That was a good game!" Kelly exclaimed.

"What did you think of your brother's touchdown, Karissa?" Jen asked.

Karissa, who had been sitting silently beside her mother, shrugged.

"I thought it was amazing," Billie said.

Cat leaned forward to see beyond Billie. "Tara, so you and the girls are going to the arcade with Seth and Steve?"

"Yeah. Pizza and games. It should be fun," Tara said.

Billie stood. "I guess we should head back to the car in case Sky and Missy get there first."

Cat, Jen and Fred also stood.

Jen addressed the girls. "So you three are going to wait for Seth and Steve, right?"

"Yes," Kelly and Tara said together.

"Be sure to stay together, okay?" Billie said.

"We will. Sheesh! Don't worry so much, Mom!" Tara complained.

Cat kissed her daughter on the cheek. "Some day, when you're a mom, you'll understand."

The adults descended the bleachers and started toward the parking lot. Billie looked over her shoulder. "Tell your brother not to keep you out too late!" she called.

Kelly watched the parents walk away. "What is it about parents? Mine act the same way. We're not little kids anymore."

"No kidding!" Tara added.

"Where are we supposed to meet Seth and Steve?" Kelly asked.

"Just outside the locker rooms," Tara replied.

"They're gonna to be a while. I need to run to the bathroom. Wait for me. I'll be right back," Karissa said.

"Okay. We'll be right here," Tara said.

Kelly waited until Karissa was out of earshot. "She's in a mood."

"I know. She hardly said a word throughout the whole game," Tara replied.

"She's gonna to be a downer at the arcade."

"We just need to cheer her up."

A half hour later, Karissa hadn't returned.

"What the heck? Where is she?" Tara complained.

"There's probably a line at the bathroom. What's up with that, anyway?" Kelly said. "There's *never* a line at the men's room."

"That's because they don't care what a mess they leave. I had to use a men's room once and it was gross. There was pee all over the floor. They don't clean up after themselves."

"Not to mention they go in there three or four at a time. Can you imagine peeing in the same room with other girls without a wall between you?" Kelly made a distasteful face.

Tara looked around. "Maybe we should go look for her."

"Maybe we should. The bathroom is on the way to the locker room anyway."

It took fifteen minutes for Kelly to push Tara across the football field to the school. By the time they reached the women's bathrooms, there was no one around.

"Wait here. I'll check it out," Kelly said. She left Tara in the hall and entered the women's bathroom. "'Rissa? Are you in here?" she called out loud.

No answer.

Kelly methodically pushed each of the stall doors open and soon realized she was the only one in the room. She quickly rejoined Tara in the hallway. "She's not in there."

"Great! She's probably given us the slip. Damn her!" Tara said.

Kelly grabbed the handles of her chair. "Let's go to the locker rooms. Maybe she's there."

A few moments later, they arrived at the locker rooms. The hallway outside was empty. While they waited, Tara pulled out her phone and called Karissa's number. It rang five times before it went to voicemail. "'Rissa, we're here waiting for you at the locker rooms. Call me when you get this message."

Kelly and Tara waited for the next fifteen minutes for Karissa to call back. The phone never rang.

"Ahh! Karissa, what the hell are you thinking?" Tara yelled.

"Calm down, Tare," Kelly said.

"What do you mean, calm down? 'Rissa has probably run off with Robert to that party!"

"I know. But panicking isn't going to help. We need to wait for Seth and Steve and then go look for her."

It was another twenty minutes before Seth and Steve exited the locker rooms. In that time, Kelly returned to the ladies' room twice to be sure they hadn't missed Karissa. Both times, she returned to Tara without their friend in tow.

Steve stepped into the hall, followed by Seth. He stopped short when he saw Kelly and Tara. "Where's 'Rissa?" he asked.

Tara fought back tears. "We don't know. She said she had to go to the bathroom, but she didn't come back."

"How long ago was that?" Steve asked.

"It's been almost an hour now," Kelly said.

Steve looked at Seth. "That's probably why Robert was in such a hurry to get out of here. Did you try calling her cell?" Steve said.

"Yes, but she didn't answer. I even left a voicemail," Tara replied.

"We need to find her," Seth said. "No doubt she's gone to the party."

"Let's go," Steve said.

***

The four teenagers piled into Seth's car. Seth looked at Steve. "The party is at Luke's house—right?"

"Yes."

"What's the address?"

Steve looked at Seth; a blank expression on his face.

"You don't know where he lives?" Seth asked incredulously.

"Do you?" Steve asked.

"Hell no!"

"That's great. Karissa's out there somewhere and we don't even know where to begin looking for her," Steve said.

"What's Luke's last name?" Tara asked from the back seat.

"Gregowski," Seth replied.

"There can't be too many people named Gregowski in this town. Let me look it up on the web," Kelly suggested. She pulled her phone out of her pocket and typed the name in. "Okay, let' see—World War I New York soldiers, Albany county records search, search public records. Let me try that one." A moment later, she cried out. "Bingo! There's one Gregowski family in Albany. Richard Gregowski, 345 Elmwood Avenue."

"That's a part of the city I'm not familiar with. Let me program the address into my GPS," Seth said.

By the time they left the school in search of Karissa, a full ninety minutes had passed. Steve held Seth's phone up so that the screen was visible to him as he drove.

"I'm going to wring her neck for ducking out on us," Steve said as they rode.

"I just hope she's okay," Tara said.

It took twenty minutes for them to reach Elmwood Avenue. They turned down the street and could tell immediately which house was Luke's, as cars lined both sides of the road in front of it. There were also groups of teenagers hanging out on the front stoop—most holding drinks in their hands—and there was loud music coming from within.

Seth pulled up behind the line of cars, as close to Luke's house as he could get. He looked into the back seat. "You two stay here. We'll be right back."

"I'm going with you," Tara demanded.

"Think, Tara! If things get rough, we'll need to get out of there fast. That won't be easy with your wheelchair," Seth said.

"Okay! Okay! Just hurry," Tara replied.

Steve was already waiting on the sidewalk by the time Seth got out of the car.

"Okay. So here's the plan..." Steve said.

Seth and Steve approached the front steps and it became readily apparent that several of the teenagers were already in various states of inebriation.

"Wow, dude, they must have started drinking even before the game ended," Steve whispered to Seth.

"Let's hope we're not too late," Seth replied. He high-fived several of his teammate who sat on the steps as he made his way into the house. Steve followed close behind. Once inside, they encountered their host.

Seth grabbed Luke's hand and chest-bumped him. "Hey, Luke. Sorry we're late. We got stuck talking to the coach in the locker room."

"Great party, dude," Steve added.

"Glad you could make it," Luke said. There's beer in the fridge, and if you're interested in something stronger, let me know and I'll hook you up."

"Beer is good for now," Seth said.

They made their way to the kitchen while keeping an eye out for Karissa. The house was crowded with many of their teammates, but they also noticed several others their age that they did not know.

Seth reached into the refrigerator and grabbed two bottles of beer. He handed one of the bottles to Steve. "Here."

"Ah, I don't really want it," Steve said.

"Neither do I, but at least carry it around."

"Got it," Steve said.

"Have you seen her yet?" Seth asked.

"No. You?"

"No. Let's mingle. Maybe she's in another room."

Seth and Steve made their way back into the dining room, clinking bottles with other partygoers along the way. They moved slowly through the dining room and into the living room.

Still no sign of Karissa.

The boys made their way back toward the front door, which opened into the vestibule in front of a set of stairs to the second story. Seth looked up the stairs and back at Steve. "Dude?" he said.

A look of fear crossed Steve's face. "Jesus, Seth. I hope to God she's not up there."

Seth and Steve quickly ascended the stairs and stood on the landing at the top.

"Shh! Listen," Steve said.

Sounds could be heard coming from a closed door to their right. It took a split second to cross the distance between the landing and the door. Seth turned the handle and threw the door open. Inside they saw a young man, clumsily fondling a girl on the bed. Steve rushed to the bed and forcefully pushed the boy off the girl and onto his back on the bed beside her.

"What the hell?" the boy exclaimed.

"Ryan?" Seth said.

"You better have a good reason for this," Ryan said angrily.

Seth looked at the girl on the bed. Thankfully, she was still fully clothed. "Amanda?" he asked.

"Hi, Seth." Amanda giggled.

It was apparent to Seth that the girl was either drunk or high. He narrowed his eyes at Ryan. "What did you do to her?" he demanded.

Ryan climbed off the bed and pushed Seth's shoulder. "None of your business."

Seth reached his hand forward to Amanda. "Come with me if you don't really want to do this."

Amanda began to cry and reached for Seth's hand. He led her into the hallway. "Wait right here," he said. He went back into the room, where he found Steve standing above Ryan, who was lying on the floor. His nose was bleeding.

"I don't know what my sister sees in you, Porter. Stay away from her," Steve warned.

Ryan wiped the blood from his nose with the back of his sleeve. "I wouldn't touch her if she was the last girl on earth," he said.

"Lucky her," Steve said and punched Ryan once more. He reached down and grabbed Ryan's shirt. He cocked his fist back, ready to strike again. "Is Karissa here?" he demanded.

"I'm guessing you're too late," Ryan said from his position on the floor.

"What the hell does that mean?"

"Johnson took her into the basement about a half hour ago."

Steve released his hold on Ryan's shirt and dropped him to the floor. He looked up at Seth.

"I'm right behind you, Steve," Seth said.

Both boys ran into the hallway, and Steve immediately noticed that Amanda was gone. With no time to look for her, he followed Steve down the stairs as he took them three at a time. They stopped at the bottom and looked around frantically for the cellar door.

"There!" Seth said. He pointed to an open door in the hallway between the living room and den.

They pushed their way through the crowded living room and quickly ran down the cellar stairs, which emptied into a large and moderately furnished family room. There on the couch, they saw Karissa lying under Robert.

"You son of a...," Steve yelled. He grabbed Robert by the shoulders, yanked him off Karissa and threw him on the floor. Steve immediately pounced on him and threw several punches at his jaw before Seth pulled him off.

"Steve! Steve, he isn't worth it. Karissa needs our help."

The sound of Karissa's name snapped Steve out of his tirade. "Karissa?"

Both boys looked at Karissa who was unconscious on the couch. She still wore all of her clothing.

Steve's fists clenched again and he looked at Robert cowering on the floor.

Seth grabbed his arm. "He's not worth it," he said again. "Come on. We need to get Karissa out of here."

Steve leaned over his sister and hefted her onto his shoulder. He followed Seth up the stairs, through the living room and out the front door. Seth did his best to clear a path through the kids on the front stoop and soon, they were on the sidewalk and on their way to the car.

"Oh, my God," Tara said when she noticed them walking quickly toward the car. "Kelly! Quick! Open the door."

Kelly scrambled across the back seat and opened the door nearest the sidewalk.

As soon as Steve reached the car, he fell to his knees and gently sat an unconscious Karissa on the seat. From inside the car, Kelly put her arm under Karissa's knees, and between them, she and Steve slid her across the seat until she was inside the car far enough for Kelly and Steve to fit on either side of her. Seth climbed into the front seat, started the car, and pulled away from the curb. No sooner had they reached the end of the road than several police cars turned onto Elmwood Avenue, with sirens blaring.

Tara did her best to turn around in her seat but was encumbered by the cast on her leg. "What's happening?" she asked. "Is 'Rissa okay?"

Kelly checked Karissa out as thoroughly as she knew how. "She's breathing, but she won't wake up," Kelly said.

Steve gently slapped Karissa's face. "Come on, sis. Wake up," he urged.

Karissa groaned and tried to shoo Steve's hand away.

He slapped her face again. "Open your eyes, Karissa."

"Nooo," she wailed.

Tara looked at her brother. "What are we going to do, Seth?"

"We're taking her home. Mama will know what to do," he replied.

"We can't! 'Rissa will be in so much trouble if we do that!"

"I'd rather she get in trouble than die," Seth said bluntly.

Tara sat back like she was slapped. "Do you really think she'll die?"

"I don't know, Tara," Seth said sharply. "We have no idea what he gave her."

"I should call Mama and let her know we're coming," Tara said.

"That's a good idea. Tell her we'll be home in about twenty minutes." Seth looked into the rearview mirror. "Steve, you might want to call your parents too."

***

Fred pulled the door open before the car came to a complete halt. Steve quickly scurried out and hefted his sister into his arms, and promptly transferred her to his father. Fred ran into Cat and Billie's house with his precious cargo and placed her on the couch. Cat was immediately by her side and in full doctor mode. Jen knelt on the floor beside her and held Karissa's hand.

Billie paced back and forth across the living room while Cat examined Karissa.

After a cursory examination, Cat looked at Fred and Jen. "Her breathing and blood pressure are normal, and her eyes dilate when exposed to light. Those are all good signs." She tapped Karissa on the side of the face. "Karissa, sweetie. Can you hear me?"

"Hmmm."

"She's somewhat responsive," Cat said.

Billie stopped pacing. She looked at the four teenagers who waited nervously. "Who wants to tell me what happened here tonight?"

"We had plans to go to the arcade tonight. I swear it," Seth said.

"So, how did Karissa end up at that party...and how did you know where to find her?" Billie asked.

"We all knew about the party," Tara admitted. "But we knew there wouldn't be parents there."

"None of you went to the party?"

"None of us—except for Karissa," Tara said.

"Why on earth did you let her go to a party all by herself?" Billie's tone of voice increased in volume and in anger.

Tara began to cry. Kelly stepped forward and put her hand on Tara's shoulder.

"We didn't let her go by herself," Kelly said. "She was supposed to go to the arcade with us. We waited for her to go to the bathroom after the game, but she didn't come back."

"Why would she go all by herself?" Jen asked.

"There's a guy she likes. She knew he would be there," Seth offered.

Fred spoke for the first time since he carried Karissa into the house. "Cat, can you tell if she's been..."

"She wasn't," Steve said. "She had all her clothes on when we found her. And by the way, the guy she was with will be wearing two black eyes at school this week."

"If he's *at* school this week. The police arrived there just after we drove away," Seth said.

"The *police* came?" Billie asked.

"Yes, but not until after we left," Seth added.

"Whose house was it?" Billie asked Seth.

"Luke Gregowski's. He lives on Elmwood Avenue."

Karissa slowly awakened and looked around. "Mom?"

Tears filled Jen's eyes and Cat moved away to allow her better access to her daughter.

"Karissa, sweetie," Jen said.

Karissa struggled to sit up. "What happened?" she asked.

"I was hoping you could tell *us*," Jen said.

Karissa looked at all the people who were gathered around her. Her gaze stopped on Tara. "Tara, I'm sorry I ran out on you."

Tara nodded and tried to smile. "I'm just glad you're okay."

Fred stepped forward. "I want to know who this boy was that Steve and Seth found you with," he demanded.

"Boy?" she asked.

"Karissa, what do you remember?" Cat asked.

"I got to the party and hooked up with Amanda. Ryan gave me a glass of water to drink. I don't remember much after that."

Steve clenched his fists. "I'm going to pound those motherfu…"

"Steve!" Jen said sharply.

"Karissa, let me take a look at you one more time," Cat said and then proceeded to check her pulse, blood pressure and reflexes. She then stood and held her hands out to the girl.

"Give me your hands, sweetie."

Karissa did, and Cat encouraged her to stand and take a few steps across the room. She walked back to the couch and sat down again.

"Whatever it was she ingested in that drink, the effects have pretty much worn off." She looked at Karissa. "You're a lucky girl. Based on the state Seth and Steve found you in, it could have been a lot worse."

"It's going to be a cold day in hell before you're allowed out of the house again, young lady," Fred said.

Jen looked at her husband. "Fred, that's not helping."

"She could have been raped...or worse, Jen." Fred looked at his daughter. "You are grounded young lady. Other than spending time with Tara and Kelly and going to school, you are to be home. Do you understand?"

"But Dad!"

"I don't want to hear it, Karissa. What you did was reckless and irresponsible. You are grounded. No argument," Fred said.

Billie returned to the living room from the kitchen. With the chaos in the living room, no one had seen her slip into the other room to make a phone call. "According to my contacts at the police department, a few arrests were made tonight at 345 Elmwood Avenue. Under-aged kids at a drunken party."

She looked at Jen and Fred. "I'll find out who was arrested. There's a good chance it might be one of the boys responsible for Karissa's condition. It'll be up to you whether you want to press charges or not."

"You're damned right we're pressing charges," Fred exclaimed.

Chapter 11

The phone rang at nine o'clock, Sunday morning. Cat picked up the receiver. "Hello?"

"May I please speak to Billie Charland? This is the Albany police department."

"Yes. Hold on, please." Cat rested the phone receiver on top of the phone and went into the yard to find Billie, who was mowing the lawn. She motioned for Billie and held her hand to her ear in the universal sign language for phone call.

Billie immediately shut off the lawn mower and jogged across the lawn toward the house. "Is it the police?" she asked.

"Yes."

Billie ran past Cat and into the house. By the time Cat returned to the kitchen, Billie was nearly finished with her phone call. "Okay. Thanks for the information. I'll be in touch," Billie hung up the phone and turned to face Cat.

"Well?" Cat said.

"They arrested two boys, Luke Gregowski and Robert Johnson. They are apparently the only legal adults that were there. They're both eighteen. The rest of the kids were released to their parents' custody."

"They arrested Robert?"

Cat and Billie turned to see their son standing in the doorway to the kitchen.

"Yes. Was he the one who assaulted Karissa?" Billie asked.

"Yeah, but I have no idea if he's the one who drugged her," Seth said.

"Who do you think may have drugged her?" Billie asked.

"I don't know for sure, but it might have been Ryan Porter."

"He was not one of the ones arrested. What makes you think he might be involved?"

"Because when we found him with Amanda, he said we might be too late to save Karissa because Robert had taken her into the basement. He obviously knew what Robert had in mind."

"Karissa also said Ryan gave her a glass of water, and that she didn't remember much after that," Billie said. She walked to the other side of the kitchen before she turned and faced her son again. "Robert and Luke are being charged as adults for providing alcohol to minors. We will need to have a restraining order placed on Johnson if you think he's a threat to Karissa. If we do that, he will face an assault charge as well and a second trial. Are you willing to testify about what you saw?"

"Will Steve get into trouble for beating him up?" Seth asked.

"Steve beat him up?"

"Yes. He got a few good shots in after he pulled him off 'Rissa. I'm betting he doesn't look very good today."

"Steve is underage and I'm guessing the judge will be lenient...if it's mentioned at all."

"When I think about what he was going to do to Karissa, it makes me wish it was *me* hitting him instead of Steve. If it comes down to me testifying or him getting away with it, I will definitely testify."

"You said this Ryan guy was with a girl named Amanda?" Billie asked.

"Yes, but it didn't look like Amanda was fighting him. She might have been there willingly."

Billie grabbed a piece of paper. "You said his name was Ryan Porter? And what is Amanda's last name?"

"Uh huh, and Amanda's last name is Jacobs."

Billie wrote the names down. "Thanks, love. I'll call Jen and Fred today to see how they feel about Steve and Karissa testifying."

"Okay, Mom. I need to get to work. I'll be home for dinner."

Cat turned to Billie once Seth had left. "You know they won't let you take this case," she said. "You're too close to it."

Billie nodded. "You're right, but that doesn't mean I can't help to investigate it."

***

News spread rapidly at school on Monday morning. The school nurse and school counselor called Karissa to their office to see if she wanted to schedule therapy sessions, which Karissa promptly declined.

Ryan Porter was conspicuously absent from school on Monday, as were Luke Gregowski and Robert Johnson.

The girls felt as though they were under a microscope in the lunchroom. They could feel the sympathetic glances and hear the whispers of gossip all around them.

At one point, as they were finishing their lunch, Amanda Jacobs approached their table and sat down next to Karissa. Kelly, Tara and Karissa all froze and waited for her to speak. "Just so you know, it's your word against theirs. You don't stand a chance in court."

Billie had advised them to say nothing to their classmates about the weekend events, so all three remained silent.

"Anyway," Amanda said. "It would be in your best interest to forget it ever happened." She stood and paused for a moment. "Oh, and by the way, Ryan is way out of your league, Tara...not to mention, he's not into lezbos."

Amanda disappeared as quickly as she had appeared.

Kelly looked at Karissa. "Did she just threaten us?"

"I believe she did," Karissa responded.

Tara sat dumbfounded. Did Ryan really think she was into him? *Oh, gag!*

Ms. Warner held them for a few minutes after volleyball class that afternoon. "Karissa, I'm here if you'd like to talk."

"Ms. Warner, I don't even remember any of it. I only know what Seth and Steve told me. It makes me sick to think of what could have happened, but thanks to my brother and Seth..."

"Thank God for small favors," Ms. Warner said. "Anyway, the offer is open if you need to talk."

"Thanks, Ms. Warner."

***

The Charland and Swenson families planned a fall cookout for that evening. Not just to celebrate the end of the season, but also to discuss the events of the weekend.

Billie and Fred were tending the grill…with a significant amount of supervision by Jen and Cat.

"You know they're just pretending to let us cook," Billie said.

"They're pretending to *let* us cook just like we're pretending to actually *be* cooking!" Fred chuckled.

Billie laughed. "They are so busted!"

"So, Billie, what do we know about the kids who attacked my little girl?" Fred asked.

"Well, we know that Robert Johnson was caught red-handed, by our sons. Seth has agreed to testify. Have you had that discussion with Steve?"

"Steve is willing."

"That's good. Because Karissa was drugged, she has no memory of the event, so Seth and Steve are our only hopes for justice. Cat will also testify from a medical point of view."

"Has anyone else been charged besides Johnson?"

"Luke Gregowski was charged with aiding and abetting delinquent behavior in minors, but he should get off with just a fine. Other than that, they are the only two charged. Unfortunately, I have to recuse myself from this one, considering one of the witnesses is my son. I expect it will be several weeks, or even months before the trial."

"How credible will Seth and Steve be? Especially Steve. I mean, Johnson's lawyers could argue he's biased since his sister was the victim," Fred pointed out.

"That's true, and I expect them to take that position. We just need to have faith in the system."

"It's hard to have faith in anything right now. Heck, I was afraid to send Karissa to school this morning."

"I wonder how school went today. I'm sure the news must have spread like wildfire." Billie scanned the yard until she located Tara and Karissa. "Hey Tara, could you come here for a minute?"

Karissa took control of Tara's chair and pushed her across the yard.

"What's up, Mom?" Tara asked.

"Fred and I were wondering how school was today."

Tara glanced up at Karissa. "It was weird, don't you agree, 'Rissa?"

"Yeah. I mean, we got stared at all day. Oh, and we were threatened too," Karissa said.

"What?" Billie said, her protective mother instinct piqued. "Who threatened you?"

"Amanda. She stopped at our table at lunch. Let me see if I can remember what she said… 'It would be in our best interest if we forgot it ever happened'."

"Amanda Jacobs?" Billie asked.

"I think that's her last name," Karissa replied.

"Did you report her to the principal?" Fred asked.

"No. Look, Dad, we already feel like we're under a microscope. I don't want to make it worse," Karissa said.

"Girls, you need to understand that this *will* get worse before it gets better," Billie pointed out.

Karissa sighed. "I just want it to be over."

***

On Tuesday, Karissa sat in her English class taking notes, when there was a knock at the classroom door. The teacher excused herself for a moment and accepted a note from the person on the other side of the door. The teacher read the note and glanced briefly at Karissa before she moved on with the rest of her lesson plan. At the end of class, she asked Karissa to stay behind.

Karissa finished loading her class materials into her backpack and walked to the front of the room. "You wanted to see me, Mrs. Brown?"

Mrs. Brown handed the note to her. "Principal Geary would like to see you during your study hall, Karissa."

Karissa looked at the note and back at her teacher. "Am I in trouble?" she asked softly.

Mrs. Brown put her hand on Karissa's shoulder. "I don't think so, dear. If you were in trouble, you would have been pulled out of class right away. I wouldn't worry about it."

"Thank you, Mrs. Brown. My next class is study hall, so I guess I'll head there now." Karissa walked out of the room and went directly to the principal's office. When she entered, the receptionist looked up and immediately jumped to her feet.

"Karissa! Come with me, dear." The receptionist led her to the principal's office and knocked on the door. "Mr. Geary, Karissa Swenson is here."

The principal rose from his chair and stood behind his desk. "Come in, Miss Swenson. Please sit."

Karissa crossed the room and sat in the chair while the receptionist left the room and closed the door behind her.

Mr. Geary sat behind his desk and clasped his hands together. "Miss Swenson, I am aware of what happened this Saturday at Luke Gregowski's house. I want you to know that Robert Johnson has been suspended from school, pending the resolution of this issue."

"I...I don't remember what happened, Mr. Geary," Karissa said meekly.

Mr. Geary leaned forward. "Karissa, no one is blaming you for what may or may not have happened. I called you in here today to let you know that pending trial, Robert has been released on bail from police custody this morning. We have no idea if he'll try to come back to school or not, so we are going to assign someone to walk with you between classes and to wait outside the door while you're in class...at least until this is resolved through legal means. Our goal is to keep you safe. Do you understand?"

Karissa looked at the hands clasped in her lap and nodded.

Mr. Geary stood once more. "Good. Do you have any questions?"

"Do my mom and dad know?"

"Yes. I called them just before I sent the note to Mrs. Brown's class. They are understandably concerned, but grateful for the protection the school is providing."

He walked around his desk and placed his hand on Karissa's shoulder. "Don't worry, Karissa, we'll do everything we can to protect you. Now, give me a minute and I'll be right back with your escort."

***

Seth and Steve had football practice that day after school. They had nearly a full roster, with the exception of Robert Johnson. Ryan Porter and Luke Gregowski were both there, having been released from custody after being processed on Sunday. Throughout the practice, the boys scowled at both Seth and Steve…especially Ryan.

Near the end of the practice, the coach called for a match and divided the boys into two teams. Steve and Seth were assigned to the same team with Steve as the designated quarterback and Seth as the wide receiver. The two teams approached the line of scrimmage and the center snapped the ball to Steve. Before Steve could take two steps backward, Ryan charged through the line and roughly slammed him to the ground. The rest of the opposing team immediately piled on top.

The coach blew his whistle. "Hey! Porter, you know better than that. If this was a real game, you'd be charged with roughing the quarterback!"

One by one, the tackling team climbed off the pile. Ryan was the last one. He placed his hand on Steve's throat and used it as leverage to push off from Steve. Before he dismounted, he hit his helmet against Steve's and growled at him. "You are toast, Swenson!"

Steve coughed uncontrollably. The coach offered his hand to help him up. Steve bent at the waist and tried to regain control.

"On the bench, Porter!" the coach bellowed.

Seth ran in from the field. He placed his hand on Steve's back. "Steve! Are you all right?"

Steve took off his helmet and dropped it to the ground. He looked sideways at Ryan on the bench. "He sucker-punched me, Seth."

"He probably thinks it's payback for what you did to him on Saturday," Seth said.

"He *deserved* what I did to him on Saturday."

"You don't need to convince me, Steve."

"Practice over," the coach yelled. "Hit the showers."

Steve and Seth walked together into the locker room. They dropped their helmets on the floor in front of their lockers, which were located at least ten feet apart.

While Seth removed his jersey, he heard a loud slamming sound just a few feet away. He yanked his jersey the rest of the way off and noticed that Ryan had Steve pinned, face first, against his locker. "Let him go, Porter!" Seth yelled. When Ryan didn't comply, Seth grabbed him by the shoulder pads and slammed him against the adjacent locker with his arm bent up behind him.

"Let go of me, asshole!" Ryan yelled.

"Big man, aren't you? What's the matter? Don't like be blindsided like you did to Steve?" Seth said. Seth grabbed him again, swung him around, and slammed his back against the lockers. He moved his face close to Ryan's. "You'd better watch your step, Porter."

"You're pretty tough for a faggot!" Ryan said.

"What did you just say?" Seth demanded.

"Word is, your moms are lezbos, so you must be a faggot."

Seth grabbed him by the throat. "My moms have more integrity in their little fingers than you do in your whole body!"

"Let him go, Seth," Steve said. "He isn't worth the trouble."

Ryan glared at Steve. "So, are you two faggots together?"

"On second thought," Steve got into Ryan's face. "How about I blacken your *other* eye?"

Seth released him. "No, Steve, you were right. He's not worth it. I think I'll change and shower at home." Seth grabbed a T-shirt from his locker and slipped it over his head. Steve did the same.

Ryan stood by, with a smirk on his face. "Are you running away, little girls?" he needled.

Steve and Seth ignored him.

"You know your moms are going to hell, right? God hates fags. My pastor says all gays should be banished to an island and nuked."

"Shut up, Porter," Seth growled.

Ryan continued to rant. "Leviticus, chapter eighteen, verse twenty-two: You shall not lie with a male as a woman. It is an abomination. Chapter twenty, verse thirteen. If a man lies with a male as with a woman, both of them have committed an abomination. They shall surely be put to death!"

Seth snapped and pushed Ryan against the lockers once more. "I've had enough of your shit. Shut your mouth before you regret it."

Ryan grinned. "Faggot! Faggot! Rot in hell!" he chanted.

"Let me deal with this," Steve said. He pushed Seth away and landed a firm punch in Ryan's solar plexus, knocking the wind out of him. "There. If you can't breathe, you can't talk." He looked at Seth. "Let's go home."

***

Billie walked into the kitchen and dropped her briefcase on the shoe tray by the back door. She could smell the aroma of spaghetti sauce wafting from the covered pan on the stove. She also noticed a stockpot of hot water heating on the stovetop beside it.

Billie was just about to help herself to a taste of the sauce when Cat caught her red-handed. "I see you!" Cat exclaimed.

"Just one bite?" Billie gave Cat puppy dog eyes until she gave in.

Billie wiped her mouth with a napkin and kissed Cat soundly. She wrapped her hands around Cat's waist. "How was work today?"

"Relatively quiet for a change. No big emergencies to deal with—just scheduled surgeries. How was your day?" Cat asked.

"It was going great until I got a call on the way home that Robert Johnson has been released on bail, pending trial."

Cat stepped back. "Are you serious? Isn't that kind of fast?"

"The kid has no other record, and he didn't actually succeed in raping Karissa, so apparently someone in our judicial system didn't think he was a threat."

"I wonder if Jen and Fred know." Cat mused.

"I would think so. It's standard practice to warn the victim…or if they're underage…the victim's parents as soon as the perpetrator is released."

"Why is it they called *you*?" Cat asked.

"In part, because I asked my connections at the police department to keep me informed...and also in part because Seth is one of the witnesses."

Cat touched Billie's arm. "Do you think Seth might be in danger?"

"Honestly, I don't know. I guess it depends on how unstable Robert Johnson is. I would hope the police wouldn't release him if they thought he was a danger to others," Billie explained. "They will have him under surveillance, for sure, so that should minimize the risk."

Just then, Tara burst into the kitchen. "OMG!" she said. "Karissa has a bodyguard at school!"

"What?" Cat exclaimed.

"Karissa has a bodyguard at school. He followed her to all her classes today, and even to lunch. She's kind of freaking out about it, and so are her mom and dad."

Billie took Tara's hand. "It's for her protection, Tare. I'm sure she's not in any immediate danger. The school is just being cautious."

"He even escorted her to the bathroom! Doesn't that seem a little over the top to you?" Tara said.

"If it was you instead of Karissa, I would welcome it," Billie said. "If Robert Johnson decided to return to the school, there is no telling what kind of mood he might be in. I'd rather Karissa has too much protection, than not enough."

"Well, it's weird," Tara said. "Do you know how hard it is to girl talk at lunch with a bodyguard nearby?"

Cat put her hand in front of her mouth to hide a grin.

Billie squeezed her hand. "Hopefully, this won't last long, Tare. Until then, suck it up and deal with it, because it's for Karissa's protection...and yours and Kelly's as well. Okay?"

Chapter 12

Ryan followed Kelly, Tara and Karissa, as well as Karissa's bodyguard, into the elevator the next morning while on their way to their first period English class on the second floor. He pushed the number two on the panel and turned to address the girls. "I want to apologize for what happened at the party on Saturday, Karissa. You gotta know not all the football players are like Robert."

Karissa nodded, but didn't reply.

An awkward silence fell over the group.

"I mean…sometimes alcohol can change the way a person acts, but Robert's not usually like that."

"I think it would be best if we didn't talk about it, Ryan," Kelly said.

"Yeah. My mom said not to discuss it with anyone until after the trial. She's a lawyer, so she knows what she's talking about," Tara added.

Ryan frowned. "I don't know why you won't talk to me. I mean, it's not like *I* did anything wrong."

"We can't talk to anyone, Ryan," Tara said, just as the elevator door opened.

Karissa and her bodyguard left the elevator first, followed by Kelly and Tara, and then Ryan.

"Is he still following us?" Tara asked when they were halfway to their classroom.

Kelly quickly glanced back. "He's right behind us."

She increased her pace and ducked into Tara's English class, but hung by the door to see Ryan's progress down the hall. She saw him linger by the door to the class for a few moments before moving on.

She looked back to Tara. "He gives me the creeps. I'm majorly shook that he thinks he has a shot with you. Like you said, it doesn't take a rocket scientist to figure out we're gay," Kelly reasoned.

"He probably thinks he's irresistible and can't imagine a girl not being interested in him," Tara said.

Kelly pushed Tara to her usual seat. "I think he's gross."

"I don't think he's gross," Tara said. "I just don't want a relationship with him."

"I'll say it again—I think he's gross," Kelly repeated. "I gotta run to my class. See you at lunch."

***

At dinner that night, Tara relayed her encounter with Ryan earlier in the day.

Seth immediately leaned forward. "Stay away from him, Tara. He's bad news."

"What do you mean?" Cat asked.

Seth sat back in his chair and fell silent.

Cat reached for his hand. "Seth, what do you mean?"

Seth looked at his mother. Steve and I kind of had it out with him at practice yesterday."

"Define, 'had it out'," Billie said.

"Mom, I'm not sure this is the right time…"

"This is exactly the right time," Cat said. "We don't keep secrets in this family."

"Okay," Seth said. "We had a scrimmage during practice yesterday, and Ryan nailed Steve much harder than he should have. Even the coach yelled at him for it. We think he did it because Steve roughed him up at the party on Saturday."

"Is that all that happened?" Billie asked.

Seth looked nervously at both his mothers. "No."

"Go on," Cat said.

Seth sighed. "In the locker room after practice, Ryan did his best to tweak both me and Steve. He called us faggots."

"He called you what?" Cat exclaimed.

"What's a faggot?" Skylar asked.

Tara answered her little sister. "That's a bad name some people call boys who like boys."

"Like Mommy and Mama?" Skylar asked.

"That's exactly what he meant, Sky," Seth said. He looked again at his mothers. "He actually called you two lezbos. He also said God hates fags."

Billie's jaw clenched.

"That's a pretty old slur. He must have heard that at home. I'm calling the principal tomorrow," Cat declared.

"Ma, don't," Seth said. "You wonder why I didn't want to say anything."

"I wonder if he knows *I'm* gay," Tara mused out loud.

"Your name didn't come up," Seth said. "I just want you to stay away from him. He's bad news."

***

After dinner, Tara retired to her room to do her homework. Once it was finished, she called Kelly. "Hey Kel. Whatcha doing?"

"Homework, ugh!" Kelly replied.

"I just finished mine. Hey, I wanted to tell you that Seth and Steve had a fight with Ryan after football practice yesterday."

"Really? About what?"

"I guess because Steve punched him out at the party on Saturday."

"Wow! Did they get in trouble?"

"No. The whole thing happened in the locker room and the coach wasn't there."

"I'm not going to say I'm sorry to hear that, Tara."

"Me either, but according to Seth, Ryan called him a faggot because of my moms."

"Seriously? Did he say anything about you?" Kelly asked.

"I asked Seth that, but he said my name didn't come up. Kel, I think we should be careful about PDAs at school. I don't want to invite any problems...especially from Ryan."

"Tara, since when are you concerned about what people think? I'm proud to call you my girl, and I don't want to hide it."

"I'm proud to *be* your girl, Kel, but I'm thinking it might be good to save our relationship for when we're not in school. I just don't want to make things difficult for us...or for Seth."

"I know you want to protect Seth, but it isn't fair," Kelly said.

"I'm asking you to understand, Kel. Please?"

Tara heard a deep sigh from the other end of the phone.

"Okay, Tara. I'll do it, but I don't like it," Kelly replied.

***

Ryan was waiting for Tara at the gym after volleyball class the next day. He sat on the bottom level of the bleachers and waited for her debriefing of the team to end. Tara had noticed him earlier, but resolved not to acknowledge him until class was through. She wheeled her chair toward the bleachers only after her classmates headed to the locker room. She acknowledged Karissa's bodyguard who was on his way to position himself outside the locker room door until Karissa came out.

"Hey, Ryan," Tara said. Secretly, she wished that Kelly would be arriving soon, but they had agreed to meet outside the school after the volleyball class.

"Hi, Tara. You know, you really have a talent for coaching," Ryan said.

"Thanks, but I'd rather be playing the game than coaching it."

"How much longer will you be in that chair?"

"Hopefully, I'll graduate to crutches in the next week or so. I'm really tired of the restrictions in this chair."

"Can't say that I blame you," Ryan said. "I'm kind of hoping you'll be on your feet before the Spring Fling dance. I'd like to take you."

Tara felt like she had been punched in the stomach. "Oh! I'm sorry, Ryan, but I already have a date for that dance."

Ryan looked as though he had been slapped. "Who's the lucky guy?" he asked.

"I'm not gonna say right now—in case things change between now and then."

"So, I still have a chance?" Ryan asked.

Karissa came out of the locker room before Tara could answer. "Hey, Tare. Are you ready to…" Karissa stopped dead when she saw Ryan with Tara.

Tara swung around quickly at the sound of Karissa's voice. "Hey, Rissa!" she said.

She looked back to Ryan. "Sorry to cut it short, but I gotta meet Seth out front so I don't make him late for work. I'll see you later."

Tara wheeled her chair toward Karissa, who stood paralyzed by the sight of Ryan. "Quick, push me!" Tara said softly.

Karissa snapped out of her inaction and took the handles of Tara's chair. She pushed Tara toward the exit, with her bodyguard walking beside them. Karissa didn't spare Ryan a glance as they walked by him.

Kelly was at the curb in front of the school, waiting for them.

"Did he follow us?" Tara said to Karissa.

Karissa covertly looked around. "I don't see him."

"Good."

"See who?" Kelly asked.

"Ryan," Tara and Karissa said together.

"Ryan?"

"Yes. He showed up at the gym near the end of volleyball class," Tara said.

"I told you I should have waited for you inside," Kelly said. "I won't make that mistake again."

The bodyguard approached the girls. "Excuse me, but I can't help but overhear. Is that young man threatening you?" he asked.

"No!" Tara exclaimed. "He just kind of likes me, but I'm already in a relationship. It's kind of weird, but I'm not afraid of him."

"Just checking," the bodyguard said. He walked a few feet away and stood by once more.

Karissa's eyes opened wide. "Ryan likes *you*?" she asked, incredulously.

Tara exchanged a grimace with Kelly, and then turned her attention to Karissa. "Unfortunately, yes. Sorry, 'Rissa."

"Some friend *you* are!" Karissa said. "You *know* I like him!"

"'Rissa, it's not like I'm encouraging him!"

"Have you even told him Kelly is your girlfriend?" Karissa asked.

"No, I haven't. That's really no one's business," Tara replied.

"I'm never going to have a chance with him unless he knows he doesn't have a shot with you," Karissa stated.

"'Rissa..."

"No, Tara. If you are really my friend, you'll tell him you prefer girls."

Kelly stepped forward. "'Rissa, part of me agrees with you, but that's Tara's decision."

Karissa turned hateful eyes on Kelly. "Doesn't it bother you that Ryan is interested in your girlfriend?"

"Yes, I'm shook about it, but I also trust Tara...and you should too."

Before the argument could escalate, Seth pulled his car up to the curb. Steve jumped out of the passenger seat to help Tara get in while Seth opened the trunk to store her wheelchair. All three girls fell silent.

Seth stepped onto the curb and looked at the girls. "Oh-oh. Trouble in bestie-land?" he teased.

Karissa stomped to the car. "What bestie?" she said as she climbed in.

***

Kelly stayed for dinner with Tara and her family. After dinner, they went to Tara's room and snuggled together on the bed to watch a movie on a popular streaming station.

When the movie was done, Kelly rolled onto her stomach and propped herself on her elbows. "Do you think 'Rissa will stay mad for very long?"

"I don't know," Tara said. "I can't blame her. She really likes Ryan."

"I don't think it's a good idea for her...or any of us...to be involved with him. I think Seth is right—he's bad news."

"I agree with you, Kel, but I don't think she'll listen to us. She's gonna have to find out for herself."

"But in the meantime, she's mad at you."

Tara shrugged. "She's been mad at me before. She'll get over it."

"I still think you need to tell him straight up."

Tara grinned. "I know. I need to grow some balls."

"Exactly." Kelly sat up again and sat cross-legged in front of Tara. Tara remained seated with her back against the headboard. "Do I have anything to worry about, Tare?" she asked seriously.

Tara leaned forward and kissed Kelly. She pulled her face away for a second and kissed her again—this time, more intensely. When the kiss ended, she looked directly into Kelly's eyes. "Does that answer your question?" she asked.

"Oh, yeah," Kelly replied. She leaned forward again for another passionate kiss.

Tara's insides felt like they were liquefied.

A knock on the door made them both jump.

"Yeah?" Tara said.

The door opened and Billie poked her head inside. "We're dishing out ice cream. Are you two interested?"

"Ice cream sounds good. Kelly?" Tara said.

"Yes! Yes—ice cream is good!" Kelly replied quickly.

"Be right back." Billie closed the door.

"Phew! That was close," Tara said.

"Maybe we should get our homework out before she gets back," Kelly suggested.

"Good idea!"

In the Blink of an Eye

Chapter 13

Karissa was still angry with Tara the next morning, and said nothing to her on the way to school. When she got out of the car in front of the school, she went immediately into the building and ignored her friends. Her bodyguard, who had been waiting for her on the curb, followed close behind.

Seth noticed the tension between them. "What's wrong with her?" he asked Tara.

"She found out that Ryan likes me instead of her."

Seth gently squeezed Tara's arm. "I've warned you about him, Tare."

"I know…and I want nothing to do with him. It's not my fault he likes me."

"Just be careful. You know how he feels about gay people."

"I will, Seth. Thanks for worrying about me."

"You're my sister, and I won't stand by and let someone hurt you. Besides, I wouldn't trust him with anyone—especially after we caught him with Amanda."

"Amanda?"

"Yeah. That night we found Karissa at the party, he was on top of Amanda in one of the bedrooms. We stopped him before anything happened."

"Seriously? And you are just *now* telling me this? Karissa needs to know."

"I'll ask Steve to have a talk with her. He cares as much about her as I do you…although he wouldn't admit it."

"I love you too, bro."

"All right. I'll see you after school."

"No you won't. I have a doctor's appointment this afternoon. Mama is coming to get me early, remember?"

Seth smiled. "That's right! You're being fitted for crutches. I bet you can't wait to get out of that chair."

"You bet I can't."

"All right, Sis. See you at home."

***

Ryan was waiting for Tara after her chemistry class. She didn't realize he was there until she felt someone take control of her wheelchair from behind. She assumed it was Kelly. "Thank you, love."

Ryan leaned forward. "You're welcome."

Tara nearly jumped out of her skin. "Oh, my God! I didn't realize it was you. I'm sorry, Ryan."

"No reason to be sorry. I don't mind. Where's your next class?"

"Algebra. Room 109."

"That happens to be right next door to my history class. Do you mind if I push you?"

A momentary feeling of panic filled Tara's chest, but she didn't want to be rude. "No. Not at all. I appreciate it."

Ryan pushed Tara in her wheelchair directly into her classroom and left to go next door to his history class. When he stepped out into the hall, he ran directly into Karissa, causing her to drop her books. He immediately stooped to collect them.

"Sorry, Karissa," he said. He handed the books back to her.

Karissa took the books from Ryan and looked directly at him. "She won't go out with you."

Ryan frowned. "What?"

"Tara. She won't go out with you." She turned to walk away.

Ryan grabbed her arm. "Wait. Why do you think she won't go out with me?"

"Because Tara is gay. Kelly is her girlfriend. You're wasting your time with her."

Karissa yanked her arm from Ryan's grasp just as her bodyguard stepped forward. She looked at her bodyguard, and walked away toward her next class.

Ryan stood frozen in place while his classmates filed into the classroom around him. He recalled what Tara had said when he came up behind her in the hallway outside her chemistry class.

Thank you, love...Oh, my God!...I didn't realize it was you. Ryan inhaled deeply. *Kelly!*

***

Mid-morning, Karissa was sitting in class when her bodyguard entered the room without knocking. The lesson immediately stopped and all eyes turned toward him. "Miss Swenson, please come with me," he said firmly.

Karissa looked back and forth between the bodyguard and her teacher, not knowing what to do.

The teacher nodded to her. "You'd better go with him, Karissa," she said.

Karissa quickly gathered her books and followed him out of the room. "What's the matter?" she asked.

"I've been told to bring you to the office. The principal will explain," he responded.

The bodyguard pushed the door to the office open and motioned for Karissa to enter before him. The principal was in the outer office waiting for her. He took Karissa's arm and ushered her into his office.

"Mr. Geary, what is this all about? Did I do something wrong?" Karissa asked.

Mr. Geary stood in the doorway with one hand on the knob. "You've done nothing wrong, Karissa. This is for your own protection. Robert Johnson was seen in the school parking lot this morning."

"He was?"

"Yes. In fact, he's still there. The police have been called. I need you to stay in here until they arrive to address the situation."

"All right, Mr. Geary."

Karissa sat in the guest chair in front of Principal Geary's desk and stared out the window. It felt like an eternity had passed before her attention was drawn to the tree just outside the window. A squirrel raced up and down a branch. Karissa rose and walked closer to get a better look. She stood in front of the window for several minutes, enjoying the squirrel's antics. She was totally caught off guard when Robert suddenly appeared in front of her. She screamed.

The door to the principal's office swung open and Karissa's bodyguard rushed in. On the other side of the window, Robert looked at him and then ran.

"Mr. Geary, Johnson is outside your office window!" the bodyguard yelled.

"Jesus!" Mr. Geary exclaimed. "Is Karissa all right?"

The bodyguard looked under Mr. Geary's desk where Karissa had crawled. "She's fine," he called to Principal Geary.

"I need to inform the police. I'll be right back," Mr. Geary disappeared into the main office.

The bodyguard looked out the window, and then reached his hand toward Karissa. "He's gone, Karissa. Give me your hand. You're safe."

Karissa allowed him to help her out from under the desk. She sat once more in the guest chair. The bodyguard sat his backside on the edge of the desk in front of her and he crossed his arms. "Are you okay?" he asked.

Karissa nodded.

"He's breaking a restraining order by being here. They'll catch him," he said.

"What if they don't?" Karissa asked.

"They will."

The door opened and Mr. Geary entered. "They've got him," he said.

Karissa visibly released a breath.

"Are you okay, Karissa?" Mr. Geary asked.

She nodded.

"Would you like us to call your mom?"

"No. I'm okay. Really. Can I go back to class now?"

***

Cat stood in the living room doorway and called to her family. "Dinner!"

Within moments, a stampede of bodies rushed toward the kitchen and filed into place around the table. Tara limped in slowly on her crutches.

"How are they working out for you, Tare?" Billie asked while she carried the casserole to the table.

"I'm getting used to them. They're way better than that chair," Tara replied.

"Are the cuffs adjusted okay?" Cat asked.

"They're making my forearms a little chafed, but I think I'll get used to them."

"I recommend you wear long sleeves. That might help. They're definitely better than underarm crutches. Talk about causing chafe!" Cat said. "I had to switch to the cuff-crutches as well."

"How much longer do you have on yours, Mama?" Tara asked.

"I should be in a walking cast in another week or so."

Their discussion was interrupted by the phone ringing.

"I'll get it," Billie said. "You all get started." Billie picked up the receiver. "Hello? Hey, Jen." Billie held the receiver to her ear. A dour expression crossed her features. "Okay, Jen. Let me make a few calls. I'll get back to you." Billie hung up the phone.

"What was that all about?" Cat asked.

Billie turned toward the table. "Tara, Seth…are you aware that Robert Johnson showed up at the school today?"

"Yeah. I heard he snuck onto school grounds and the police arrested him," Tara said.

"Why didn't you tell me?" Billie asked.

"It was no big deal, Mom," Seth said. "The cops caught him. He didn't hurt anyone."

"Well, Jen just said the police have released him already. She also said Karissa was sequestered in the principal's office during this whole thing."

"Yeah. She told us about it on the way home after school," Seth said.

"Why would they release him so soon?" Cat asked.

"That's what I intend to find out." Billie pulled out her cell phone.

"Billie, your dinner will get cold," Cat complained.

"I'll nuke it. I need to make a few calls."

***

Jen and Karissa stood in Billie and Cat's kitchen after dinner that evening.

"Mom, it was really nothing. He was just on the school grounds," Karissa said.

"Obviously, Principal Geary thought it was serious enough to take you out of class for your own protection," Jen countered.

"The police said he was cooperative, and that he was unarmed," Billie said. "Yes, he violated the restraining order, but he was nonviolent. That's the main reason they didn't hold him."

"He was nonviolent, *this* time," Jen said."

Karissa rolled her eyes. "Mom, you're really making this bigger than it is."

Jen stood nose to nose with her daughter and shook her finger at her. "Nothing is too big when you, or your brother, are in danger, Karissa." She looked at Billie. "They never even called me. I'm just across the parking lot, for Christ's sake!"

"They didn't call you 'cause I asked them not to," Karissa said.

"You what? For crying out loud, Karissa. I'm your mother. I have a right to know."

Billie interrupted the encounter. "Karissa, Tara is in her room. Why don't you go see what she's up to?" She watched Karissa stomp away then took Jen by the shoulders. "Jen, the hardest thing in the world for parents to do is to let our kids make their own decisions. I struggle with that every day, but if Karissa felt safe, maybe it was okay for her to go back to class."

"How would you feel if it was Tara in that position instead of Karissa?" Jen challenged.

"I would most likely feel exactly the way you do right now...and it would be *you* trying to talk sense into *me*."

Jen couldn't help but grin. "What would I do without you, big guy?" she asked.

Billie pulled her friend in for a hug. "I don't plan to let you find out," she replied.

***

"Tare, can I come in?" Karissa asked.

Tara opened the door. "Sure." She shuffled back a few steps on her crutches.

"Wow! I forgot you were getting your crutches today!"

"Yes. I'm finally out of that horrible chair."

Karissa looked around. "Where's Kelly?"

"She's home with her family. It's her dad's birthday."

Karissa nodded and walked into the room. She sat on the edge of the bed. "Tare, I'm sorry for being so savage about Ryan. I know you're not flirting with him."

"I'm glad you finally realize that, 'Rissa."

"I was jealous that he likes you and not me."

"'Rissa, Seth told me to stay away from him. Apparently, he doesn't like gay people very much."

The color drained from Karissa's face. "Really? How does Seth know that?"

"He went on a major bender in the locker room about how God hates fags. I mean, even if I wasn't gay, I could never like someone who thinks like that," Tara said.

"I didn't know. He seems so nice."

"Well, as my English teacher says...don't judge a book by its cover."

Both girls heard Jen call out Karissa's name.

"Sounds like it's time to go home. My mom is really freaking out about Robert being at school today, and your mom is helping her find out information from the police."

"Cut her a break, 'Rissa. Your mom is cool...and she really loves you."

"I know she does. She just goes all extra over things sometimes."

"That's her job, 'Rissa...and she's really good at it! You'd better get going."

Karissa stood and hugged Tara. "I'll see you in the morning."

Chapter 14

The next morning, Tara climbed out of Seth's car and held onto the open door until she pulled her book bag onto her back and took the crutches that Kelly held for her. Carefully, she maneuvered her way toward the front door of the school with Kelly on one side of her and Karissa on the other.

"It feels weird to be walking beside you instead of behind you," Kelly said.

Tara stopped and looked at Kelly. She shifted her weight to her good leg and reached with the opposite hand to stroke Kelly's arm. "It feels good to be face to face with you again."

Their gazes locked for a few short moments without either speaking.

Karissa reached for the door handle and held it open. She watched her two friends visually devour one another. "You two need to get a room!" she joked.

Tara leaned her head back and laughed. "Funny, 'Rissa. Very funny!"

She looked beyond Karissa and through the door into the school lobby. "Looks like your new boyfriend is waiting for you."

Karissa's head snapped around. "My new boyfriend?" she said.

"Yeah. He's waiting to walk you to class," Tara said, a teasing lilt to her voice.

Karissa scanned the lobby. "Where?" she asked.

"Right there. Tall, dark and handsome. He's a little old for you, though."

Karissa suddenly realized that Tara was referring to her bodyguard. She punched Tara in the arm. "You're lucky you're on crutches, or I'd kick your…"

"Happy Thursday morning, ladies."

The three friends turned to see Principal Geary walk up from behind them.

"Let me get that door for you," he said. He took the door from Karissa and held it open for all three to pass through. Once inside the lobby, he turned to Karissa. "Let's hope we don't have a repeat of yesterday."

"You got that right!" Karissa said.

The three girls stood there, not knowing what else to say to their principal.

Karissa's bodyguard rescued them from the awkward silence. "Are you ready to go to class, Ms. Swenson?" he asked.

"Yes!" Karissa said, too enthusiastically.

"I have to get to work anyway," Mr. Geary said. "Have a good day, ladies."

The girls watched him walk away and grinned. "*That* was weird!" Tara said.

Karissa looked at her bodyguard. "Thanks for saving us."

"Any time." He motioned toward the elevators to the second floor. "After you."

When the group exited the elevator, Karissa and her bodyguard walked toward Karissa's Spanish class, while Kelly walked Tara toward her class, in the opposite direction. They stopped in front of the lockers, just short of the classroom door. The hallway was crowded with students on their way to their first period class.

Tara leaned heavily on the handgrips of her new crutches. Kelly reached forward and covered Tara's hand with her own. "Tare, can I come over to your house after school tonight"?"

"Sure. You can come over any time you want," Tara replied. She watched Kelly's eyes closely and sensed she had something to say. "Are you okay, Kel?"

Kelly was looking at their interlocked hands. At the sound of Tara's voice, Kelly's gaze moved to her face. She didn't say anything right away.

Tara cupped Kelly's face in her palm. "Kel?"

Kelly closed her eyes and took a deep breath. "I…"

"Kelly, if you have something to say…just say it," Tara insisted.

"I love you."

Tara's head snapped back. "Really?" She couldn't stop the grin from spreading across her face.

A mist of tears filled Kelly's eyes. "Yeah...really."

Tara pivoted and pressed her back into the lockers. "Oh, wow!" she said. Her breathing came in quick pants and an intense anxious feeling filled her chest.

Kelly shifted from foot to foot, and looked everywhere but at Tara's face. "Ah...I'm sorry. I shouldn't have said anything," she finally said.

"Oh, shut up!" Tara suddenly disregarded all thoughts of keeping her sexuality secret. She grabbed the front of Kelly's jacket and pulled her close.

Kelly had to place her hands against the lockers on either side of Tara to avoid crushing her.

Nose to nose, Tara whispered, "Kiss me."

Kelly did just that.

Tara felt her insides explode as a warmth unlike anything else she had ever experienced, spread throughout her whole body. So engrossed was she in the kiss, that she didn't hear the *Ooos* and *Ahhs* emanating from the other students in the hall.

When it ended, Tara felt like her lifeline had been suddenly severed.

Kelly leaned her forehead against Tara's. "I gotta get to class she whispered."

"I know," Tara whispered back. "Tonight?" she asked.

"Tonight," Kelly said.

Tara watched her walk away toward her own class, and struggled to regain her composure. The bell for first period rang and she quickly slipped into her classroom.

In the Blink of an Eye

Chapter 15

Tara

Tara was *so* not into listening to her teacher drone on and on about dangling participles. Her only thoughts were of Kelly pressing her into the lockers, and the feel of Kelly's mouth on hers just a half-hour earlier. Tara ran her fingertips across her lips. Her breath caught in her throat, and she felt an unfamiliar spasm in her abdomen.

She said she loves me. Do I love her too? Is that why I'm totally wrecked right now?

Tara thought about how she had felt the first time she saw Kelly. She and Karissa had been on their way to the mall and they walked by Kelly's house hand in hand. There was a moving van in front of the house down the street from where she lived.

Just as they approached the corner of the property, a girl came out of the moving van carrying a box that was so large, she could barely see over it. Tara's heart was in her throat when the girl walked down the ramp and came precariously close to the edge of it before finally touching down on the pavement.

The girl didn't notice them until she stepped onto the sidewalk and realized she had cut them off.

"I'm sorry," she said.

"No problem," Tara had responded. "Do you need help with that?"

"Nope! Got it covered, but thanks."

An awkward silence fell, and they stood gawking at one another…Tara and Karissa still hand in hand, and the girl, holding the large clumsy box.

"My name is Kelly Barkum. I'd shake your hand, but, I'm kind of tied up here."

Tara laughed. "Tara Charland…and this is Karissa Swenson. We live a few houses down the road."

"Kelly! There'll be time enough for socializing later," a man had called out from the porch.

Kelly blushed. "That's my dad. I gotta go. Maybe I'll see you later?"

"Sure!" Tara said brightly. She and Karissa continued down the sidewalk. They stopped several feet beyond Kelly's property and looked back. "She's cute!" Tara said.

"Yeah...if you're into girls," Karissa replied.

"Which I am!"

Tara was absorbed in her thoughts. So much so, that her mind almost didn't register the odd, repeating sounds coming from some distant place on campus. She looked around her classroom and realized other students had heard the sounds as well. Everyone sat frozen in their seats. Her gaze darted next, to her teacher, who also stood motionless.

The surreal moment was suddenly intruded on by the deafening peal of the fire alarm.

Oh, great! Tara thought. *Just what I need—an evacuation drill on crutches!*

"All right students. You know what to do. Line up orderly at the door and follow me along the evacuation route to the parking lot," the teacher yelled above the alarm.

"Is this for real?" a student shouted out.

"We did not have an evacuation drill planned for today, so we need to assume it is real," the teacher replied.

Tara took her place at the end of the line so she wouldn't hold anyone up, and waited for the teacher to open the door.

The fire alarm suddenly stopped.

The repetitious popping sound grew louder.

A series of three peals came from the intercom.

Screams could be heard coming from the hallway.

Tara watched a look of terror cross her teacher's face, and suddenly, she understood what was happening.

***

Karissa

Karissa entered her Spanish class while her bodyguard stood in the hall. She found her seat and pulled her tablet out of her backpack. While she waited for class to begin, she thought about her conversation with Tara the night before about Ryan hating gay people.

He went on a major bender in the locker room about how God hates fags. I mean, even if I wasn't gay, I could never like someone who thinks like that.

She'd told Ryan that Tara was gay.

Should I have done that? Tara is my best friend. I don't care that she's gay. If I was Ryan's girlfriend, would he want me to end my friendship with Tara? I don't think I could do that. I love her like she was my sister. Is it fair for me to have to choose between Ryan and Tara?

Karissa was pulled out of her own thoughts by the sound of the teacher's voice. "Okay, folks, plug in your ear buds and listen to lesson number sixteen. The dialogue is roughly twenty minutes long. Everyone in this class is a second-year Spanish student, so I expect you'll be able to understand what is being said. After the dialogue is finished, we'll discuss it."

Karissa took notes while she listened to the lesson. She was totally immersed in the dialogue when the fire alarm sounded. The sudden, loud peal startled her so, that she literally jumped to her feet. She pulled the ear buds out of her ears and looked around the room. All of her classmates had nearly identical reactions to hers. Interestingly, her teacher was no longer in the room.

Karissa and her classmates automatically gathered on one side of the room to form an evacuation line…just as they had been taught during fire drills.

The alarm stopped just as suddenly as it had started, and the door to their classroom flew open to admit their teacher.

When the door was opened, a series of repeated popping sounds could be heard as clear as day.

All eyes turned toward the door.

"I heard the popping sounds. I went to investigate," the teacher said to explain why he had left his students alone.

The teacher hastily closed the door just as a series of three peals came from the intercom.

Screams could be heard coming from the hallway.

At that moment, Karissa immediately knew her choice would be clear. She would choose Tara.

***

Kelly

The kiss Kelly shared with Tara just before going to first period class shook her to her very core. She knew without a doubt that she was totally in love with Tara. To hear Tara say she loved her back was something she hoped for, but hadn't expected.

She had tried not to fall in love with Tara. She knew that someday, she might have to leave if her father moved again with the military. She fought what she felt, but her heart was stronger than her mind. And now it was too late. She loved her. She loved her with everything she was.

Kelly knew she wouldn't be able to concentrate in class. All she could think about was Tara. So, she decided to skip. She decided to go to the library to think and to work through her feelings.

The library was on the second floor and was located just above the front lobby of the school. Kelly walked directly past her first period classroom to the end of the hall—toward the front of the building. She slipped into the library and found a table in the far corner, near the windows. It was quiet and secluded there. From her perch, she could see the whole library. She was actually surprised at the number of people in the library during first period. She guessed most of them were there for study hall.

Kelly settled in and stared out the window. Her thoughts immediately turned to Tara. She had been kind of surprised that Tara agreed to be her girlfriend. After all, she was pretty butch and so was Tara.

When Kelly first knew she was attracted to girls, she read everything she could get her hands on about LGBTQ youth. From everything she'd read, butch girls were more attracted to femme girls. Tara was anything but femme. In a lot of ways, she's an even bigger tomboy than Kelly. And she was tough. She'd been through a lot.

Kelly pulled her phone out of her pocket and for the next half hour, she looked through all of the pictures and texts she had from Tara. When she was finished, she wiped tears from the corners of both eyes. *Damn, I've got it bad.*

Kelly's reverie was abruptly shattered by a familiar sound. She sat straight up and looked around, wide-eyed. She knew that sound from time spent practicing with her father.

The fire alarm startled everyone in the library. Kelly was on her feet in an instant and heading for the door.

The librarian reached the door before anyone else. "You know the drill, people. Form an orderly line."

The fire alarm stopped suddenly, followed by very loud, repeated, popping sounds. *It sounds like it's just below us...in the lobby*, Kelly thought.

Before Kelly could act, three loud peals sounded on the intercom. More loud popping...and screams followed.

This can't be happening. Not now!

***

Seth

Seth followed Amanda into his physiology class and sat behind her, in the back of the class. "Hey, Amanda," he said in a low voice.

Amanda sneered at him.

"Whoa! What's with the 'tude? All I did was say hello," Seth said.

"After what you and Steve did to Ryan...I can't even!"

"The shape you were in on Saturday makes me wonder how you even know what we did to Ryan."

"I was fine!" Amanda argued.

"You were drugged...probably by Ryan."

"You don't know that."

"So...what do you *think* we did to Ryan?" Seth asked.

"You called the police. Do you know how much trouble he was in with his dad?"

"No, Amanda. We didn't call the police. We were driving away when the police got there."

"Ryan said you and Steve are gay."

Seth shook his head. "In his warped mind, he thinks that because my moms are gay, that I am, too. He has some pretty twisted ideas, Amanda."

"They aren't *ideas*, Seth. They're beliefs. He has a right to believe what he wants."

"He's using his *beliefs* to judge people. Wake up and smell the coffee, Amanda. He's bad news. Where is he, anyway? I haven't seen him in school today."

"Not that it's any of your business, but he's home sick," Amanda shot back at him.

"All right, class. Please go to chapter twelve of your physiology app," the teacher instructed.

Seth turned on his tablet and opened the app for his physiology class. He clicked on chapter twelve in the table of contents. He read the chapter title, and felt the heat rise into his face. He looked around the room and noticed the subject of today's class also made several other students in the room a little uncomfortable.

The teacher walked around the room. "Sexual arousal," he said, "is one of the most natural functions of the human body."

Seth slinked down in his seat and avoided looking at anyone else in the class.

"Sexual arousal is as much a physical reaction as it is an emotional one," the teacher continued as he walked up and down the aisles.

Seth leaned forward in his seat and whispered hoarsely to Amanda, "Is this guy for real?"

The teacher turned around abruptly. "Do you have an issue with the topic of chapter twelve, Mr. Charland?"

"No. I have no problem with sexual arousal, sir." Seth regretted it as soon as it left his mouth. "Ah...that didn't come out right," he added quickly.

The class erupted in laughter while Seth's face turned multiple shades of red.

The laughter was interrupted by the sound of repeated popping sounds. The room immediately fell silent.

"Oh, shit," the boy beside Seth said.

Suddenly, the fire alarm sounded.

Everyone in the room froze.

"Let's go folks," the teacher said. "Fire drill. You know what to do."

As soon as the teacher made his statement, then the alarm stopped. Again, popping sounds came from the hallway, followed by screaming.

The teacher walked to the door to look through the window into the hallway.

Three loud peals sounded on the intercom at the same time the teacher fell to the floor. A red pool quickly formed beneath his head.

***

Steve

Steve sat in his first period math class and waited for the other students to file in. He busied himself by playing a game on his cell phone. From the corner of his eye, he watched Luke enter the room. Luke walked down the aisle Steve sat in, and intentionally bumped into him...hard. Steve nearly fell out of his chair.

"Knock it off, Gregowski," Steve growled.

"Or what, little girl?" Luke replied.

"Is there a problem, gentlemen?"

Steve and Luke turned to look at their teacher.

"No problem at all, Ms. Fletcher," Luke said. He continued past Steve, but not before he kicked Steve's feet out of the aisle.

Steve bit his tongue and said nothing. The last thing he wanted was to appear as a whiny baby. He would take care of Luke later.

He watched Luke walk down the aisle and sit in a seat two rows in front of him. Luke reached his right hand up and ran it through his hair, and allowed his hand to linger on the back of his head, with his middle finger displayed prominently in Steve's line of vision.

Steve wanted to tell Luke to crawl out of his cave and join the human race. He was one of those guys who tried to act all cool in front of the girls, but when he was with the guys, he was a big old redneck. More than once, Steve had overheard conversations in the locker room about him using squirrels and rabbits for target practice. Steve had no issue with hunting. He was a hunter himself, but his father had taught him to use what he took—not to leave it to die and rot in the field.

Steve's attention was drawn to Ms. Fletcher as she distributed a piece of paper to each student in the room.

"Pop quiz today, class," Ms. Fletcher said.

The whole room released a collective groan.

"None of that," she added. "If you've been paying attention, you'll do fine. You have twenty minutes to complete it…beginning now."

Steve turned his paper and began solving the mathematical equations. Math was one of Steve's favorite subjects and he progressed through the list of problems with ease. He finished quickly and looked around the room at nearly all of his classmates, who still toiled on the quiz. *Maybe I'll just review my answers,* he thought. *I don't wanna look too much like a geek.*

Steve was halfway through reviewing his answers when he heard the first repetitious popping sounds. He looked up to see he wasn't the only one in the room to notice the sounds.

"No way!" Luke exclaimed.

Suddenly, the fire alarm sounded, and everyone in the room rose to their feet.

"Leave your quizzes on your desks, class," Ms. Fletcher said. "Don't think for a moment that a fire drill is going to get you out of taking this quiz. Now line up!"

"This is not a fire drill," Luke yelled.

"What did you say, Mr. Gregowski?" Ms. Fletcher asked.

Before Luke could answer, the alarm stopped. Again, popping sounds could be heard outside of the classroom.

"That is a…" Luke was cut off by three short peals on the intercom.

Screaming in the hallway increased the anxiety in the room exponentially.

***

Jen

Jen hadn't slept well the night before. She was worried about the upcoming trial of Robert Johnson, and what both Karissa and Steve would have to go through in court.

Due to lack of sleep, she arrived in her classroom that morning with a slight headache. She hoped the kids would behave. Fifth graders could be a real pain in the backside when they wanted to be.

Jen checked in with the office for any call-outs, and picked up her attendance sheets and mail. She went to her class and sat down to review her lesson plans for the day. Before she knew it, it was time to meet the buses in front of the school.

Jen stood on the sidewalk in front of the main office and looked across the parking lot toward the high school. Thoughts of Steve and Karissa immediately came to mind, and once again, she began to fret about the upcoming trial.

Soon, the buses arrived. Most of the students in her class came in on the first three buses. She enjoyed greeting the children as they stepped off the bus, and she sent each one into the classroom after a cheery good morning.

She took attendance and started the day with the pledge of allegiance, after which, they immediately got to work on a new language arts module.

They were about a half-hour into their lesson, when the alarm rang…three peals on the intercom. Jen knew immediately what that meant. *Is this an unannounced drill?* she wondered.

Jen went to the door, locked it, and then pulled the shade. She turned to the children. "Okay kids, you know what to do. We've practiced this countless times."

The children immediately took action. The larger boys pulled several of the tables to the door, while others piled their chairs on top of them. They did their best to barricade the door with as much furniture as possible—including Jen's desk. They armed themselves with pencils, scissors, rulers, and any other object they might use to defend themselves, and they retreated to the back of the room and piled into a small, locked safe room.

Jen was terrified. She had no idea if this was real…or just a drill. They had practiced this many times, but nothing prepared her for actually having a real lockdown. She pulled her phone out of her pocket and put it on vibrate to avoid revealing their location should it ring. When she looked at the phone, she noted a text message. It was from Karissa. It said simply…*Active shooter. I love you, Mom! Tell Dad I love him, too.*

Chapter 16

"911…what is your emergency?" Dispatcher Monica Harris asked.

"We have a shooter!"

Monica immediately put the caller on speaker. "Ma'am, where is your emergency located?"

"At Nassau High School. Oh, my God! He just shot Mr. Geary! Please! Please send help."

"I am dispatching a police car right now," Monica said.

"You don't understand. He has a gun!"

By this time, several other dispatchers had gathered around and were listening to gunshots clearly coming through on the call. Monica muted her microphone and looked over her shoulder. "John, call the police. We have an active shooter at Nassau High School."

She un-muted her mike and turned her attention back to the woman on the phone. "Ma'am, I need to know who you are."

"Linda Collins. I'm Principal Geary's secretary. Please send help! Oh, my God! More gunshots! He's killing the students!"

"We have help on the way, Linda. Stay with me. Where are you in the school?"

"I'm…I'm in the office."

"Are you safe right now, Linda?"

"Yes. I hid under the desk when I heard the first shots. He shot out the glass doors in the front of the school. Principal Geary tried to stop him in the lobby and now he's dead. There's blood everywhere."

"Did you see the shooter, ma'am? Could you identify him?"

"He has a ski mask on. I don't know who he is. Oh, my God! Mr. Geary tried to stop him, and now he's dead. I panicked and pushed the fire alarm instead of the intruder alert."

"Do you know where the shooter is now, Linda?"

"He went toward the science wing. God, please help us! I hear more shots. My, God! My, God! He's shooting the children."

Monica turned to her co-workers. "Jane, call the state police...now!"

***

New York State Police

Captain John Spencer paced back and forth in front of the emergency gathering. When he spoke, his tone was fast-paced and urgent.

"We don't have a lot of time here, but we have reports of an active shooter at Nassau High School. You know the drill...the Situational Assessment Team goes in first. It's your job to determine the number and description of suspects, as well as their location. You also need to determine if the physical site is free of booby traps, such as IEDs. Contact Team, your job is to intercept and immobilize the suspect and to minimize the casualties— especially the children. Rescue Team, it is up to you to retrieve the victims, beginning with the injured, followed by the deceased, but only if the site is contained, otherwise, they will be recovered later. The local police department will set up the Unified Command. They will secure the inner and outer perimeters, facilitate the evacuation of neighboring locations, arrange med-evac and notify the media. In the event backup is needed, they will also assist in the apprehension of the suspect. Are there any questions?"

Captain Spencer looked at the solemn faces of his fellow officers. "Okay, then. These are children we are talking about. Let's take this bastard down!"

***

Seth

Seth watched his teacher fall and he instinctively knew he was dead before he hit the floor. He felt like he was going to throw up.

Everyone scrambled to hide under desks.

The door suddenly burst open and slammed into the wall behind it.

The girl closest to the door screamed.

The gunman stepped into the room and looked around. He aimed his automatic rifle at the screaming girl. Several shots later, she fell silent.

A scurry of bodies moved as one to get as far away as possible from the shooter…toward the back of the room…where Seth was.

Seth found himself pinned up against the back wall. He fought for breath under the throng of bodies pressing against him. The sickening sound of bullets hitting flesh surrounded him. One by one, he heard, rather than saw, his classmates fall. Seth had the presence of mind to slink down the wall, so by the time the shooter had finished, he lay motionless beneath his classmates.

Suddenly, a deafening silence descended on the room, except for the moaning and crying of those around him who were still alive. Seth held his breath and lay as still as possible until he was forced to inhale or pass out. Finally, he opened one eye and came face to face with Amanda, staring directly at him…unblinking. She had a bullet hole in the middle of her forehead and the back of her head was no longer there. He had an intense urge to scurry out from beneath the pile of bodies on top of him, but he knew if he moved too soon, he was as good as dead.

Seth scanned what little of the room he could see through the bodies around him. When he was satisfied that the shooter had left, he pushed his way out of the tangle of bodies and immediately checked on his classmates who were still alive.

Out of a class of fifteen students, six were alive, including himself. He tried desperately to find the pulse of the nine who died, but to no avail. Seth fought to keep the contents of his stomach intact while he checked them out. Their injuries were devastating, and in some cases, grotesque.

Nearly all of the survivors were at the bottom of the pile, and, like him, they were saved by the sacrifices of their classmates.

None of the five other survivors was injured critically. Two others, like himself, weren't injured at all. The remaining three received minor gunshot wounds, mostly to arms or legs.

Once the injured were attended to, Seth rushed to the front of the classroom and closed the door. He locked it, and had to drag his teacher's body out of the way so he could flip the teacher's desk on end and push it up against the door. He pulled out his cell phone and called 911.

***

Albany 911 Dispatch

Monica was still on the phone with Linda when the second call came in. "Jane, can you get that?"

"911...what is your emergency?" Jane asked. "Whoa...slow down. What is your name?"

"Seth Charland."

"Okay, Seth, where are you?"

"Nassau High School. A shooter just murdered nine of my classmates. There's a lot of blood."

"Where are you in the school, Seth?"

"In the science wing...first floor...room 101. You need to send help. He's still shooting. I can hear the gunshots."

"Are there other survivors with you Seth?"

"Yes. Five. Some of them are shot, but they're still alive."

"Help is on the way, Seth. I want you to barricade the door, and whatever you do, don't move from where you are. Do you understand?"

"My sister is out there. I need to help her."

"No, Seth. You're safe where you are. Do not leave! The police are on their way."

"Okay...okay! Please hurry. He is still out there killing kids."

"I have the number of the phone you called me on, Seth. I will call you back soon to check on you," Jane said.

***

Seth

Seth hung up the phone and called his mother. His hands were shaking so violently, he could barely dial her number. His voice broke when she answered the phone. "Mom?"

"Seth? Seth, is that you?" Billie asked.

"Mom…there's a shooter in the school."

"What? Oh, my God, Seth. Are you okay?"

"Yeah, but I don't know about Tara." Seth began to cry. "Mom, he killed nine kids in my classroom. There's blood everywhere!"

"Seth, stay right where you are. Do you hear me? I am on my way."

"I love you, Mom."

"I love you too, baby."

***

Cat

Cat left the operating room and headed to the cafeteria for a midmorning coffee, just as her back pocket vibrated. She reached for her phone and looked at the screen. She saw it was a missed call from Billie and quickly pressed the dial-back number and waited for Billie to answer.

"Cat! Cat—there's a shooter at the high school!" Billie sounded like she was out of breath.

Cat froze. "What did you say?"

"There's a shooter at the high school. Seth called me two minutes ago."

Cat reached for the closest wall for support. "Oh, my God, Billie. Is he okay?"

"He's alive, but the shooter killed nine kids in his class. My poor baby." Billie was crying.

"What about Tara?"

"I...I don't know. I'm on my way to the school, and I have a call into the police department. Cat...what are we going to do if..."

"Don't say it, Billie! Please don't say it. I'll be there as soon as I can."

"You can't, Cat. The hospital will need you. Cat, my heart is breaking for so many young lives. God, please let Tara be okay...and Karissa, Kelly and Steve." Billie was sobbing and couldn't go on.

"Billie, is the middle school safe?"

"Sky!" Billie suddenly said. "I think so. The news feed I'm listening to said it was the high school. Cat, I will die if we lose them."

"Please don't say that, love. We need to pray that they survive this. We can't give up hope."

"I'll call you as soon as I have news."

"I'll be waiting. I love you, Billie. Tell our kids I love them too."

"I will."

Cat hung up the phone and immediately ran toward the emergency room to deliver the news of incoming casualties.

***

Jen

Jen stared at her phone. *Active shooter. I love you, Mom! Tell Dad I love him too.*

Jen covered her mouth with her hand to prevent herself from crying out and scaring her students more than they were already. *Karissa...Steve!*

It seemed like an eternity that Jen had hid with her fifth grade students in the safe room. That was the last place she wanted to be at that moment, but she knew she couldn't desert them. She knew it was her duty to protect them...with her own life if necessary. She only hoped the teachers in the high school—where her children faced undoubtedly the most traumatic event of their young lives—felt the same way.

About thirty minutes after the intruder alert sounded, Jen heard movement in the classroom beyond the wall of their safe room. Twenty pairs of terrified eyes looked to her for guidance. She motioned for all of them to be quiet, and she continued to listen intently for the safe-phrase.

"Ms. Swenson. Time to clear the dance floor."

Jen released the breath she hadn't realized she'd been holding. "Okay, kids, it's safe to go back to our classroom." Jen led the way out of the small closet-like room. A police officer was waiting for them.

"Ms. Swenson, I'm Officer Minor. I'm here to lead you and your students out of the school. We are evacuating the grounds."

"You heard the officer, kids. Single file. Let's go," Jen said.

Once they reached the far end of the parking lot, Jen noticed her room aide standing nearby. "Kathy! Kathy, over here!"

Kathy ran to Jen and embraced her warmly. "Thank God you're okay!"

"Kathy, my kids are in that high school. I need to go. Please stay with the students until their parents come."

"Yes! Yes, of course," Kathy said. "Go!"

Jen headed toward the parking lot that separated the middle and high schools, and ran directly into a reporter from the local news that shoved a microphone in her face.

"Ma'am, Megan Cross, Channel Five News. We have reason to believe there is an active shooter on campus. Is that true?"

"I don't have time for this. My son and daughter are in danger," Jen replied.

The reporter looked across the parking lot at the high school. "So the shooter is in the high school, then."

"I gotta go." Jen broke free of the reporter and ran across the parking lot.

***

"It has been verified by Channel Five news that there is an active shooter at Nassau High School." The camera panned across the parking lot and filmed the arrival of the state police SWAT team, in full bulletproof gear and armed with military grade weapons. "Stay tuned for breaking news, which we will bring to you as the situation develops. This is Megan Cross, Channel Five News, Albany."

The young man, who had been home watching the news, shut off the television and headed out the door.

***

Kelly

Chaos erupted in the library as soon as the three peals sounded, signaling an intruder. The librarian stood in their way and did her best to regain control.

"The last place you want to go is out there. Take cover in the stock room at the back of the library. The shots sound close. Go quickly!"

In the confusion caused by the mass exodus to the back of the library, Kelly ducked behind a bookcase and waited for her fellow students and the librarian to vacate the area. Once she was alone, she ran straight for the door and into the hall.

Kelly walked a few feet down the hall. All was quiet, and completely deserted. She walked a few more feet and froze when she heard footsteps on the stairs. She quickly ran into the girls' restroom and stood behind the door with it cracked open just enough for her to see into the hall. She held her breath and remained as still as possible so as to not give her presence away.

***

Steve

"This is not a fire drill," Luke yelled.

"What did you say, Mr. Gregowski?" Ms. Fletcher asked.

"Those are gunshots. I've shot enough guns to know."

Ms. Fletcher ran to the door, closed and locked it, and pulled down the shade. "Carl, Luke, David…move my desk in front of the door. John, Steve, Michael, move the file cabinet close to my desk and then tip it on top. Quickly! The rest of you, move to the wall adjacent to the door, out of the range of the shooter. Stay down. Please stay down, and be very quiet."

The students did as they were instructed, but not soon enough. A spray of gunfire shattered the window in the door just as the three boys hefted the file cabinet onto the desk. Michael was shot in the chest and fell to the floor. Steve and John dropped to the floor and dragged Michael away from the line of fire.

Michael clung to Steve's arm. "I'm hit. Steve, I'm hit!" Michael said.

Steve did the only thing he could think of; he pressed his hands onto Michael's wound and held them there. "Hold on, Mike. Hold on. Don't give up."

A burst of gunfire shattered the door handle and the shooter tried to open the door. It stopped short when it hit the desk. He screamed out in frustration and peppered the door with bullets, and kicked it once more. The students on the inside huddled close to the floor and covered their heads as their barricade continued to hold.

Ms. Fletcher dialed 911.

***

Albany 911 Dispatch

"911...what is your emergency?"

"There is a shooter at Nassau High School. My student has just been shot in the chest."

The dispatcher covered the receiver with his hand and called out to Monica Harris. "Monica! We have another call from inside the high school." He turned his attention back to the caller. "Ma'am, I need to know your name and your location in the school."

"Cherilynn Fletcher. We are on the second floor, room 248. I have a student shot in the chest. Please...we need help right away."

"Ms. Fletcher, is the door locked?"

"Yes, but that didn't stop him from shooting the window out."

"Is he still shooting?"

"Yes. For Christ's sake, will you listen to me? I have a boy dying here! He's been shot in the chest. We need an ambulance right now!"

"Ma'am, are you or the other students in any imminent danger?"

"What part of active shooter do you *not* understand? Yes! We are all in danger. Every student in this school is in danger. He stopped shooting into this classroom, but he's still out there in the hall firing that gun. This boy will die if we don't get help soon. Do you understand me?"'

"The SWAT team is on campus, Ma'am. Keep as much pressure as you can on the boy's wound and stay low. Do not—I repeat—do *not* move from your location. Help is on the way."

***

Kelly

From her hiding place inside the girls' bathroom, Kelly watched a man in a ski mask ascend the stairs to the second story, and slowly walk down the hall. Karissa's bodyguard was sitting outside her classroom…still on duty, despite the shootings going on elsewhere in the school.

"You don't really want to do this," the bodyguard said.

"You have no idea what I want," the shooter said. He aimed the rifle at the bodyguard and pulled the trigger.

The shooter continued down the hall and stopped to look through the window on several classrooms, until he reached Ms. Fletcher's math class. He leveled the barrel of the rifle at the door and shattered the window. Kelly could hear screams from inside the classroom.

The man tried to push the door open, but it was locked. He shot out the lock with a flurry of bullets, and again attempted to open the door, but the furniture the students had piled against it, held. The shooter was clearly angry and he took his frustration out on the door with a spray of bullets that easily pierced the thin sheet metal. He kicked the door, but again the barricade held. Finally, he gave up and moved down the hall.

No! Kelly agonized. *He's heading toward Tara's class!*

In the Blink of an Eye

Chapter 17

Albany State Police SWAT Team

"Go! Go! Go!" the squadron commander yelled. Forty SWAT team commandos ran into the school lobby with their weapons at the ready. The first thing they saw was the body of a man, lying in a pool of blood. A quick check of the man's pulse confirmed that he was dead. The commander sent ten men down the wing toward the gym, and another ten down the science wing. The remaining men secured the lobby. Three of the men moved toward the main office. They kicked open the door and were immediately met with a scream.

Linda Collins stood up with her hands in the air. "Don't shoot. Please don't shoot!" she said.

"Identify yourself!" one of the officers shouted.

"Linda Collins. I'm Mr. Geary's secretary."

"Are you the only one here?" another officer asked.

"Yes…except for Mr. Geary. He's on the lobby floor. I think he's dead."

"Yes, ma'am, we verified he is deceased. Come with me, ma'am," the lead officer said. "We'll get you out of here safely."

By the time the group of three officers led Ms. Collins from the office, the group of ten who had gone to investigate the gym had returned. "All clear," they said.

"Commander!" A loud voice was heard coming from the science wing. "We have casualties."

***

Seth

Seth huddled in the far corner of the room with his injured classmates. He froze when he heard a voice in the hallway outside his classroom.

"No!" one of the injured girls whispered. "Please don't kill us."

"Shhh," Seth said. "Maybe if we're quiet he'll go away."

The door handle suddenly rattled and the door opened as far as the barricade would allow. Then, very slowly, the barricade moved and the door opened wider. The next thing Seth saw was the point of an automatic rifle extending through the open door.

Seth squeezed his eyes closed and hoped for it to be over quickly.

"Son? Son, we're here to help."

Seth opened his eyes and saw what he thought were several soldiers...all dressed in combat gear. He immediately dropped his face into his hands and sobbed.

***

Albany State Police SWAT Team

"Shots fired!"

Five members of the SWAT team held back to assist Seth and his classmates while the remaining squadron quickly regrouped in the lobby to assess the new rounds of gunfire. The commander motioned to the ceiling, indicating the gunfire was coming from the floor above them. They moved as one, slowly toward the stairway, with their rifles ready for anything that might move.

***

Tara

There were limited options in Tara's classroom to provide protection from a lunatic with a gun. Instead of desks, there were large round tables, big enough to seat eight students. There was no safe room…and there was no closet. They barricaded the door as best as they could, and hid under the tables and waited.

The waiting was excruciating. The first round of gunfire had happened just before the fire alarm sounded. Another round happened just minutes after that. Both were muted and distant. The third round sounded as if it was just outside their classroom door. The shooter was getting closer.

Suddenly, a loud bang against the door pushed it open far enough for the shooter to get inside. He stood there in his ski mask and loaded a new clip into his rifle. He looked round the room and his eyes stopped directly on Tara. Tara's teacher suddenly jumped up and drew a handgun she had taken from her desk earlier.

"Stop right now or I'll shoot you. I swear I will!" the teacher warned.

The shooter simply raised the barrel of his rifle and shot her three times. She fell into a heap at his feet. Several girls screamed, and were met with the same fate. He turned again in Tara's direction and walked directly toward her. She was huddled between two of her classmates against the back wall. He stopped in front of her and raised his rifle. Within seconds, the two teenagers book-ending Tara were dead, despite their efforts to move away while his attention was on Tara. Several of the students scurried out of the room while he stood in front of Tara with his back to them.

The shooter put the barrel of the gun directly on Tara's forehead. She closed her eyes and tried not to move, despite the burning sensation on her skin from the hot barrel.

Please make it quick.

The shooter stood there, very still for several long moments. Finally he spoke and simply said, "Bang."

"No!" Kelly burst into the classroom.

The shooter quickly turned around and shot Kelly in the stomach.

"Kelly!" Tara scrambled to her feet and limped to Kelly.

The shooter walked directly past them and out the door.

Tara gathered Kelly into her arms. "Kel. Kel, talk to me."

"It hurts," Kelly whispered. She clutched her stomach with both hands.

Tara laid her flat on the floor and took her shirt off. She folded it into a small square and placed it directly on Kelly's wound. She pressed hard. Kelly winced.

Tara wept. "I'm sorry, Kel. I know it hurts. Please don't die. I need you. I love you. Please don't die." Tara pressed even harder.

"Help us!" she screamed. "Help!"

***

Karissa

Karissa sat huddled in the corner with her knees drawn to her chest. She could hear the gunshots coming from the classroom directly next to hers...Tara's classroom. Everything seemed so surreal. Her teacher instructed the class to hide against the far wall while he waited beside the door to ambush the shooter. He chose not to lock or barricade the door. Instead, he chose to rely on the element of surprise.

Karissa was sure they would all die. One teacher was no match for a loaded rifle...especially one that could shoot so many bullets so fast. She found herself swimming in a sea of mental anguish. She was sure her best friend was dead or lay dying in the next room. She was sure she would never see her parents again. She was afraid her brother had met the same fate she was about to. She wasn't afraid to die, but she was afraid to *not* live.

***

Albany State Police SWAT Team

Part way up the stairs, a second round of gunfire stopped the SWAT team mid-step. On command, they increased their ascent and reached the top in time to see several students run out of one of the classrooms with their arms straight up in the air.

"The shooter is in there!" one of the students yelled. "He shot David and Michelle in the head. He's gonna kill Tara!"

The commander assigned one of the officers to escort the students to the lower level, while the rest of them proceeded down the hall.

The shooter exited Tara's classroom and saw the SWAT team. He went back into the room and grabbed a student. He used the student as a shield and made his way down the hall toward Karissa's classroom.

"If you try to stop me, I'll kill him!" he shouted.

"You won't get away with this, son," the commander said. "Give yourself up and end this bloodshed."

"They have to be stopped. They are corrupting everyone they come in contact with." The shooter moved farther down the hall, still holding the student in front of him as a shield. Finally, he made it to Karissa's classroom, pushed the student away, and reached for the door handle.

"Don't do it son!" the commander yelled, "Drop the gun or I will be forced to shoot."

The shooter turned around at the same moment a figure sprung from the exit door just opposite the classroom. The figure launched himself at the shooter and tackled him to the floor, but not before the shooter set off a round of bullets, most of which sprayed across the lockers and ceiling…and one of which embedded itself in the tackler's thigh.

Within seconds, the SWAT team was on top of them, holding both the shooter and the tackler at gun point. "Don't move! Don't move!" The commander yelled.

He motioned for individual troops to check the other classrooms while he restrained the shooter.

Just then, the door to Karissa's classroom opened and the teacher walked out, still holding the baseball bat he had planned to use on the shooter. Some members of the SWAT team trained their guns on him as well.

The teacher dropped the bat and put his hands in the air. "Whoa! I'm one of the good guys," he said.

Soon, several of the students came to the open doorway…including Karissa. "Robert?" she said.

"Karissa," the tackler said.

"The commander reached down and pulled the ski mask off the shooter.

"Ryan Porter!" the teacher said.

"Go to hell," Ryan spat.

One of the officers rolled Ryan onto his stomach and handcuffed his wrists behind him.

"From the beginning of creation, God made them male and female. For this cause a man shall leave his father and mother, and shall cleave to his wife, and the two shall become one flesh...," Ryan ranted.

The officer pulled Ryan to his feet.

"Leviticus, chapter eighteen, verse twenty-two. You shall not lie with a male as a woman; it is an abomination. Chapter twenty, verse thirteen. If a man lies with a male as with a woman, both of them have committed an abomination. They shall surely be put to death!"

"Shut up, Porter," the commander warned him.

Ryan looked directly at Karissa. "Your friends, Tara and Kelly are going to hell. They are an abomination. This is all their fault. They will rot in hell for their heinous crimes against God."

"Get him outta here," the commander said.

As soon as Ryan was dragged away, Karissa ran to Robert and dropped to her knees. His leg wound was being tended to by one of the SWAT team members.

"I don't know what to say, Robert. Thank you. You saved my life. You saved all our lives," Karissa said.

"I couldn't let him hurt you, Karissa. I just couldn't let him do it."

"We have casualties here!" the offer called out from the next classroom. "We need an ambulance."

"We have one here as well," the officer who checked on Ms. Fletcher's math class said.

"Tara! Steve!" Karissa yelled. She ran down the hall toward Tara's classroom and found her sitting on the floor holding Kelly in her arms while one of the SWAT team members applied pressure to Kelly's stomach wound.

She dropped to her knees and wept. "Please don't die, Kel." She looked around the room and realized there were several other victims who were not as lucky as Kelly. Most of them had been shot point-blank in the head. Karissa looked at Tara and noticed the blood covering her face and clothes. "Are you okay?"

All Tara could do was nod through her tears.

"I need to check on Steve."

"I'm here, 'Rissa."

Karissa turned sharply and saw her brother standing in the doorway. She jumped to her feet and ran into his arms. "Stevie! Stevie…you're okay!"

"I'm fine, and considering the circumstances, I will let you off the hook for calling me, Stevie, you little dweeb."

Tara looked up at her friends. "Seth?"

"Seth is okay. He texted me a few minutes ago. The medics are checking him out in the nurse's office before they release him. I'm betting they'll want to see all of us."

Karissa took her brother's hand. "Steve, it was Ryan. He was the shooter."

A commotion at the door drew the attention of all those still in the room.

"Coming through," the paramedics said. They pushed a stretcher into the room in front of them, and immediately took control of Kelly's care from the SWAT team officer. "You need to let go of her, sweetie," one of the female paramedics said to Tara. "I promise, we'll take good care of her."

Tara leaned forward and kissed Kelly on the forehead. "Don't you dare die on me, Kelly Barkum. Do you hear me?" she scolded.

Kelly forced a smile onto her face. She lifted one hand and gently touched the circular mark on Tara's forehead, causing Tara to flinch.

"Kelly, promise me you won't die."

"Yes, ma'am!"

"I love you."

"I love you more," Kelly replied.

***

Billie, Jen and Fred waited for word of their children, along with the rest of the parents in the back of the parking lot. The scene was still unsecured, so they were not allowed to get any closer. They had seen several ambulances come and go, but they had no idea if their children were in them.

Billie held her phone in her hand and furiously texted Cat, as well as her contact at the police department. The anxiety she felt in the pit of her stomach was making her physically ill.

She already knew Seth was okay—physically anyway—but she still had no word about Tara...nor about Karissa, Steve or Kelly.

Suddenly Billie's phone rang. "Seth!" Billie said quickly.

"Mom, it's Tara. I lost my phone."

"Tara! Oh, my God. You're all right!" Billie looked at Jen and Fred who had hopefully expectant expressions on their faces. "Sweetie, are Karissa..."

"Karissa and Steve are both okay. We all are...except Kelly."

"What happened?" Billie asked.

Jen and Fred immediately looked alarmed.

"Hold on a sec, Tare." Billie turned to Jen and Fred. "Karissa and Steve are okay, but apparently Kelly isn't." She returned to her daughter. "What happened to Kelly, sweetheart?"

"He shot her in the stomach. The ambulance just took her to the hospital," Tara explained.

"Sweetie, Mama is at the hospital to help out in the emergency room. I'll call her right away and let her know Kelly is on her way in."

"Mom?"

"Yes, love?"

"It was horrible." Tara's voice broke. "I need you."

Billie choked back a sob. "Sweetheart, Mama and I are here for you. My arms are waiting for you as soon as they let you leave. I'm so sorry you had to go through this, love. I'm sorry all of you had to go through it."

"I'm worried about Kelly."

"I know you are, Tare. I will call Mama as soon as we hang up. Do you know when they'll let you go?"

"We're coming out now."

"Good. We are at the back of the parking lot near the football field. We'll be watching for you."

"I love you, Mom."

"I love you too, sweetheart."

Billie hung up the phone and immediately fell into Jen and Fred's arms. "They're okay. They're okay," she said. She pulled back and composed herself. "They're okay, except for Kelly. Tara said she was shot in the stomach. I need to call Cat."

Billie dialed Cat's number. She answered on the first ring. "Billie?"

"They're okay, Cat…except for Kelly. She was shot in the stomach and she's on the way to the hospital right now."

"They're okay?"

Billie could hear Cat sobbing on the other end of the line.

"Have you seen them yet?" Cat asked.

"They are on their way out of the school now. Tara asked me to let you know about Kelly."

"There's an ambulance docking right now. I'll check it out. Tell Tara I will do everything I can to see that Kelly gets the best care possible."

"She was shot in the stomach, Cat. How bad is that?" Billie asked.

"It depends on what the bullet did once it entered her abdominal cavity. I'll know more when I see her. They're wheeling a stretcher in right now. I'll call you back soon."

Billie hung up the phone and slipped it into her pocket. She looked at Jen and Fred, who stood arm in arm beside her, and she wrapped her arm around Jen's shoulder. Together, they waited for their children to come out of the school.

"There they are!" Fred exclaimed.

Billie's gaze followed the trajectory of Fred's arm. Her breath caught in her throat when she saw them. Seth, Steve and Tara were all covered in blood. Considering they were uninjured, she concluded the blood belonged to their classmates. Steve, Seth and Karissa patiently slowed their pace so that Tara could keep up with them on her crutches.

Had it not been for the yellow crime scene tape holding them back, Billie, Jen and Fred would have run toward them, but they were forced to wait patiently. Finally, they were reunited. There were no words exchanged during the reunion—just love communicated through hugs and tears.

Before they left, Karissa took her mother's hand. "Mom, Robert saved me."

"What are you talking about?" Jen asked.

"Robert saved me. He tackled the shooter and stopped him from going into my classroom."

"Robert *wasn't* the shooter?" Fred asked.

"No. It was Ryan Porter."

Billie turned to Seth. "Isn't that the kid who ranted homophobic slurs at you and Steve in the locker room?"

"That's him," Seth said. "Like I said—he's bad news."

Billie draped one arm over Seth and the other over Tara. "I, for one, have had enough bad news for one day. Let's go get your sister at Grammy and Grampa's and go home."

***

It was nearly dark by the time Billie arrived home with all three of her children. Seth headed directly to the bathroom to shower the blood from his body, while Tara went to her bedroom and sat on the edge of the bed.

Billie followed her into her room and sat beside her. "Wanna talk about it?"

"Why did he do it, Mom? Why would someone do something like that? Those kids he killed didn't do anything to him. I was sitting against the back wall in the middle of two other kids and he killed both of them and not me. He just shot them in the head without a second thought. Then, he put the gun to my head and said 'bang', but he didn't pull the trigger. Why would he do that?"

Billie's heart broke at the thought of what her daughter had lived through. She pulled Tara close to her. "I don't know, Tara. I wish I did, then maybe we could make sense of this, but I just don't know."

Billie took Tara's face between her palms and studied the mark on her forehead. "Tara, this looks like a burn."

Tara touched the mark and winced. "It is. The barrel of Ryan's gun was hot 'cause he just shot the other two kids." Tara's voice broke. "Mom, there was blood everywhere. He

152

shot them in the head. It…it was like their heads just exploded everywhere."

Billie gathered Tara into her arms and she began to cry. "My poor baby. No child should have to live through that. I am so sorry, love." For a long time, mother and daughter clung to one another as sobs wracked their bodies. Finally, their breathing returned to normal.

Billie released her daughter and looked again at the burn on her forehead. "We'll need to bandage that after your shower." She examined Tara once more. "Where did you get that shirt? I don't recognize it."

"I took my shirt off and used it to put pressure on Kelly's stomach when she was shot. I had only my sports bra on, so the school nurse gave it to me to wear."

"I see. You're covered in blood. Did you want to get out of those clothes?"

"Not until I know how Kelly is. It's her blood."

Billie nodded her understanding. "I see."

As if on cue, Billie's phone rang. It was Cat. "Cat? Can I put you on speaker? Tara is here with me."

"Yes." Cat waited until Billie confirmed she was on speaker.

"Hi, Mama," Tara said.

"Hi, my love. I can't wait to get home to hug and kiss and spoil you and your brother. I was on pins and needles all day worrying about you. I have never been so scared in my life. I can only image what you all went through."

"Mama, how is Kelly?"

"It looks like Kelly will be okay. I was worried that she might have damage to her spinal cord, but remarkably, the bullet only nicked her intestines and her reproductive organs…all of which should heal. She's lost a lot of blood and required a transfusion, but she'll be fine. Healing will take several months, but I predict a full recovery."

Tara looked at Billie and smiled through her tears. "When can I see her?"

"How does tomorrow sound?"

Tara released a visible sigh. "Tomorrow sounds great. Thanks for taking care of her, Mama."

"You're welcome, love."

"Mama, all of this made me realize that I love Kelly. I *really* love her...like you love Mom. I was so scared when I thought she was dying."

"What you feel for Kelly is very special, love," Cat said. "Not everyone is lucky enough to experience that."

"Are you sure she'll be okay?"

"I am sure, sweet pea. You'll see for yourself tomorrow. Her mom and dad are with her now, and she's awake already."

Tara wiped the tears from her eyes. "Thanks, Mom. I love you."

"I love you too, baby girl."

***

True to her word, when Cat arrived home that night, she showered hugs and kisses on all three of her children. They spent the evening together as a family, sadly talking about the traumatic day all of them had lived through. That night Cat and Billie tucked them all into bed—just like they had done when they were small.

In the morning, they awoke to find both Seth and Tara had climbed into bed with them some time during the night.

Chapter 18

The next morning, Seth and Tara sat on the couch in front of the television and watched news reports about the shooting. Billie stood behind the couch nursing a cup of coffee and watching over her children's shoulders. Needless to say school was closed for the day…and quite possibly, well into the next week.

Tara was tucked into her brother's side, with his arm wrapped securely around her. Their attention was glued to the television screen.

"Channel Five News reports that the gunman in yesterday's high school shooting killed sixteen people, including two teachers and the school's principal. Six others were also injured in the incident. The SWAT team, composed of members of the Albany City Police Department, Albany County Police and the Albany State Police apprehended the assailant with the help of another student, Robert Johnson.

"The shooter has been identified as Ryan Michael Porter, seventeen, a senior at the high school. Porter entered the school wearing a ski mask, and carrying an AR-15 semiautomatic rifle. By the time he was apprehended, he had gone through all but two spare clips, containing thirty rounds each.

"Porter was a relatively new student at Nassau High School, having transferred from Syracuse at the beginning of his senior year. Sources say that Porter's transfer to Nassau was due to religious conflicts he had with other students at his previous high school."

"Oh, my God!" Tara exclaimed. "He told me about that. He said he got into some trouble at his last school because of his beliefs."

"Amanda said the same to me just minutes before he came in and killed her and eight others in our class," Seth added. "What a freaking hypocrite he is!"

"What do you mean, Seth," Billie asked.

"That night we went to find Karissa at the party, we found Ryan clearly assaulting Amanda. Apparently, his *religion* allows rape, but not homosexuality."

"Hey, I just realized something," Tara said.

"What's that," Billie asked.

"He only hit the classrooms that *we* were all in…Seth, then Steve, then mine and finally, Karissa's," Tara said.

"What about Kelly's class? He didn't hit hers," Billie replied.

"That's because Kelly's class was *after* Karissa's. He would have hit hers if he hadn't already shot her in my classroom," Tara explained.

"What do you mean?" Billie asked.

"If you get me a piece of paper and a pen, I'll show you," Tara said.

Billie retrieved a sheet of paper from the printer, along with a pen, and gave them to Tara.

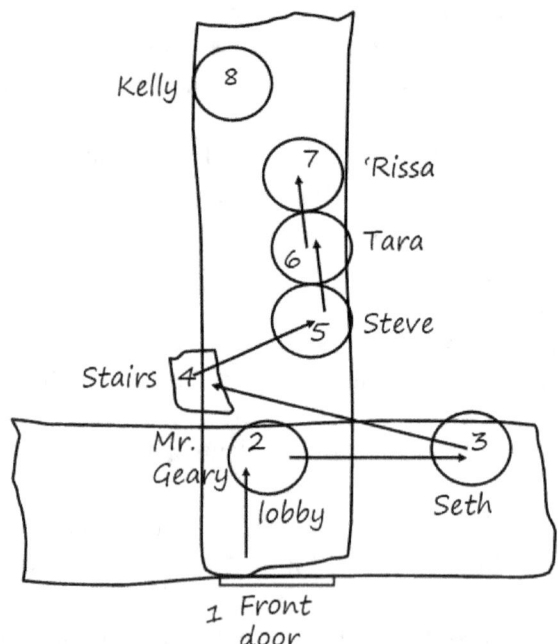

"Okay, the school kinds of looks like a cross…" Tara drew a crude layout of the school. "And here's the order he did the shooting in. See? Kelly's class was *after* Karissa's. While we were waiting for the school nurse to check us out, we talked to the other kids there, and all of them were in our classrooms. Ryan was after *us!*"

***

"Chief Bergman, please. Billie Charland calling," Billie said into her phone. "I'll wait." Billie paced back and forth across the kitchen while she waited for the chief of police to answer the phone.

Her attention was suddenly drawn to the back door when Jen and her children entered.

"The kids are in the living room watching the news," she said to the teenagers."

"I'll make coffee," Jen whispered.

"I'm on hold, Jen. Coffee would be great."

"Where's Cat?"

"She had surgeries this morning. I'm supposed to take Tara to see Kelly this afternoon, and then we're planning to do dinner. Want to join us?"

"That sounds great! We'll pick up Seth and Sky on the way so you don't have to come back to get them."

"Perfect! Ah, yes, Jeff, this is Billie Charland," she said as the chief's voice on the phone commanded her attention. "Thanks for taking my call. Jeff, I have reason to believe the shooting was a hate crime. I'd like to come in to talk to you about it. Yes, Monday is fine. How is nine o'clock? Great. I'll see you then."

"Hate crime?" Jen asked.

"Yes. Look at this diagram Tara drew for me earlier. See these circles? They represent the classrooms our kids were in. There are many other classrooms all around them, but Porter only went to *our kids'* classes."

"How does that make it a hate crime?"

"Seth said he and Steve had an encounter with Porter in the locker room a couple of weeks ago. Didn't Steve tell you about it?"

"No, he didn't."

"Apparently, Porter started quoting bible verses about homosexuality, and he accused Seth of being gay, because, of course…having gay moms means he's just *got* to be gay as well…and then he accused Seth and Steve of being a gay couple."

"He did what?" Jen exclaimed.

"My reaction, exactly!" Billie said.

"So what's that got to do with Karissa, Tara and Kelly?"

"The only thing I can think of is that he's figured out Tara and Kelly…and he assumed Karissa is gay by association."

"It's my fault."

Billie and Jen turned sharply toward the living room. Karissa was standing in the doorway, crying.

"What did you say, Karissa?" Jen asked.

"It's my fault. I told Ryan that Tara and Kelly are gay."

Tara walked up behind Karissa on her crutches. "'Rissa…how could you?"

"Okay, before we have an all-out war, let's all sit around the table and discuss this," Billie suggested. She led the girls to one side of the table, while she and Jen sat opposite them. "All right. Tell me what happened."

Karissa looked at the stern, angry look on Tara's face. "I'm sorry, Tare. It was that morning I was angry at you because Ryan liked you and not me."

"I *told* you, 'Rissa, that I had no interest in him!" Tara said.

"I know. I guess I needed someone to blame besides myself that he didn't like me."

"You should be damned happy that he didn't like you," Jen said.

Karissa looked at her hands and fought to hold back tears. "Anyway, I saw him push you in your wheelchair into your class, and I ran into him on purpose when he came out. I told him you wouldn't go out with him because you were gay and that Kelly was your girlfriend. I'm sorry, Tare."

Tara didn't say anything for a few moments. Then, she looked at her friend and shoulder-bumped her. "Like I said to Kel, it doesn't take a rocket scientist to figure us out. It's okay, 'Rissa."

"No! It's not okay. Don't you see? Because of me, sixteen people are dead!"

"No, no, no, no no!" Jen said. "You are *not* responsible for his choices, Karissa."

"I agree with your mom," Billie added. "Even if he hadn't heard it from you, he would have heard it from someone else, or he would have figured it out himself. Don't blame yourself for this. The point is—he did this because he hates gay people. Apparently, his religion teaches him that homosexuals are evil and deserve to die. I'll be damned if I will let him get away with an insanity defense. This is a hate crime, pure and simple."

***

Billie and Tara approached the nurse's station and asked for Kelly's room number. Moments later, they stood in the doorway to Kelly's room and saw two other visitors were already there...an attractive forty-something woman with long blond hair and wearing a color coordinated outfit, complete with pearls, and a fifty-something gentleman in a military uniform with a variety of ribbons and badges above his left breast. He was clean-shaven and was tall and broad-shouldered with close cropped sandy-blond hair.

As soon as Tara saw Kelly, the other people in the room no longer existed for her. She made a beeline straight to Kelly's bed and took her hand. She fought to keep the quiver from her voice. "Kel, my mom says you're gonna be okay. I was so scared. How are you feeling?"

Kelly looked nervously at Tara and then at her parents. "Hey, Tare. I've been better."

Tara leaned down to whisper in Kelly's ear. "I love you."

Kelly smiled, but didn't respond. Again, her gaze darted toward her parents.

Tara stood erect again and frowned. "They don't know, do they?" she whispered.

Kelly looked directly at her. "I'm sorry," she said softly.

"So, I assume this is Tara," Kelly's father said.

"Yes. Tara Charland, and this is her mom, Billie," Kelly said.

Kelly's father extended his hand to Tara for a handshake. Tara's hand disappeared into his.

"It's nice to meet you, Mr. Barkum," Tara said.

"And that's my mom," Kelly added.

Mrs. Barkum waved. "Hi, Tara."

Mr. Barkum turned to Billie and extended his hand. "Roger Barkum."

"Billie Charland," Billie said. "Nice to meet you, Colonel."

"You're familiar with military ranks?"

"Yes, sir. When I earned my law degree, I was especially interested in studying military law. Thank you for your service, Sir."

"My wife, Cindy," Colonel Barkum said.

Billie shook her hand. "Nice to meet you, Cindy."

Colonel Barkum took Billie's arm and led her to the other side of the room. "My wife and I are pretty shaken by the shooting at the school yesterday."

"My wife and I are as well," Billie replied. "I for one, believe it was a hate crime, and I am pursuing that angle with the chief of police."

"A hate crime?"

"I have reason to believe that our children were targeted in this attack."

"Why on earth would they be targeted?"

"The suspect has been known to have verbally attacked the LGBTQ community at his last high school. I intend to make sure an insanity defense does not hold in this case."

"LGBTQ?" Colonel Barkum looked at his daughter and then back at Billie. "You think...?"

Billie dropped her chin to her chest and rubbed her forehead. She looked at Colonel Barkum again. "I'm sorry. I thought you knew."

He sighed deeply. "To be honest, I have suspected it for a while now, but no—she hasn't said anything to me. I assume Tara...?"

"Yes, Tara is gay. She cares very much for Kelly."

"I see."

Colonel Barkum walked to the window and looked out across the parking lot for a few moments. Finally, he turned around to face Billie once more. "Cindy and I will do whatever we can to prevent people like Ryan Porter from marginalizing our daughter, and people like her. She has the right to live a happy and fulfilling life—just like anyone else—regardless of who she loves. You can count on us."

Billie extended her hand. "You are a good man, Colonel Barkum. Kelly is lucky to have you and Cindy for parents."

"We love our daughter. It's just that simple."

Colonel Barkum walked to Kelly's bedside. Tara took a step back. He reached for Kelly's hand. "I think it's about time you introduce us to your girlfriend, young lady."

Chapter 19

"Yay! Pizza!" Skylar yelled when the waitress delivered three large pies to their table.

They sat in the middle of the pizza parlor with three tables pulled together. The five kids sat on one end, while the four parents sat on the other.

"I'm sorry Kelly's parents couldn't join us, but I understand they want to spend time with her while she's in the hospital," Cat said.

"I like Kelly's dad. He seems like a fair guy…and he obviously loves his daughter," Billie added.

"He kind of scares me," Tara said.

"Really? How so," Billie asked.

"I don't know. He's…"

"Intimidating?" Cat suggested.

"Yeah. That's the word. I'm kind of bummed that Kelly didn't tell her parents about us."

Billie covered Tara's hand with her own. "Cut her some slack, Tare. It's not easy to come out—especially to your parents."

"I didn't find it that hard," Tara said.

Cat chuckled. "I would hope not! Especially considering who we are."

"It was weird…and awkward at the hospital," Tara said.

"I know what you mean. I think I unintentionally spilled the beans with her dad. I hope Kelly's not upset about that," Billie said.

"I guess I was just surprised she didn't tell them. When we first admitted we liked each other, Kelly thought her parents would be okay with it 'cause her dad supported getting rid of Don't Ask, Don't Tell. I thought she told them."

"I hate to say it, but it's people like Ryan that make it scary to be different," Seth said. "I mean, you can be killed for just being who you are."

"Ryan's mind has been poisoned with beliefs that have been drilled into him—probably for years," Billie said.

"We're in your corner, Billie," Fred said. "This truly is a hate crime and it needs to be prosecuted as one. We can't have him claiming mental illness and getting off after a few years in an institution."

"I can't believe I actually liked him," Karissa added.

Tara reached for Karissa's hand. "You didn't know, 'Rissa. None of us did. The first time I met him, I thought he was really nice too. In fact, Kelly and I were trying to think of ways to get him to like you. I'm glad now that we failed."

"You know, Ryan's beliefs are only part of the problem," Jen said.

"Guns," Steve and Seth said together.

"Exactly," Jen replied.

Tara became animated. "We need to do something about that."

"Define 'something,'" Billie said.

"I don't know...protests, rallies, and letter-writing campaigns. Our school isn't the first one to have a shooting, and it probably won't be the last one," Tara said.

"Again, the gun advocates will try to turn this into a mental health issue instead of a gun problem," Billie said. "Fighting the gun lobby is a huge undertaking, but we don't stand a chance of changing the laws if they continue to ignore the hatred that is running rampant in this country."

"The racist, hateful rhetoric will not get better as long as the people at the top continue to encourage it," Cat pointed out.

"Then we need to get out and campaign to change our leadership, *as well as* fighting to restrict access to certain weapons," Jen said adamantly. "There's an election next year— right? It's not too early to start campaigning *against* the hate and *for* people who have the guts enough to take on the gun violence issue."

"I agree," Fred said. "I'm against banning all guns, but no one needs an AR-15 to hunt. Hell, there'd be nothing left to eat if you emptied an AR-15 clip into a deer. Weapons like that were made for only one reason – killing as many people, as fast as possible."

"I agree, wholeheartedly!" The voice came from behind the moms.

Cat and Billie turned around quickly and saw Colonel Barkum and his wife, Cindy, standing behind them. Billie immediately rose to her feet, as did Fred. She extended her hand for a firm handshake. "Colonel Barkum," she said.

"Roger. Call me Roger. Do you mind if we join you? Kelly insisted we go get a bite to eat."

"No! Not at all." Billie and Fred dragged another nearby table to theirs. "Please, have a seat."

Once seated, Billie made introductions. "Roger, this is my wife, Cat."

"Colonel Barkum shook hands with Cat. "Didn't I see you in Kelly's room earlier today?" he asked.

"Yes. I anesthetized her during her surgery. I was just checking in on her."

"We want to thank you for taking such good care of her," Cindy said.

"She's a special young lady. We're very fond of her," Cat replied.

Billie continued with the introductions. "This is Fred and Jen Swenson. They're Karissa and Steve's parents."

They shook hands with both Roger and Cindy.

"Karissa. We've heard a lot about her," Cindy said, and she acknowledged both Karissa and Steve.

"The girls are inseparable," Jen pointed out. "We have come to really enjoy Kelly."

"Finally, these are our other kids…Skylar and Seth, and of course, you've already met Tara."

Colonel Barkum looked at the children. "It hits home to put faces on the victims of yesterday's tragedy. His gaze stopped on Skylar. I'll bet even you were affected, little one."

"We had to hide in the safe room," Skylar said. "It was kind of scary."

"Jen teaches at the middle school," Fred said. "Imagine hiding in a closet with your students while your own son and daughter are in danger just across the parking lot."

"Our hearts go out to all the victims and their families…and make no bones about it…we are all victims, whether you survived or not," Cindy added. "We heard you talking about protesting the lack of gun control. We want to help."

"Seriously?" Tara asked.

"Seriously," Colonel Barkum replied. "Don't let this uniform fool you. I support a strong military, but the kinds of weapons being used in this shooting epidemic have no business in the hands of ordinary citizens."

"The fight for gun legislation will not be easy," Billie said. "The gun lobby is very strong."

"We may need to divide and conquer to focus our efforts on both gun violence and the trial," Roger said.

"I suspect the trial will not happen for several months yet." Billie said. "Any lawyer worth his salt will recommend Porter enters an insanity defense. That will push the trial out for months for the psychological analyses alone. I will keep an eye on the legal aspects of this case, but we'll have plenty of time to focus on gun control in the meantime."

The new friends said their goodbyes in the parking lot after dinner.

"Roger, I want to apologize again for outing Kelly. I truly thought you knew," Billie said.

"Think nothing of it, Billie. Like I said, I've suspected it for a while now. I just wish she had felt comfortable enough to tell me herself."

"For what it's worth, I understand her reluctance. I never really did come out to my own parents, and now they're both gone. It sounds much easier than it really is—no matter how good a relationship you have with your parents."

Roger nodded. "I'm just glad to know. I won't pretend to understand it, but I want Kelly to feel she has the right to love who she loves, without ridicule."

"Anyway, it wasn't my place to out her, as unintentional as it was. I will apologize to her as well."

Roger shook her hand. "You're a woman with integrity. I like that!"

"Thank you. I'm sure we'll be in touch when the kids have organized their grassroots campaign. Cat and I are looking forward to working with you and Cindy. Hopefully, we'll be able to make a difference."

***

Billie awoke in the middle of the night and looked at her clock. Two in the morning. She frowned and wondered what had awakened her. She closed her eyes and tried to fall back asleep, but her subconscious mind registered a sound that was out of place. She opened her eyes again and looked at the ceiling while she strained to listen.

Thud, thud, thud.

Billie sat up in bed and looked around. "What the hell?" she whispered into the dark.

Thud, thud, thud.

Thud, thud, thud.

She threw the covers back, swung her legs around and placed her feet on the floor. A moment later, she tied her bathrobe closed, slipped her feet into her slippers and headed into the hallway. She noticed Seth's door was open as she passed by. Billie peeked in and saw it was empty.

Thud, thud, thud.

Thud, thud, thud.

Billie followed the sound and descended the stairs to the living room. The volume increased as she approached the kitchen. Finally, she realized it was coming from outdoors. Billie reached for the door handle and stepped onto the porch. The motion light was on above the garage door, and there was Seth, shooting baskets. *Thud, thud, thud, swoosh.*

Billie leaned against the post. "Hey love. Can't sleep?" she asked.

Seth looked up to see his mother and acted as though it was perfectly normal to be up shooting baskets in the middle of the night. "Yeah."

Billie stepped off the porch and held her hands out for the ball. Seth threw it to her.

For the next ten minutes, it was a one-on-one scrimmage between mother and son. Seth appeared to become more and more aggressive with each basket he dunked. Finally, he slammed the ball through the basket hard enough for him to lose his balance and to crash into the garage door. He slid down the door and sat on the ground with his back against it, and buried his head in his hands and sobbed.

Billie sat beside him and wrapped her arm around his shoulder. It didn't take long for him to lay his head in her lap, while she stroked his hair.

"Talk to me, love," Billie encouraged him.

"I don't understand it, Mom. I don't understand how anyone could do what Ryan did. He destroyed so many lives."

"I know. Ryan's mind is filled with all kind of evil beliefs that he was taught all his life. I have seen so much hatred taught in the name of religion. It is sometimes beyond my comprehension."

"It was horrible, Mom. I had to lie under the bodies of my classmates and pretend to be dead so he would leave us alone. I will never forget that for as long as I live."

Tears rolled down Billie's cheeks and her heart broke for her son. "I know, sweetie. I know. That's why we need to get you some help...you and Tara. You two have seen things that kids your age should never see. We will get through this...I promise."

"I love you Mom. I love you and Mama, and my sisters too. I can't imagine how I would feel if Tara was killed. I just can't imagine it."

"Mama and I love you too, scout." Billie continued to stroke Seth's hair until he stopped crying. "Do you think you might be able to sleep now?" she asked.

Seth sat up with his back against the door once more. He looked at his mother with a crooked grin on his face. "I feel like a baby."

Billie took his hand. "It's perfectly okay to feel vulnerable, Seth...and besides, you'll always be my baby—no matter how old you are." She bumped shoulders with him. "Come on—time for bed."

***

Tara went with Cat to the hospital bright and early the next morning to visit with Kelly while her mother completed some paperwork from the trauma cases the day before. She approached Kelly's room and peeked inside. Her heart soared when she realized Kelly was alone.

"Hey, Kel!" she said brightly as she entered the room.

Kelly smiled broadly. "Tara!"

Tara crossed the room, and tenderly kissed Kelly on the lips. Although their lips parted, their gazes did not. They couldn't stop looking at one another. Emotions flowed freely between them.

"I was so afraid of losing you when he put that gun to your head," Kelly whispered.

"When he turned around and shot you instead, my heart sank into my stomach. I would have wanted to die as well if I lost you," Tara replied.

Kelly touched the burn on Tara's forehead. "Does it hurt?"

"It stings a little, but it's nothing compared to what you're going through."

A few tears escaped Kelly's eyes. "Tare, what are we going to do if my dad wants to move away because of this?"

Tara smiled and wiped the tears from Kelly's cheeks. "I don't' think we have to worry about that for a while."

"What do you mean?"

"Your parents joined us for pizza last night, and they both volunteered to help us fight this."

"Fight what?"

"The insanity around guns. Your dad is really against the public having semiautomatic weapons. We made plans last night to start a campaign for gun control."

"You mean, like those kids in Florida?"

"That's exactly what I mean. All our parents are on board, but *we* need to be the face of the campaign…you and me, and Seth, Steve and Karissa. Even Skylar wants to join in. We need to get the kids at school on board too. We need to make the government listen to us—starting with our own state senators."

"My dad wants to help?" Kelly said, disbelief coloring her words.

"Both your parents. I know! I was shocked too. I thought that since he's military, that he would be all *for* guns, but he's not—at least not the kinds of guns used in war. If we can get just the semiautomatic weapons banned, that will be a good start."

"Wow! I'm shocked."

"Me too! Oh, and my mom says she's going to make sure what Ryan did is considered a hate crime, and not because of mental illness...although, I do think he's nuts!"

"Hate crime?"

"Yeah. She said he did it out of hatred for gay people—not because he's mentally ill. She said it will help our case to ban semiautomatic weapons if it's considered a hate crime."

Kelly reached up and cupped the side of Tara's face. "Are you ready for this, Tare? I mean, everyone will know we're gay."

Tara lowered her lips to Kelly's once more and for several long moments, she savored the taste and feel of Kelly. When the kiss ended, she placed her forehead on Kelly's and closed her eyes. "This feels amazing, Kel. How can I admit it to myself, and at the same time, deny it to everyone else? This is our chance to show everyone just how wonderful this is. I don't care if they like it or not."

Kelly also closed her eyes. "I love you, Tare."

"Hey, you two!"

The girls looked up to see Kelly's mom breeze into the room. They quickly parted and put a little distance between them. Both girls wore pretty shades of pink on their faces, having been caught in a romantic position.

"Good morning, Mrs. Barkum," Tara said.

"Hi, Mom!" Kelly added.

"I just spoke with your doctors, and it looks like they plan to release you tomorrow," Mrs. Barkum said.

"Already?" Kelly exclaimed.

"Apparently, they are pleased with your progress. Of course, you'll be under strict limitations for a while, but yes—you go home tomorrow. Of course, that depends on you getting out of bed today, and on you pooping."

"Mom!" Kelly complained. "Did you have to say that in front of Tara?"

Mrs. Barkum approached the girls. She took one of Kelly's hands in hers, and then placed her other hand on Tara's arm. "Get used to it. Pooping is something couples do in front of one another all the time."

"Jeez, mom! That's gross!" Kelly's face was beet red.

Tara just grinned.

Cat walked into the room at the tail end of the conversation. "Are we talking about pooping in front of our significant others?" she asked.

"Yes, we are, in fact," Cindy replied, a hint of mischief in her voice.

"Billie and I do it in front of each other all the time," Cat said.

Cindy laughed. "You two are lucky. Guy poop is toxic! When Roger poops, the smell is bad enough to mold bread!"

"Eww!" the girls exclaimed together.

Chapter 20

On Monday morning, Billie took Seth and Tara with her to her appointment with Chief Bergman. Her intent was to convince the police chief that there was enough evidence to at least consider what Ryan Porter did as essentially a hate crime, done with intent.

Seth provided a verbal description of his encounter with Ryan in the locker room.

"So he called you and Steve faggots?" the chief asked.

"And he quoted some bible verses that basically said gay people were abominations and should die," Seth said.

"And Steve Swenson will collaborate your story?"

"Yes."

"Did anyone else witness this?" the chief asked.

"I honestly don't know. The only people close by when it happened were me and Steve. And of course, Ryan. There could have been others in the locker room, but if there were, they didn't say anything. Oh, the coach will back up the unnecessary roughness stuff during practice. He actually benched Ryan for doing it."

"This is helpful, Seth. I'll speak with the coach as well." The police chief turned to Tara. "So what do you have for me, young lady?"

Tara explained her drawing with the shooting sequence to the police chief to convey her belief that Ryan's goal was to kill her, Seth, Steve, Karissa and Kelly. "There were a lot of other classrooms he could have gone into, but he only chose the ones that me and my friends were in. He's been kind of stalking me since the beginning of the year. He also told me he was kicked out of his last school because of his beliefs."

"So you think he planned all of this," the police chief said.

"It looks that way to me," Tara said.

Chief Bergman sat back in his chair. "You've both given me something to think about. I'll start an investigation into Porter's last high school right away, and I'll have my guys interview everyone on the football team. Some of them might have been in the locker room when your confrontation went down, Seth. I want to thank both of you for coming in."

***

Later that morning, Billie, Cat, Seth and Tara sat in the waiting room of Justin Martin, the prosecuting attorney assigned to the trial of Ryan Porter.

"Mom, why can't *you* be our lawyer?" Tara asked.

"Because I have a conflict of interest," Billie explained. "I'm too close to it. We can't introduce any doubt in the jurors' minds that might lead to a mistrial."

"But…"

"Tara, I can't. It just isn't allowed. The defense attorney could say that I'm biased…and you know what? He would be right. Don't worry. I've been working with the attorney general to choose the right person for the job, and I will work closely with them to be sure all the bases are covered. Okay?"

"Is there a chance Ryan will get away with this?" Seth asked.

"No. There's no way he would technically get away with what he did. The real question is whether he'll be convicted based on cognitive intent…or mental illness. The penalty based on a proven mental disability defense is much less severe and much shorter than proving he knowingly and intentionally planned and executed it."

"I still don't know why you can't be our lawyer." Tara pouted.

Cat spoke up. "Sweetheart, it raises the same ethical questions around surgeons who operate on their own family members. It's just not done unless there is no other option."

Tara crossed her arms in front of her chest. "It isn't fair."

The door to the inner office opened—effectively putting an end to the ethics debate.

"I assume you're the Charlands?"

"Yes," Billie replied.

"Come in. Have a seat."

The family filed into the room and sat in the four chairs that were arranged in front of Martin's desk. Mr. Martin shook hands with each of them then circled his desk and sat down. He opened the folder on his desk and shuffled through the papers.

Cat reached for Billie's hand and squeezed. She raised her eyebrows at Billie and smiled. Billie nodded almost imperceptibly when Cat mouthed the word *'trans.'*

Mr. Martin found the page he was looking for. He sat back in his chair and looked at the family before him. "The first thing I want to do is express my condolences that you had to go through this horrific event. Especially you, Tara and Seth. I can only imagine how traumatic that must have been."

"Thank you, Mr. Martin," Billie said. "It's something I hope we never have to experience again."

"Justin. Please call me Justin." He looked at the paper in his hand. "I've read the legal details of the case and I have to say that it may not be as easy a win as it might look on the surface. There is no doubt he did what he did. What is in question here— and what the defense will argue—is that he was not in his right mind when he did it."

He put the paper on his desk and looked directly at the family. "What we need to determine here is whether this is a hate crime, or a crime of passion."

Tara raised her hand.

"You have a question?" Justin said.

"How can it be a crime of passion? What he did was evil, not passionate," Tara said.

"That is a very good question," Justin replied. "When we say a crime of passion, we mean the person was not in their right mind, kind of like when you have a boyfriend or a girlfriend and what you feel for them makes you do things you wouldn't normally do. A crime of passion is another way of saying they were under mental distress at the time and they may not be responsible for what they did."

Tara looked quickly at Billie. "That can't happen here, Mom. Ryan can't get away with this."

"Let's not get ahead of ourselves," Justin said. "After reading the police report, there is no doubt Mr. Porter did what he did. We just need to present enough evidence to prove he did it with intent. That's where all of you come in, as well as several other witnesses I will need to interview."

"We'll help in any way we can," Billie said. "I am prepared to act in the capacity of paralegal for you if necessary, although I have to avoid anything that might be misconstrued as legal representation."

Justin looked at the paperwork in front of him. "Ah...you're Billie Charland. You have quite a reputation with the courts."

"Guilty! A little lawyer humor there," Billie said.

"That was so corny, Mom!" Seth added.

Justin grinned and shook his head. He looked at Cat. "So you must be Caitlain O'Grady of the famous "Charland-O'Grady versus the State of New York same-sex marriage case."

"Also guilty," Cat confirmed.

"Well, I'm happy to meet you both—and yes, I will accept any help on this case you can give me, Billie."

"Okay, so when do we get started?" Billie asked.

"How about right now? Do you have time?"

"We have as much time as you need."

***

Tara lay side by side on her bed with Karissa, holding her tablet above them so that both of them could see Kelly on the other end of the video chat.

"So, what was it like?" Kelly asked.

"At first, we were all in his office talking about the trial and stuff like that, and then he sent Seth out of the room and questioned me, with my moms there," Tara said. "He brought Seth in and questioned him after he was done with me."

"What kind of questions did he ask?" Karissa said.

"He asked about how long I've known Ryan, and what I thought of him. Oh, and he asked if Ryan has done anything that was uncomfortable for me. We talked a lot about what happened during the shooting. He also asked me if Ryan ever talked about gay people around me. I didn't tell him I was gay, but I think he might suspect I am."

"What makes you think that?" Kelly asked.

"I'm pretty sure he's trans. I kind of got those vibes from him. I assume he caught my vibes too."

"You mean gaydar?"

"Yes. Anyway, he asked me a lot of questions about Ryan and the shooting. He said he would be sharing the questions with us that he'll ask at the trial so we can prepare ahead of time."

"So, he's going to interview *all* of us?" Karissa asked.

"Yes. He's probably already called your parents, and he plans to talk to the other kids in our classes and to the SWAT team officers who arrested him."

"I'm kind of nervous about testifying," Karissa said.

"Me too," Kelly agreed.

"We just need to tell the truth," Tara said.

"I wonder if Ryan will be in the room when we testify," Kelly said.

"Probably," Tara replied.

"That will be creepy," Karissa added.

"What *I'm* worried about is when Ryan's lawyer cross-examines us. Justin said he will be brutal."

"On TV shows, the other lawyer tries to make you look bad, or make you look like you're lying," Karissa pointed out.

"Just tell the truth—and don't cry!" Kelly said. "You can't look weak."

"That's what my mom said," Tara added. "She said they will try to break us, so we need to be strong and to stick to our story."

"I am not looking forward to this," Kelly said.

"Me neither, but we can't let Ryan get away with this," Tara replied. "And besides, my mom thinks the trial won't happen for a while yet…maybe even a year…so we have plenty of time to prepare."

Karissa pulled her phone out of her pocket. "My mom just texted me. I gotta go home for dinner."

"All right, 'Rissa. Call me later," Tara said.

"Bye, 'Rissa!" Kelly said on the other end of the video chat.

Tara waited for Karissa to leave before she addressed Kelly again. "How are you feeling, Kel?"

"I've only been home for one day and I'm already bored out of my mind. Can you come over?"

"Maybe after dinner."

"I can ask my parents if you can stay over."

"Do you think they'll let me? I mean, they haven't had a lot of time to get used to the gay idea."

"I have a hole in my stomach. It's not like we're gonna have hot monkey sex in my bed!"

That visual made Tara laugh so hard, she literally rolled off the bed and onto the floor.

"Oh, my God. You are hilarious!" Kelly said once Tara righted herself. "Don't make me laugh. It hurts!"

"Sheesh! That was graceful! Call me back after you talk to your parents. I'll go clear it with my moms."

***

Kelly called Tara back before she even had a chance to make her way into the kitchen for dinner. "Hey, Kelly," Tara said into her phone.

"Mom and Dad said you can stay over, but you have to sleep on the floor. They are blaming it on my injury, but I suspect there's much more behind it, if you know what I mean."

"I'll take it," Tara said. "Just knowing I'm there with you will be enough."

"I know it sucks, Tare. You don't have to if you don't really want to."

"I *really* want to, Kelly. I still need to ask my moms. I'll text you thumbs up or down in a few minutes. If it's thumbs up, what time should I come over?"

"We're getting ready to have dinner right now, so maybe in an hour?" Kelly replied.

"That sounds good. I'll let you know. Love you!"

"Love you too!"

Tara hung up her phone and slipped it into her pocket. *Love you, too!* The feeling of euphoria almost overshadowed the anguish and trauma she had lived through just four days earlier. Almost.

***

Tara arranged a pile of pillows and blankets on the floor beside Kelly's bed and spread herself out on them to try it out. "This isn't so bad," she said.

Kelly looked over the edge of her bed at her. "I'm sorry, Tare. I'd rather have you up here with me."

Tara raised her hand to touch Kelly. "I'd rather be up there with you too, but maybe your mom and dad are right. I'd feel horrible if I rolled over in my sleep and hit your incision."

"You know they'll be in and out of here all night, checking on me. I'm not sure how much sleep either of us will get."

"I can't blame them, Kel. After all, you were shot in the stomach only four days ago."

"I guess. We're just not going to have a lot of privacy tonight."

Tara climbed to her knees and leaned on the bed toward Kelly. "Kel, it's okay. Really. I'm happy just to be here with you."

"Okay…okay! I believe you. So, when do you think school will start again?"

Tara sat back on her heels. "I don't know. I'm guessing there's a lot of clean-up to do. There were bodies everywhere, and a lot of blood, not to mention the damage to the walls from bullets."

"And there are all the funerals. I can't imagine they'll start classes again until all the funerals are over," Kelly said.

"My mom said it will be an active crime scene for a while. The police need to take pictures and collect evidence, so it might take a while before they even start the clean-up."

"I read somewhere that at some school shootings, they actually close or tear down the school buildings the shootings happened in. I'm kind of worried about how we're gonna finish our sophomore year," Kelly said.

"I hope they don't make us go to school all summer to make up the time. That would suck."

"That would suck, big time!" Kelly agreed.

***

The shooter raised the barrel of his rifle and shot her teacher three times. She fell into a heap at his feet. Several girls screamed. He shot them as well…shot them in the head.

He turned again walked directly toward Tara. She was huddled between two of her classmates against the back wall. He stopped in front of her and raised his rifle. Suddenly, he looked at the girl on Tara's right. Bang! She was dead. The shooter watched her slump and turned his attention to the boy on her left. Bang! He was dead.

Tara was paralyzed with fear, the blood of her classmates splattered on her face and clothes. She couldn't run. She couldn't even scream. The shooter put the barrel of the gun directly on Tara's forehead and held it there for a long time. Finally, he spoke. "Bang." He threw his head back and laughed when Tara realized she was still alive.

Tara watched Kelly burst into the classroom.

"No!"

The shooter quickly turned around and shot Kelly in the stomach.

"Kelly!"

"Tara! Tare, wake up! You're having a nightmare." Kelly did her best to reach Tara from her position on the bed, to no avail. Finally, she grabbed one of her pillows and hit Tara with it.

Tara immediately sat up. "What! What happened!"

Kelly was crying. "Tara, it's me. Kelly. Tare, you were having a nightmare."

Tara looked around, her eyes wide open and wild with fear. Her body shook. "Kelly?"

"I'm here, love. You were having a nightmare," Kelly said.

Tara pulled her knees into her chest and rested her elbows on them. She dropped her face into her hands and wept.

"Tare, come here," Kelly said.

Tara looked up at Kelly from her position on the floor. "But your parents…"

"You need me right now more than I need to obey the rules. Come up here." Kelly did her best to make room for Tara to climb in beside her.

Tara very gently lay beside Kelly, with her head on Kelly's shoulder.

Kelly pulled the sheet over both of them and ran her fingertips back and forth on the arm Tara had draped over her chest. "You're safe, Tare. I've got you. You're safe," she said repeatedly until they both fell asleep.

Unknown to the girls, Kelly's bedroom door slowly opened and Colonel Barkum looked in. He saw Tara and Kelly in bed together and Kelly was stroking Tara's arm.

"You're safe, Tare. I've got you. You're safe," he heard Kelly say.

His eyes brimmed with tears when he saw Tara's distressed state. *PTSD.* His heart went out to her. His gaze moved to his daughter.

You are turning into a compassionate young woman, Kelly. I'm proud so of you.

Slowly, he backed out of the room and closed the door.

In the Blink of an Eye

Chapter 21

After dinner, the Swensons retreated to their family room to watch movies and to unwind before heading to bed. Karissa sat tucked into Jen's side on the couch.

"Mom?" Karissa said.

"Yes love?"

"The funerals should be happening soon."

"Funerals?"

"Yes. For the kids and teachers who were killed in the shooting."

Jen turned to face Karissa. "I'm sorry, love. I never even gave it a thought. They were your friends? Of course, we'll go."

"Mom, I want to go to *all* of them."

"All? All sixteen funerals?" Jen asked.

"Yes."

"Why would you want to do that, sweetie? I can understand the ones in your class, but why all of them?"

Karissa began to cry. "Because I still feel like this is my fault. If I didn't tell Ryan about Tara and Kelly…"

Fred leaned forward on the couch when he realized Karissa was crying. "Whoa…what's going on?"

Jen took Karissa by the shoulders. "Karissa, you are not responsible for Ryan's actions. You are not. Sweetie, if your brother robbed a bank because you wanted a new pair of shoes, would it be your fault or his?"

"Leave me out of this," Steve said from the overstuffed chair.

"Steve, please!" Jen shot back. "Whose fault would it be, Karissa?"

"Steve's?"

"Yes—Steve's. Ryan did what he did because he wanted to…not because you made him do it, or encouraged him to do it. If you want to go to all of the funerals, we can do that. It would be good for the whole community to go, but do it because you want to pay your respects, not because you feel guilty. The guilt is Ryan's to feel—not yours."

"I still feel like it's my fault. I can't sleep at night because all I can do is think about it."

Jen looked closely at her daughter and noticed the dark circles under her eyes. "Sweetie, maybe we should get some therapy for you." She looked at her son. "And for you as well, Steve. Are you having problems sleeping?"

Steve shrugged. "Kind of. I've been waking up at night 'cause I keep seeing Mike getting shot in the chest. I keep wondering why it was him and not me."

Fred clenched his fists. "This whole family has suffered because of Ryan Porter. Just imagine how the families feel who lost loved ones. I think we should all go to therapy, Jen."

***

For the next two weeks, the Charland, Swenson and Barkum families attended funeral after funeral. There seemed to be an endless stream of tears shed by the entire community. There was also a great deal of discussion about starting a political action group to address the issue of gun violence. Based on her previous activism and his military experience, Billie and Roger were encouraged by the community to lead the effort to form such a group. Plans were made to organize as soon as possible.

***

It took several weeks for the damage at the school to be repaired. All of the affected classrooms were repainted, and a memorial plaque was mounted on the wall inside the lobby. It listed the names of all twenty-two victims, with special emphasis on those who did not survive. Pictures of each victim were mounted around the plaque to preserve their memories.

After three weeks, classes resumed. The first thing Steve, Seth, Tara, Karissa and Kelly noticed when they entered the campus, was the overwhelming array of flowers, teddy bears, crosses, hearts and candles that lined the entryway of the school.

It was literally a shrine to all those who were lost or injured in the shooting. All three girls shed tears as they walked through the tribute and into the lobby.

There were reminders everywhere that things would forever be changed. Metal detectors were installed just inside the front doors. There was a heavy police presence on campus, including several uniformed officers patrolling all of the hallways throughout the day. Cars were prohibited from being parked in front of the school for more than a simple drop-off or pick-up. And last, but certainly not least, was the replacement of the now-deceased Principal Geary with the former vice principal Calloway.

The staff of the school tried hard to resume business as usual; however, the new normal now included the metal detectors and a requirement for all backpacks to be made of clear, see-through plastic. Counseling sessions were also arranged for any student who felt the need to talk through their trauma.

And the silence was deafening. A feeling of reverence followed the students from class to class. In many ways, it felt more like a church than a school. Students even opened and closed their lockers more softly than usual.

Through extraordinary effort from the department of education, all traces of the tragedy were erased. Gone were the bodies of their classmates. Gone were all traces of blood from the walls and floors. Gone were the broken doors and bullet holes in the walls. All evidence of the tragedy was gone, except, perhaps, the most visual sign of all—the caution and fear in the students' eyes as they walked from classroom to classroom. It would be a long time before any of them felt safe again.

***

On a Friday night, shortly after school resumed, Billie and Cat invited the Swensons and Barkums to their house for dinner. The discussion during and after dinner was about moving forward with their lives and in some way, trying to restore the feeling of safety and security to their community.

They retired to the family room after dinner.

"There is a lot of healing to do," Jen said. She pulled Karissa to her side and kissed her on the temple.

"I'm just happy we're all safe. This could have turned out so differently," Billie pointed out.

"I don't want to rain on anyone's parade, but you're right, Billie. This *could* have turned out differently," Roger said. "That's why we need to act soon. There's a whole war to be waged ahead of us with the gun control issue."

"Agreed," Billie said. "We need to strike while the iron is hot and the memories of this horrific event are fresh. We are not a family that shies away from activism or challenges. Based on the conversations we had at the funerals, it appears we will have a lot of community support as well. I'm in. Who's with me?"

Billie thrust her arm forward, palm down. She was soon joined by Seth, who placed his hand on top of hers. Karissa was next, followed by Tara, Steve and Kelly. At that point, it became a race between Jen, Fred, Roger and Cindy to see who would be next.

"Hey! What about me?" Skylar exclaimed.

Billie opened a space for her younger daughter to fit into. "Get in here, rug rat. Together, we are like a small pebble in a large pond. We might not make a huge splash, but our ripples will carry far, and the pond will be forever changed. We can do this!"

"Okay," Cat said. "Let's get this party started. First things first…we need to make protest posters. Who's up for going to the office supply store with me?"

Several hands shot into the air.

***

That evening, after all the excitement died down, Tara climbed into her bed and held the covers open for Kelly to join her. They lay on their sides, face to face. Tara took Kelly's hand and placed it on her chest between her breasts.

"Do you feel it?" Tara asked after several moments.

"I do. I can feel your heartbeat," Kelly replied.

"When I think of how close I came to losing you, Kel. I don't know what I would have done if you died."

Kelly kissed Tara's forehead. "I felt the same way when Ryan put that gun to your head."

"We need to do something to stop this, Kelly. These school shootings are happening more and more often."

"I know. Since the shooting, I can't even concentrate in class. I find myself listening for every noise. My mom and dad have me in therapy."

"My moms have me and Seth and therapy too. Do you really think we can make a difference?" Tara asked. "I know our parents are in our corner, and a lot of people in the community want to help too, but we're only one school."

"The kids in Florida are making a difference, Tare. They're pushing for new laws, and they're convincing people to register to vote. It won't hurt for us to add our voices to theirs and to all the other schools that have gone through this."

"What I know is that things can't continue this way. Too many kids are dying. If it continues like this, can you imagine how life will be for *our* kids?" Tara said.

"*Our* kids? Do you think we'll still be together when we're old enough to have kids?" Kelly asked.

Tara traced her fingertip down the side of Kelly's face and stopped on her lips. "I hope so," she said.

Kelly kissed Tara, tentatively at first, but then with increasing intensity. Tara opened her mouth and allowed Kelly's tongue to delve inside. An intense spasm ripped through her abdomen.

"Kel, I can't get enough of you. You make my body feel things I've never felt before."

Kelly pulled back. "Are you telling me you've never…you know…done it yourself before?"

"Well, duh. Of course, but this feels so much better than what I can do for myself."

"But we haven't really done anything yet, except kiss," Kelly said.

"But even your kisses drive me nearly over the edge."

"Do you *want* to do more?" Kelly asked.

"Yeah, I do, but it needs to be right for both of us, Kel. Until then, I am happy to just hold you, and to be close to you."

"I love you, Tare."

"I love you too, Kel." Tara yawned.

Kelly kissed Tara's eyelids. "It's after one. I can't believe we worked on the posters until midnight! Time to sleep. We have a big day ahead of us tomorrow."

"Sweet dreams, Kel."

"Sweet dreams to you too, Tare."

Chapter 22

The next morning, Billie peeked her head into Tara's room and found her and Kelly sitting on the bed, busily typing away on their phones. "Hey, girls. Mom is making breakfast before we head out. She's taking egg orders."

Tara looked up. "Scrambled works for me."

"Me too," Kelly said.

Both immediately turned their attention back to their phones.

Billie walked over to the bed. "What's so interesting on your phones?"

"Social media," Tara said. "We've been posting about the rally at the school gym this morning to all our friends. Our friends are posting to their friends, and so on...and so on."

"Steve, Seth and Karissa are also posting," Kelly added.

"That's not a bad idea," Billie said.

"Yeah. I already have more than five hundred likes on the first note I posted last night," Tara said.

"You've been doing this all night?" Billie asked, incredulously.

"Not all night. Just for an hour or so after we went to bed."

"Seriously? Tara, you went to bed around midnight. Are you telling me you stayed up until after one posting on social media sites?"

"Yeah. Mama said we needed to get the word out."

"I think she meant we needed to increase awareness of our movement. You didn't need to do it all in one night."

"We gotta start somewhere," Tara reasoned.

"I guess you're right." Billie walked back toward the door. "Breakfast in about ten minutes. Okay?"

"Thanks, Mom."

"Oh, and dress warm. It *is* November, after all."

"Got it," Tara said without looking up from her phone.

***

Strategy was discussed around the breakfast table about how to structure the rally.

"Do we really need to plan this?" Tara asked. "I thought we would just wing it and see where it goes."

"I think we can do a certain amount of that, Tara," Cat said. "But we need to have a goal. What do you want to achieve with this rally?"

"Better gun control?" Kelly suggested.

"Actually, I did some research on gun laws last night, and it turns out, New York has some of the strictest gun laws in the country...and they became even stricter after the Sandy Hook shooting," Billie said.

"That didn't stop Ryan from shooting our school up," Seth pointed out. "There must be a hole in the gun laws somewhere."

"Hold on. I'm going to grab my laptop. I bookmarked the site on New York gun laws," Billie said.

While Billie was gone, Cat dished out the large pan of scrambled eggs she had cooked. "Toast is on the table. Sky, would you please grab the jelly from the fridge?"

A moment later, Billie returned carrying her laptop, which she had already turned on and was in the process of booting up. "Okay. It says here that New York requires background checks on nearly all gun purchases, including private sales. Handguns require permits, but long guns do not. You also have to be at least twenty-one to purchase a gun or ammunition in New York."

"Are assault rifles considered long guns, Mom?" Seth asked.

Billie scanned the text before her. "No, they're not. It says here that there's a ban on assault rifles, unless you already owned one before January fifteenth, twenty-thirteen. It looks like New York passed something called the NY SAFE Act that requires grandfathered assault weapons to be registered by January fifteenth, twenty-fourteen. It also says the clips used in assault weapons can't hold any more than ten rounds."

"Ryan had way more than ten rounds in his clips, Mom," Tara pointed out.

"I'll have to ask Justin about that...and to check on whether Ryan's assault weapon was registered." Billie took a bite of the eggs Cat had placed onto her plate. "These are good! Thanks for cooking, love." She continued to read the information on her laptop. "Oh, wow! It looks like there's a total ban on assault weapons in New York City, Buffalo, Albany, and Rochester."

"So, Ryan's gun may be totally illegal?" Cat asked.

"Maybe," Billie replied.

"Can I see your laptop, Mom?" Tara asked.

Billie swung her laptop around so Tara could see it.

"Hmm. It says here that if someone has a history of violence, the police can take their guns. Also, if they're mentally unstable or the police think they'll commit a crime with them." Tara looked at her mother. "Mom, Ryan was thrown out of his old school for the way he treated LGBTQ students. How's he allowed to have a gun?"

"I suspect the gun belongs to his father, or someone else, love. But you're right. If Ryan tried to buy a gun in New York, the background check should catch his expulsion from his old high school. By the way, where was that?"

"I think he said Syracuse," Tara replied.

"Interesting. Syracuse is not on the list of cities that has banned assault weapons. One more thing for Justin to check into."

"So, we'll need a goal for this rally this morning," Cat said.

"I think assault weapons should be banned in the entire country...even if you've owned them for a long time," Tara suggested.

"My dad says those types of weapons shouldn't be in the hands of civilians because they're weapons of war. I agree with Tara," Kelly said.

"I think gun laws need to be the same for all states," Seth suggested. "What's to stop someone from bringing an assault rifle to New York that is legal in another state?"

"That's exactly what Ryan might have done if he got the gun while they still lived in Syracuse," Billie pointed out.

"Not that I'm defending what he did, but how would he know it was illegal in Albany, unless he intentionally looked up the gun laws when they moved here? Who would think to do that?" Cat said. "I agree with Seth. I think gun laws should be consistent everywhere in the country."

"That'll be a hard sell for a lot of people," Billie said. "But I guess we need to start somewhere."

Their conversation was suddenly interrupted by a knock on the front door.

"I'll get it!" Skylar said.

Cat walked to the doorway between the kitchen and living room while Skylar opened the door. "Roger, Cindy! Come in. You kind of startled us. We almost never hear a knock on that door. Traffic sort of naturally flows in and out the kitchen door, and seldom do our neighbors knock."

No sooner had the words left Cat's mouth than Jen, Fred, Steve and Karissa let themselves into the kitchen. "Good morning, neighbors! Are we ready to rally?" Jen called out.

"I rest my case," Cat said to the Barkums. "How about a cup of coffee?"

"I'd love some," Cindy said.

"So, to be clear about this, our goal is to standardize the gun laws across the country, correct?" Roger asked.

"And to ban assault weapons across the board. No grandfather clauses," Billie added.

"People won't take kindly to the government confiscating their guns, Billie."

"I know. What we need is a very lucrative buy-back program. Look, Roger, by far, gun owners are good and law-abiding people. We're not talking about taking people's handguns away, or their hunting rifles. What we *are* talking about is taking weapons of war out of the hands of everyday people."

"I agree with you, but it won't be an easy fight."

"No, but it *is* a battle worth fighting."

***

The rally was scheduled to begin at nine. By the time the Charlands, Swensons and Barkums arrived at the school at eight-forty-five, there was no place to park. They ended up parking on the grass median between the two parking lots.

"Oh, my lord," Cindy exclaimed. "Where did all these people come from?"

"These are your neighbors, Cindy," Billie commented. "This is your community."

"How on earth did they all find out about the rally?" Cat asked.

"Social media!" Tara and Kelly said together.

"We've all been sending notes out since last night."

"It looks like they're all headed to the football field," Fred said.

"I can see why. This many people wouldn't fit in the gym," Roger added.

"Tara! Tara! Over here. Everyone is excited to begin."

Tara turned and saw her gym teacher waving at her. "Ms. Warner?"

"I moved them from the gym to the football field. There are more than a thousand people here. Most of them have been here for almost an hour. I talked the maintenance crew into running the PA system to the edge of the field. Oh, and they've erected a small stage with a podium for you to stand on."

"Me? You want *me* to start the rally?" Tara said.

"Of course. You...Kelly, Karissa, Seth and Steve...and anyone else who wants to speak," Ms. Warner said.

Billie squeezed Tara's shoulder. "You can do it love. You all can. You've lived through this. You are the face of this movement. I have faith in all of you."

"I'll go first, if you want, Tare," Seth volunteered.

"Really?"

"Really."

Chapter 23

Seth stood at the podium and looked out across the crowd. There were countless posters being waved around with various gun control slogans.

Protect our Kids—Not our Guns!
Am I Next?...Books—Not Bullets!
Never Again!
You Can Put A Silencer On A Gun, But Not On Me!
We Want Regulations—Not Thoughts And Prayers!
Enough Is Enough!

Seth took a deep breath and stepped up to the microphone. "My name is Seth Charland, and I'm seventeen years old. I am a senior at Nassau High School. A few weeks ago, a shooter broke through the barricade we had set up in my science classroom and he shot my teacher in the head. He stepped into the room and sprayed the room with bullets. In an attempt to get away from him, my entire class rushed to the back of the room and crushed me against the wall.

"You might think being crushed against the wall is a bad thing, but the truth is—it saved my life. As horrible as it is, the bodies of my classmates protected me from the bullets. As long as I live, I'll never forget the screams, or the sounds of bullets ripping through flesh."

Seth paused to compose himself and to wipe the tears that flowed freely down his cheeks.

Cat and Billie clung to one another as every word their son spoke ripped through their souls.

"I was one of six lucky students who were saved by being crushed by the nine students who died that day," Seth continued. "We had to lie under a stack of dead bodies for what felt like an eternity—just to be sure the shooter had left the room before we moved."

Seth paused again, his shoulders shaking. When he returned to the microphone, there was an intensity of anger in his voice that could not be contained. "Those students sacrificed their lives for the rest of us. Many of them died before they were even old enough to vote. Their voices have been silenced by senseless violence. *We* must now speak for them! *We* must fix this! *We* can't let their deaths be for nothing!"

The clapping and cheering overwhelmed Seth's voice on the loudspeakers. He waited for the response to subside and took advantage of the opportunity to once more get his emotions under control. Finally, the din died down enough for him to continue.

"I am calling on all of you to let your voices be heard. Call your senators. Call your representatives. Call the governor, and most importantly, let your vote speak for you at the polls next November. If those in power won't fix this, we need to replace them with people who will.

"We need to get semiautomatic assault weapons out of the hands of ordinary people. We need to make sure every state in the country follows the same set of rules. We have the power of our vote. Don't let them take that power away from you like they have from the sixteen people who died in this school."

Seth thrust his fist into the air. "Who's with me?"

The crown erupted into a deafening roar that continued for several minutes. Finally, Tara walked across the stage on her crutches and joined her brother at the podium. She embraced him in a firm hug and then stepped up to the microphone.

"My name is Tara Charland, and I'm fifteen years old. I am a sophomore at Nassau High School. The shooter also broke into my classroom. He was carrying one of those AR-15 rifles. He shot my teacher three times, and he shot a few other kids as he made his way across the room toward me. Their only crime was screaming in fear. When he reached me, I was huddled in the back of the room with my other classmates. He stopped directly in front of me and shot the students who sat on either side of me. He shot them in the head. Their heads exploded and splattered all over me and the wall behind us."

Like her brother, Tara had to pause to compose herself.

"After he killed Michelle and David, he put the barrel of the gun directly on my forehead and held it there. I was never so scared in my entire life. I prayed that it would be over quickly and that it wouldn't hurt too much. I silently said goodbye to my moms, my brother and sister, my friends, and my girlfriend, Kelly. I closed my eyes and prepared to die. It seemed like forever before he just said 'bang', and dropped the barrel of the gun from my head.

"Things happened so fast after that. My girlfriend, Kelly, ran into the room.' He turned around and shot her in the stomach." Tara looked to the left side of the stage where Kelly was standing with Karissa and Steve. "All I could think about was Kelly. I ran to her. I didn't care if he shot me at that point because if Kelly died, I wanted to die with her. But instead of killing either of us, he just walked out of the room."

The crowd chanted, *Kelly! Kelly!"*

Tara reached her hand toward Kelly, prompting her to walk gingerly across the stage to join Tara and Seth, still not able to move quickly because of the wound in her stomach. Tara embraced her warmly. The crowd cheered even louder.

Tara faced the microphone once more. She raised their clasped hands into the air. "*This* is why he did what he did. He could not tolerate the kind of love I share with Kelly. The assault weapon he carried allowed him to act on his hatred. My biggest regret is that others died because of who Kelly and I are. They were innocent victims…and he allowed *us* to live, to carry that knowledge of their sacrifices with us for the rest of our lives. I have nightmares about it almost every night."

Tara's voice was hoarse with anger. "I am as mad as hell! We *cannot* sit by and continue to let this happen. Orlando, Las Vegas, San Bernardino, Parkland, Sandy Hook…those innocent five and six-year-olds at Sandy Hook." Tara sobbed. "They were just babies. They didn't deserve to die. None of us deserve to die like this!"

Kelly wrapped her arm around Tara's waist for support as she cried uncontrollably. Billie and Cat, as well as Fred, Jen, Roger and Cindy were crying openly, as were many members of the crowd.

Kelly motioned for Tara to let her speak. Tara stepped aside and Kelly approached the microphone. "What do all of those killings have in common? All of the shooters used semiautomatic assault weapons. Those weapons can shoot dozens of rounds in a matter of seconds. Their victims didn't stand a chance. They are weapons of war and they should not be in the hands of ordinary people."

The crowd chanted loudly, *'Never Again.'*

Kelly waited patiently for the crowd noise to subside.

"The state of New York has some of the strictest gun control regulations in the country, but more can be done. For example, there is an assault weapon ban in this state, but assault weapons owned before the ban went into effect are exempt. Some cities in the state have banned them altogether—including Albany—but what happens when someone moves to Albany from a city that *hasn't* banned them…and the gun owner just isn't aware of the law? And what if someone brings an assault weapon into the state from another state where they are legal?"

A wave of boos surged from the crowd. Kelly waited for them to die down before continuing.

"Assault weapons must be banned from every state in this country, and every state must follow the same set of rules. These changes will remove excuses based on ignorance of the law. Assault weapons in this country were banned between nineteen-ninety-five and two-thousand-four, but that ban was allowed to expire at the end of two-thousand-four. Since then, the average number of shootings per year has doubled and the number of victims has tripled.

"We're just kids, and we will *not* be silenced, but we need your help. We need your vote to help restore sanity to this nation. We should not be afraid to go to school. We should not be afraid to go to nightclubs, or to church or to the mall. The gun lobby is holding all of us hostage. They are also holding many of our representatives hostage. Your votes count. Let your voices be heard. Help us to stop this madness."

Steve and Karissa approached the podium, hand in hand while the crowd erupted in chants of *'Albany Strong.'*

Karissa huddled with Kelly and Tara while Steve stood before the microphone.

"My name is Steve Swenson and I'm a seventeen-year-old senior at Nassau High School. We've all heard the phrase: 'guns don't kill people – people kill people!' Well, Duh! We need mandatory safety courses for people—not guns! We need more thorough background checks for people—not guns! We need stricter negligence penalties imposed on people—not guns!

"No one is trying to take your hunting guns or handguns away, but we do need common sense legislation to remove weapons of war from our streets. No one needs a gun that shoots thirty rounds in twenty seconds to shoot a deer. Assault weapons were designed for war. They were designed specifically to kill a lot of people...as fast as possible. They have no place in our society. I am *not* anti-gun...but I *am* anti-assault weapons.

A loud cheer erupted from the crowd and lasted for several moments.

"I was one of the lucky ones a few weeks ago. I managed to escape without being shot, but I did not escape the trauma of having to press my bare hands into the chest wound of one of my classmates until the paramedics arrived. I did not escape the trauma of wondering if I would live to see another day. My parents did not escape the fear that they would never see their children alive again.

"If any of you have had near-death experiences at the hands of others, you'll understand what I am saying. We are at war here. If you have served in the military, you may have witnessed what an assault rifle bullet can do to the human body. The victims of this shooting are casualties of war, pure and simple...and those of us who survived are the walking wounded. We will forever carry those wounds with us—physical and emotional—until the day we die.

"You've already heard this from my friends, but we need your help. We need you all to rise up...register to vote and then to get out there and let your voices be heard. For those of you who will turn eighteen before the next election...please register to vote! Together, we can make a difference.

The crowd chanted, *'Vote! Vote! Vote!*

"We are Albany Strong, and we need to stand our ground and do what we can to stop this madness before more children and teachers are lost. We're planning a march to the capitol as soon as it can be arranged. We will post notices on social media when we have more information. We urge you to join us."

Seth approached the microphone once more while the crowd chanted their support. He patiently waited for several minutes until he was able to be heard above the crowd. "Before we open the stage to anyone else who wants to share their experiences, we want to thank you for listening…and for participating in this rally. We need to fight like our lives depend on it—because, they do. Thank you."

Seth stepped back and all five of the teenagers locked hands and raised their arms into the air in solidarity. The crowd went wild with their applause and support. The teens hurried off the stage into the arms of their parents.

Ms. Warner was also there waiting for them. "Come with me," she said.

She quickly ushered them toward the school and into her office in the gym. The press followed close behind. "We'll be ready for statements soon," she said to the press, and closed her office door. She turned toward the group. "Wow! Who knew you had that in you. I am so proud of all of you," she said to the teenagers.

"Can you believe the size of that crowd?" Tara said.

"Sometimes it takes a tragedy to pull a community together," Ms. Warner said. "I hope you're all ready to become celebrities."

"We don't want to be celebrities," Seth said. "We just want better gun control."

"I get that, but it can't be helped. You saw what happened with the Parkland kids. You also need to be prepared for criticism."

"I agree," Billie said. "There'll be a lot of reaction from the gun lobby and gun-rights advocates, and it won't all be nice."

"But, Mom, we're not suggesting all guns be banned," Tara said.

"I know, but there are those who believe that a ban on any one type of gun will be a steppingstone toward banning all weapons. Don't get me wrong, kids. I'm not trying to talk you out of this. We're all very proud of you, but you need to be prepared for some push-back," Billie explained.

"So, I brought you in here to let you know that I'm in your corner and I'm willing to help," Ms. Warner said.

"Thank you, Ms. Warner. We'll take all the help we can get," Roger replied.

"And you are?" Ms. Warner asked.

"Roger Barkum. I'm Kelly's father, and this is my wife, Cindy."

After a full round of introductions, Ms. Warner turned to the group. "Are you ready to face the music? The press will be on you as soon as I open the door."

Chapter 24

The Charland family gathered in the family room that evening to watch the local news.

Seth stared at the television and watched the coverage of his speech. "Wow! I didn't realize how angry I sound," he said.

"Now that you've seen this, would you change anything?" Billie asked.

"No. I *am* angry. I'm kind of glad it came off that way."

"I'm hoping it makes other people angry as well...angry enough to take action," Billie added.

"Hey look! There you are, Tare!" Skylar exclaimed.

"Ugh! I'm an ugly crier," Tara said.

"You are beautiful," Cat replied. "Besides, what people will see is your passion and your determination."

Tara looked at the social media sites on her phone. "My phone is exploding with reactions. This is a lot bigger response than I thought it would be."

"So, Steve mentioned a march on the capitol. You realize we'll need to get a permit for that," Billie said.

Seth sat forward. "Really?" he said.

"Yes. I'll get my paralegal to start working on it on Monday. If I remember right, it might take a couple of weeks to get through the approval process. In fact, let me take a quick look on the Albany city website." Billie quickly searched for the permitting process on her cell phone. "Ah, here it is." She quickly scanned through the steps. "Yeah, it's just as I thought. We need to submit a permit application, show proof of liability, provide information on the purpose of the event, provide the route information if it's a march, oh, and we even need to provide our own recycling and trash bins and stage."

"That seems like a lot of work," Tara moaned.

"Actually, most of it is paperwork, except for the trash bins and stage if we need one," Billie said. "Like I said, I'll ask my paralegal to start the permitting process next week. If all goes well, we'll be able to hold the march just before Thanksgiving."

"That's almost three weeks away. Won't we risk losing momentum between now and then?" Cat asked.

"That's certainly a risk. I'll make a few calls on Monday to see if I can shorten the approval process. In the meantime, we need to do what we can to keep this in front of the voting public," Billie said.

***

Tara dialed Kelly's phone number the next morning.

"Hey Tare," Kelly answered.

"I missed you last night," Tara said.

"I missed you too. I'm glad you called. I wanna talk to you about the rally yesterday."

"Yeah. I wanna talk to you too. We need to plan what to do next. My mom said it might take a couple of weeks to get a permit for the march," Tara said.

"I know. My dad said the same thing."

"I was thinking that maybe we could go to the mall and stand outside with posters. What do you think?"

"We might want one of our parents there. My dad is concerned about us being alone in case someone attacks us."

"Or maybe the press will show up again. We definitely need parents there for that. I can talk to my moms."

"Okay. If they say yes, maybe we can get some other kids from the school to join us," Kelly suggested.

"I'll call you back."

***

"Hi, Kel. I talked to my moms. They're willing to work in shifts so we're not alone at the mall," Tara said. "I also talked to 'Rissa, and her parents will help too."

"Cool! My mom and dad also said they'd help. I'm gonna send a note out to our friends to see if anyone else wants to do it."

"I'll send a note, too," Tara said.

204

***

"Hi, Tare. We're gonna have lots of help at the mall. I've told some kids to come at noon and some at two o'clock and another group to come at four o'clock. I think we should get there this morning around ten. They all said their parents would come too."

"Maybe we should get there around nine-thirty so we'll have time to set up before shoppers start showing up at ten."

"Okay. I think we can do that. I'll see you there."

***

"This is Megan Cross, Channel Five News in Albany, New York. We are at the Colonie Center Mall where a large group of nearly two hundred demonstrators are protesting for improved gun control legislation. These protesters are motivated by the recent shooting at Nassau High School in which sixteen students and teachers were killed, and another six injured. The leaders of this protest appear to be Nassau High School students, Seth and Tara Charland, Steven and Karissa Swenson and Kelly Barkum, all of whom were in the classrooms attacked by the alleged shooter, Ryan Porter, also a student at the high school. With me here, is Tara Charland. Miss Charland, what do you hope to accomplish with this protest?"

"This is a peaceful protest to demand a total ban of all semiautomatic assault weapons, not just in this state, but across the entire country," Tara said. "The politicians who make our laws need to work together, regardless of which party they belong to. We are talking about the lives of children, here. If we can save even one child, it'll make living through this nightmare worth it. We can't give up. The future depends on us."

"What do you have to say to those who believe it's our government's responsibility to protect second amendment rights?" Megan asked.

"I say, your right to own an assault weapon does not override my right to live…and to feel safe in my own school. No one is talking about taking all weapons away. We are only demanding weapons of war be banned. Our goal is *not* to get rid of the second amendment, but to get rid of *one* type of gun that didn't even exist when our founding fathers wrote the Constitution."

"My sources tell me you are organizing a march on the capitol. Do you have any more information for us on that event?"

"We're organizing the March of Hope right now—and we're calling for a nationwide march on each of the fifty state capitols to show solidarity across the entire country. We'll be making an official statement as soon as we have the plans finalized," Tara said.

"For how long do you plan to demonstrate here today, Miss Charland?"

"We'll be here all day, and we encourage everyone who supports us to come out and join us. This madness has to stop. The killing has to stop. Together, we can make our voices heard."

"There you have it. The young people of Nassau High School, in a day-long protest for the abolition of semiautomatic assault weapons. This is Megan Cross, Channel Five News, Albany, New York."

***

Tara rejoined her group after giving the interview to Channel Five News.

"March of Hope, huh?" Billie said. "I like it."

Tara looked at the large crowd that was carrying banners and walking back and forth in front of the mall entrance. "I can't believe how many people have come out to join us. And this is just the first shift!"

"The first shift?" Cat asked.

"Yeah. Kelly arranged for groups of kids to show up at noon, two o'clock and four o'clock. If the people who are here now stay, the crowd is going to be huge!"

"That might be a problem," Billie said. "If the group becomes too large, the police may be called in to do crowd-control. If things remain peaceful, that won't be a problem, but it won't take much for things to get out of control."

No sooner had the words left Billie's lips, than a police car pulled up alongside them. A police officer exited the car and approached them on the sidewalk.

"Ma'am, do you know who is in charge here?" the officer asked.

Tara stepped forward. "I am."

Seth, Steve, Kelly and Karissa also stepped forward. "We are too," they said together.

The officer looked at them over his glasses. "You're the kids from Nassau," he said.

"Yes, sir," Tara said.

"Are your parents around?"

"We are," Billie said. Cat stood by her side. Within moments, Jen, Fred, Roger and Cindy joined them.

"Ma'am," the officer said, addressing Billie, "I see the protest is peaceful…at least up until now, but it's becoming too large to be held here in front of the mall entrance. We're receiving complaints from the property owners that shoppers are having problems gaining entrance into the facility."

"Where do you suggest we go?" Roger asked.

The police officer put his hands on his hips. "Off the record?"

The adults nodded.

"I recommend you protest on the sidewalk lining the entrance to the mall. You'll have exposure to every holiday shopper entering the mall instead of just those who come in through the entrance you're currently protesting at."

Cat smiled broadly and offered her hand to the officer. "Thank you. We appreciate your advice."

"My daughter was in that school, Ma'am. Luckily, she wasn't in one of the rooms the shooter visited. Just keep it peaceful and there shouldn't be a problem." The officer walked toward his car and stopped to turned around. "Good luck with your fight. I hope you win."

***

The Charland, Swenson and Barkum crews remained at the demonstration until six when the protesters finally dispersed.

Kelly's parents brought a lawn chair with them for Kelly to rest in periodically throughout the day, as she was still recovering from her gunshot wound. Between the four waves of protesters, they estimated up to six hundred participants. Overall, it was peaceful, despite the few sneers or negative remarks from random passersby. By far, the comments they received from shoppers were largely supportive and encouraging.

By the end of the day, they were exhausted and they dragged their weary bodies into the house.

"I vote we order pizza delivery," Billie said.

"I second that," Seth replied.

"Me too!" said Skylar, Tara and Cat in unison.

Tara limped to the table and sat down heavily. "I'm beat."

Cat came up behind her and enveloped her daughter in a hug. "I'm proud of you, kiddo. I'm proud of all of you."

"This is probably gonna be a long battle," Tara said.

"I think you're right, rug rat," Billie replied. "Be prepared for a lot of rallies and interviews. Heck, you may even be asked to appear before congress."

"What?" Tara said.

"What?" Seth echoed.

"Be prepared for that. If this gets enough national attention, you may have to testify before a congressional committee."

"Will that do any good, Mom?" Seth asked. "I mean, will it be enough to convince them to vote for better gun laws?"

"That's a good question, scout. With enough pressure from the voting public—maybe. It certainly won't hurt."

"If it doesn't, we need to vote them out of office next November," Cat said.

"Mama is right. That should be part of our message at all future rallies. Getting people out to vote is a critical part of this," Billie said. "In any case, even if they are willing to change the gun laws, it's a long and slow process."

"And in the meantime, more kids could be dying in schools," Seth said.

"That is an unfortunate possibility," Billie said.

Chapter 25

Kelly and Tara lay on their backs, side by side on Tara's bed the next day after school. They held their tablets above them as they played an interactive video game.

"Turn, turn, turn! You're gonna get us killed!" Tara exclaimed.

Both girls tilted their tablets sharply to the left.

"I'm trying!" Kelly said.

"Aagh! We crashed!" Tara complained.

"Sorry! I never claimed to be a good driver."

Tara looked at Kelly. "It's okay. It's just a game." She continued to look directly into Kelly's eyes. "Have I ever told you that you have amazing eyes?"

"Are you flirting with little 'ol me?" Kelly fluttered her eyes at Tara.

Tara rolled onto her side to face Kelly. "I'd like to do a whole lot more than flirt," she teased.

Kelly cupped the side of Tara's face in her palm. "What are you waiting for?"

Tara lowered her lips to Kelly's while Kelly's hand wrapped around the back of Tara's head. The kiss deepened, and soon, Tara's hand moved to caress Kelly's left breast.

Kelly shuddered.

Tara pulled her hand back quickly. "I'm sorry. I shouldn't have done that."

"Don't say that. I'm the one who's sorry. My body just spazzed out. I didn't do that on purpose."

"You liked it then?"

"Yes, I did."

Tara looked at Kelly's breast and with one very shaky hand, she reached forward and cupped it gently in her palm. She looked at Kelly and grinned.

Kelly's breath was ragged.

"You are so beautiful," Tara said.

"Kiss me," Kelly demanded.

Tara lowered her lips to Kelly's and gently squeezed her breast.

Kelly moaned.

"Oh, my God," Tara said as her own body spasmed.

Both girls nearly jumped off the bed when a knock sounded at the door.

"Jesus!" Tara said under her breath.

Kelly buried her face in Tara's shoulder.

They quickly lay side by side again and held their tablets in front of them.

"Come in," Tara said.

Billie opened the door. "The national news just came on and one of the feature stories is our demonstration at the mall today. There's a commercial on right now. If you hurry, you won't miss it."

"National news? Okay. We'll be right out," Tara said. She watched Billie close the door and turned to Kelly. "That was close."

Kelly pushed Tara back onto the bed and rolled on top of her so they were nose to nose. Tara's hands instinctively wrapped around Kelly's back.

"You mom has amazing timing," Kelly said.

Tara grinned up at her. "Yeah, she does."

"We'd better get out there before she comes back. Is the red gone from my face yet?"

"Almost. How about mine?"

"Let's just say you look good in pink."

***

Billie returned to the living room and sat beside Cat on the couch. "They were so making out," she said.

"Awkward!" Cat said.

"What's awkward?"

Billie and Cat turned to see Seth descend the last step into the living room.

"Your sister and Kelly."

Seth stopped and put his hands on his hips. "Tell me you didn't walk in on them."

"Almost," Billie admitted. "Shh…here they come."

"You're just in time, girls," Cat said. "You too, Seth. Our protest is featured on the news."

The girls sat beside Billie and Cat while Seth stood behind the couch.

"Mom…this is national news, not local," Seth said.

"Exciting, huh? Apparently word of our movement is spreading. This is exactly what we need," Billie said.

The entire interview Tara had given to the local news was aired. Afterward, the anchors highlighted Tara's comment about the March of Hope and promised the listening audience more information as soon as it became available.

"Wow!" Tara said. "We need to let them know as soon as we have a date for the march. Wouldn't it be awesome if we really could get others to organize marches across the country at the same time?"

***

Billie managed to shave a few days off the processing time for the event permit, bringing it down from seventeen to twelve days and making it valid beginning on Friday, November fifteenth. The March of Hope was scheduled for the following Monday, November eighteenth and the date was immediately released to the media.

For the next ten days, the kids worked on new protest posters and on getting the word out that the March of Hope would be scheduled for November eighteenth. With the help of their parents, they mapped out the route between the high school and the capitol building, and even walked it a few times to determine how long the march might take if the crowd was as large as they expected it to be.

At least a week ahead of the march, Jen worked with the teens to design a flyer that they could hand out at school and in other public places. The flyer advertised the meeting place and the start time for the march. It also mapped out the march route and provided suggestions for parking and public transportation.

Finally, Tara worked with Ms. Warner to borrow electronic megaphones from the gym departments of various high schools in the area so their voices could be heard from the steps of the capitol building.

They were ready...and the best part was that their parents fully supported them skipping school on Monday, November eighteenth!

***

During these ten days, Billie met with Justin to identify witnesses and to review a list of potential jurors for Ryan Porter's trial.

As expected, during his arraignment Ryan entered a plea of not guilty due to insanity, after which the judge ordered a thirty-day assessment period.

Billie and Justin knew it would be months before Ryan Porter's case actually went to trial. Considering the number of witnesses and the psychological assessments Ryan's lawyers would insist on, they estimated the trial would be scheduled for June in the following year...just in time for the school year to end, and for Seth and Steve to graduate.

Although the actual trial was several months away, Billie and Justin interviewed all of the witnesses in order to select those who would be important to their building a solid case against Ryan Porter. One of the first witnesses they spoke to was Robert Johnson. One part of Robert's interview concerned Billie. Under oath and knowing he was being recorded, Robert explained what had happened at the party that Steve and Seth rescued Karissa from:

I took Karissa to the senior party and we got separated. I asked Ryan if he knew where she was and he said in the basement. He told me he put something in her water to make her 'more receptive' to my advances. I was really worried about her. I found her passed out on the couch in the basement. I knelt on the floor beside her and checked to see if she was breathing. The next thing I knew, I was on my back and Steve was punching me. I would never hurt Karissa. I swear it.

When Billie arrived home that same day, she asked Seth to call Steve, and she relayed the essence of Robert's testimony that he gave willingly, knowing he was being recorded.

Steve and Seth looked at one another from their position on the couch. Seth leaned into Steve. "Dude! Could he be right?"

"I don't know. It happened so fast. I don't actually remember," Steve said. "All I saw was him on top of Karissa. And he did risk his life to save her from Ryan. I suppose he could have been trying to help her that night at the party."

Billie nodded. "He's been suspended from school for about a month now, mostly based on your accusations."

Seth stood and paced across the room. "I know. Damn. I'm not absolutely sure he assaulted her, Mom."

"I'm not absolutely sure either," Steve admitted.

"Okay. I'll talk to the police chief and see what we can do about getting the charge dropped and the restraining order lifted." Billie paused for a few moments. "You realize you owe Robert an apology."

Both boys nodded. "We know. We'll do the right thing, Mom. We promise," Seth said.

***

Robert Johnson returned to school two days later. Steve and Seth intentionally intercepted him in the locker room before football practice. Understandably, Robert was somewhat wary of the confrontation.

"What do you want?" Robert asked

"We need to talk to you," Steve said.

"What do you want to talk to me about?"

"Robert, we owe you an apology," Steve said. "Especially me."

"Yeah. We know now that you didn't assault Karissa," Seth added.

"Dude, I'm sorry. All I saw was my sister unconscious and you leaning over her. I didn't even stop to ask, I just reacted. I'm sorry."

"I would never hurt, Karissa," Robert said.

"We know that now," Seth said again. "Dude, what you did during the shooting was the bravest and most honorable thing ever."

"You saved Karissa, and God knows how many other kids. You're a hero, man!" Steve added. "I can't thank you enough."

Robert nodded. "Like I said, I would never hurt Karissa."

"Are we good then?" Steve asked.

Robert looked at them and extended his hand. "If Karissa was my sister, I would have done the same thing."

Both boys shook his hand firmly.

"Thank you, Robert," Steve said. "You're okay."

Seth and Steve walked toward the locker room door, but Seth stopped after a few feet and turned around. Robert was still watching them. "Hey, Robert, Steve and I just started a new ass-kicking video game. We play each other online. Care to join us?"

"That would be awesome," Robert said.

"Give me your phone number. I'll text you and then we'll have each other's numbers," Seth said.

Robert quickly pulled his cell phone out of his locker and then recited his number for Seth. He couldn't keep the grin from his face when his phone signaled Seth's incoming text. "Cool! I'll catch you dudes later," Robert said.

Chapter 26

On the morning of November eighteenth, Billie turned on the television in the living room and went into the kitchen to make coffee. While she stood at the counter waiting for her coffee to brew, she listened to the words coming from the living room.

Crowds are gathering at state capitols all around the country this morning in preparation for the March of Hope.

She ran into the living room and threw herself onto the couch in time to see a collage of pictures on the screen, all depicting snapshots of crowds clearly preparing to march. She looked at her watch. "But it's only seven!"

Billie jumped up from the couch and ran all around the house to wake up her family members. "Get up! The crowds are already forming! We need to get moving!"

Seth came running down the stairs in his boxers and T-shirt. "Crowds are already forming?" he asked.

"Look!" Billie pointed to the television. "Hartford, Dover, Atlanta, Tallahassee, Augusta, Boston, Trenton, Concord, Montpelier, Richmond, Charleston, Harrisburg, Raleigh…the whole east coast is already on the move."

"Mommy, what's going on?" Skylar said.

"Change of plans, Sky. We need to get to the march earlier than expected."

Tara, walked sleepily into the living room on her crutches. "What's going on? It's only seven. The march doesn't start for another two hours."

Billie grabbed Tara by the shoulders. "Look, sweetie! You did it. All of you did it. You've awakened the sleeping giant. Crowds are already forming in capitols all along the east coast."

Tara sat on the couch and watched the news coverage. "Wow! I need to call Kelly."

"Stay right there. I'll get your phone," Billie said. Seconds later, she handed Tara's phone to her. "You call Kelly and I'll call Jen. This is so exciting!"

Cat finally made it down the stairs. "What's all the commotion about?" she asked.

"We need to get moving a lot sooner than planned," Billie said. "The entire east coast is already assembling at their meeting points. They did it, Cat. The kids did it. The whole country is participating in the March of Hope!"

Cat's eyes filled will tears and she went around and kissed each of her children. "I'm so proud of you. I knew you could do it."

Billie hung up the phone after calling Jen and looked at her family, all of whom were still hanging out in the living room. "News flash, family! We need to get moving! Let's go!"

"Coffee. I need coffee. Then I'll get moving," Cat said.

***

The march from Nassau High School to the capitol in Albany took longer than expected due to the massive number of people who arrived to march. The Charland, Swenson and Barkum families arrived before eight, and there were already nearly ten thousand people mulling around on the sports fields and parking lots. They met up with Ms. Warner and her partner, Mariana in her office, where she passed out a half-dozen megaphones she had managed to borrow from nearby high schools.

With megaphones in hand, they all lined up in front of the crowd and at nine, they set out on their march, carrying their posters, chanting slogans and singing songs of solidarity. Kelly and Billie pushed both Tara and Cat to the capitol in wheelchairs so they would not have to make the trek on crutches.

Thanks to arrangements Billie had made ahead of time, the police force managed traffic patterns along their route, and as one collective hive, they flowed through the streets of Albany, picking up more and more marchers along the way. By the time they reached the capitol steps, the crowd had nearly doubled in size.

To their surprise, there was already a crowd of equal size assembled in front of the capitol by the time they arrived. All five of the teenagers climbed the steps of the capitol.

Tara was the first to speak.

"Good morning, Albany! I am Tara Charland."

The crowd went crazy as a roar rose from the masses.

"As my mom said to me this morning—we have awakened the sleeping giant! According to the news, the entire country is on the move and marching for hope!"

Again, the crowd roared and shook their signs.

"I don't know how to thank all of you for being here. Most of us aren't even old enough to vote, but with your help, we will make a difference. We are angry, and we will not be silenced. This is our story. The threat of school shootings has been hanging over our heads since kindergarten. This is all we've known. *This* is our truth."

Again, the crowd drowned her out with their cheers.

"Your presence here gives us the power to speak up and demand that our representatives do what is right…and if they refuse, we have the power to vote them out and to replace them with people who will.

"We need common sense gun control. We need to stop the murder of innocent children and teachers. School shootings are increasing at an alarming rate with one hundred twenty seven victims in twenty-eighteen alone. If nothing changes, we could have at least ninety-two more shootings this year. On the news just four days ago, there was another shooting at Saugus High School in Southern California. Three students were killed in that shooting, including the shooter, and three more were injured. In the three years of this administration, there have been more school shooting victims than in the entire eight years of the past administration. Hatred starts at the top. That situation must change."

Tara had to pause for several minutes while the crowd volume increased exponentially.

"You can argue that our state bans assault weapons, but what you may not know is that all assault weapons owned before the ban went into effect in twenty-fourteen are exempt from the ban.

"You can argue that the city of Albany has a total ban on assault weapons with no exceptions. That is true, but we have reason to believe the assault weapon used to kill sixteen students and teachers at Nassau High School came from outside of Albany.

"We need to ban semiautomatic assault weapons from every state in this country, without exception, and we need the laws governing gun control to come from the federal level so the rules are the same across the whole country."

Again, the volume of the crowd increased as they cheered their support for what Tara was saying.

"A semiautomatic assault weapon was used to kill sixteen people at Nassau High School and injure six more—despite the ban on these weapons in our city. They need to be banned nationwide to minimize them being carried across state lines, or city lines. Did you know that the ten states with the highest gun death rate have some of the weakest gun laws in the nation? Did you know that almost fifteen-hundred kids are killed every year by guns? Did you know that more kids have died by guns since Sandy Hook than the number of soldiers who have died in military combat in the same time frame? Did you know that nearly forty-thousand Americans die every year from gun violence?

"We can't do this alone. As I said, most of us aren't old enough to vote, so we need your help to see this through, and to help stop this madness. You have the power with your votes and we *all* have the power of our voices. We are dying in our schools. We are dying in our churches. We are dying in our movie theaters. We are tired of growing up hiding under our desks. Please see this for what it is—a cry for help. Thank you."

Tara lowered her megaphone and the crowd cheered for three minutes before Seth interrupted them.

"My name is Seth Charland, and we are Albany Strong!" he said, prompting another round of applause.

"We've heard on the news that the gun lobby is calling us puppets. Tara is right. Most of us are not even adults yet, so they question how we can organize and pull off such a massive event as we have today. I promise you that every word that comes out of our mouths are *our* words...*our* stories...*our* truths. We are not pawns. Everything we have done has been done by us, or through small donations from individuals who feel as strongly as we do about stopping this madness.

"You might wonder why we are doing this. I'm here to tell you, we're doing this because we don't want to be shot and killed in our classrooms. We are doing this for our sixteen classmates and teachers who were violently gunned down. We are doing this because never again, do I want to lie beneath a pile of dead classmates, pretending to be dead myself, so the shooter will not actually kill me. We are doing this because no fifteen year old girl should have to witness a shooter blowing her classmates' heads off like my sister had to witness."

Seth's voice broke and he fought back sobs. "We are doing this because we are tired of hiding under our desks, or in safe rooms. We are doing this because no one should have to deal with the horrors of a school shooting again and again—and then again in their dreams."

Seth welcomed the applause as he stepped back to wipe the tears from his cheeks and to compose himself.

"I am only seventeen years old, although I feel like I've aged twenty years since the shooting. I am still not old enough to vote. If I sound angry, it's because I am…and you should be too. We are here to ask for your help. We need you to use your voice on our behalf, and on behalf of all the students and teachers that have been murdered in their own classrooms, including almost two dozen five and six year olds in the horror that was Sandy Hook. We need you to use your vote to force the changes we so desperately need. As long as our representatives are in the pockets of the gun lobbies, change will never come."

The volume of the crowd increased as they chanted, *'never again…never again.'* Seth patiently waited until the din had died down.

"Your superpower is your vote. You have two choices…use your vote to promote change, or do nothing and support the status quo. Here's a newsflash for you people…status quo is killing us in our classrooms. You know what to do. Thank you."

Seth lowered his megaphone and walked over to hug Tara.

"Citizens of Albany," Kelly said through her megaphone once the crowd noise subsided. "My name is Kelly Barkum. For all intents and purposes, I shouldn't be here today. I shouldn't be here today because I was shot, point-blank, in the stomach by the Nassau High School shooter. If it wasn't for my girlfriend, Tara, I could have bled to death on that classroom floor.

"I am also one of the reasons we even *had* a shooting. I am gay, and as it turns out, the shooter hates gay people. You see, the shooter went on his rampage because he had a thing for my girlfriend, and when he found out he would never have her, he decided she and I shouldn't be together either. So he shot me, and I can only assume he thought I would die. Mission accomplished. But I didn't die. It was love that got me shot, and it was love that saved me. Ladies and gentlemen...I choose love!" Kelly threw her fist in the air.

A roar rose up from the crowd and chants of *"love, love, love"* filled the air.

"Tara and Steve are right. We need change. We need to stop the hatred and we need to stop giving the haters permission to kill. Change starts at the top. You have the power to make change happen with your vote and your voice. We need leaders who care more about people than about their own pockets, and we need leaders with the balls enough to stand up against the gun lobbies. Your vote counts. Please use it wisely. Thank you."

Karissa waited for the crowd to settle down before she spoke.

"Hi. I'm Karissa Swenson. Ummm. I'm not very good at this kind of thing, but I can't sit by any longer and let my friends do all the work. For me, it's not easy to push my fear aside and take action. Sometimes you are paralyzed with fear, and sometimes it takes something horrible like one of your best friends being shot, to give you the courage to push your fear aside.

"I sat in my classroom during the shooting at Nassau High School, listening to the screams and the gunshots. I was terrified that my brother was already dead and that my best friend was already dead in the classroom next to mine. I was terrified that I would never see my mom and dad again. I was paralyzed by fear.

"What this experience has taught me is that when you are paralyzed by fear, you can't move, and if you can't move, you can't grow and if you can't grow, you can't live. This experience made me realize that I needed to do what my friend Kelly told me to do…grow a pair."

Karissa paused as the crowd laughed and cheered at her analogy.

"So that's what I'm doing. I'm growing a pair, and I'm gaining the courage to stand up here to ask for your help. We need your vote and we need your support to stop the killing. New York may already have some of the strictest gun laws in the country, but the shooter found a way to break those laws anyway. We need to do more, and we need your help."

Karissa lowered her megaphone and walked directly toward Kelly who enveloped her in a big hug while the crowd cheered her on.

Finally, it was Steve's turn to speak.

"Good morning. My name is Steve Swenson, and I am a hunter, but I do *not* believe semiautomatic assault weapons should be in the hands of ordinary citizens. Assault weapons were designed for one thing only…to quickly kill a lot of people on the battlefield. No hunter needs an assault weapon to go deer hunting. And if anyone believes they need assault weapons to protect their families from the government, I've got news for you…your little assault weapon will be no match for the firepower of the army, marines, air force or navy. Assault rifles are weapons of war, pure and simple. When they find their way into society, they find their way into schools, and churches and nightclubs and shopping malls."

Steve paused to allow the crowd to express their solidarity with what he had said.

"Do you know that more than two-hundred thousand kids have been exposed to gun violence in schools since Columbine? That is four times more than the number of soldiers who died in Vietnam. How many kids have to be exposed to this kind of violence before our government takes action? I say even *one* is too many. All five of us on these steps are part of that two-hundred thousand. Many of your children are part of that two-hundred thousand. If we sound angry, it's because we are! We the people, including all of you, need to take the action our government is unwilling to. We need to use our voices and votes to pressure our representatives to do the right thing. *Your* kids will continue to die if they don't. Thanks for listening."

Again, all five of them clasped hands and raised them into the air. The crowd's reaction was loud and long. After a full five minutes of cheering, Ms. Warner took the megaphone from Tara and addressed the crowd. "Let's give these brave young people a round of applause for sharing their passion with us."

The five teenagers waived and thanked the crowd for their support while the cheering once more increased in volume and intensity, before dying down several minutes later.

"If anyone else would like to share their story or support for the victims of gun violence, please come forward," Ms. Warner said.

Tara, Kelly, Karissa, Seth and Steve took this opportunity to rejoin their parents in the crowd.

For two more hours, several members of the crowd took the opportunity to speak their minds and pledge their support to end gun violence. So engaged were the participants in the rally that they didn't notice five tired teenagers and their families slip away from the crowd to return to the safety of their homes.

Chapter 27

With the March of Hope behind them, Billie and Justin renewed their focus on interviewing the witnesses to the horrific circumstances surrounding the shooting at Nassau High School a month earlier.

Billie felt the case they were building against Ryan Porter was strong and indefensible. The evidence was clear and irrefutable. There were sixteen dead and six injured. And there were dozens of others who had witnessed the carnage without injury to themselves. Ryan Porter was clearly responsible for the deaths and injuries of twenty-two people. The only unanswered question was whether Ryan would be found guilty of premeditated murder, or if he would be declared innocent by reason of insanity.

The process of witness interviews took a full three months, including face to face interviews and background checks on dozens of firsthand witnesses of the shooting and additional witnesses on the list provided by the defense,

The biggest challenges that both the prosecution and defense faced during jury selection was finding suitable candidates that had limited knowledge of the shooting. The extensive media coverage of the shooting, the rallies, the protests and the March of Hope demonstration significantly reduced the pool of potential jurors.

Once a list of potential jurors was put together, they all had to be interviewed to determine if they had any biases that might make them favor one side or the other. For example, jurors who had strong feelings about homosexuality or fundamentalist religions were generally excused, since both of those issues would feature prominently in the trial. Once the pool of jurors was reduced to twelve plus two alternates, each one had to go through an extensive background check to determine if there was anything in their past experiences that might introduce biases.

Because of these issues, the jury selection process took two additional months.

The final delay in starting the trial was the defense's insistence on multiple psychological assessments for Ryan Porter. Billie and Justin were concerned that multiple assessments could mean the defense planned to have more than one expert declare Ryan to be insane. On the other hand, they hoped it meant that the defense was having trouble finding psychologists that would declare Ryan insane.

***

The seven months between the March of Hope rally and the start of Ryan Porter's trial were very busy for the Charland, Swenson and Barkum families. Between going to school, protesting on the weekends and interviews with the local and national news networks, the months flew by in what felt like record time to the teenagers.

During this time, a deep friendship developed between Seth, Steve and Robert. Seth and Steve did their best to help Robert recover from the month of school he missed during his suspension as they all worked their way toward graduation. They also tactfully taught him how to get over his awkwardness in social situations. Even Karissa had come around to believe he was not such a bad guy.

During this time, both Seth and Steve turned eighteen, and Kelly turned sixteen. What a difference seven months made in the maturity level of all of them.

Tara, Kelly and Karissa's friendship blossomed under their shared emotional experiences during the shooting, and Tara and Kelly were able to help Karissa get past her feelings of guilt for telling Ryan about their sexual preference. Karissa soon came to realize that what Ryan did was his choice alone, and had Karissa *not* told him about Tara and Kelly's relationship, he would have found out some other way. After that kiss in the hallway on the day of the shooting, Tara and Kelly certainly were not keeping it a secret.

Tara also celebrated her graduation from crutches to a walking cast, and then, to no cast at all. Finally, she felt normal again.

One month before the trial was scheduled to begin, official letters from the United States Attorney General appeared in their mailboxes. Tara tore into her letter when she got home from school and immediately called her mother.

"Hello, this is Billie Charland."

"Mom! We're going to Washington!"

"Tara? What do you mean, you're going to Washington?"

"I got a letter in the mail today. Seth and the others got one too. It's from the attorney general. They want us to testify in front of congress."

"Really? Wow! Are you ready for that, Tare?"

"I don't think we have a choice, Mom. We need to do something about the shootings."

"Okay. When do you need to be there?"

Tara took a moment to scan through the letter. "May fourteenth. That's in two weeks."

"That's two weeks before your brother's graduation. Ryan's trial also starts the first week in June. It looks like we're going to have a busy spring."

"So, we can go?" Tara asked.

"Like you said, love. I don't think we have a choice."

***

Seth, Tara, Kelly, Karissa and Steve sat at a table in front of the U.S. Department of Justice's Bureau of Alcohol, Tobacco, Firearms and Explosives Committee as well as the House Committee on Oversight and Reform, while their parents sat nervously in the balcony. Both boys wore starched white shirts and ties. Karissa wore a dress, and Tara and Kelly wore slacks, button down shirts and neck ties, with the knots pulled below their open collars.

The ranking committee member opened the proceedings.

"Good afternoon. I understand you are here to testify about events that happened in your high school in Albany, New York in early October of last year."

Seth leaned forward to speak into the microphone. "That is correct, your honor."

The committee member chuckled. "I'm not a judge, son. Sir will be good enough."

"Yes, sir," Seth said.

"I would like to begin by asking you to state your names and ages."

"Seth Charland, age eighteen."

"Tara Charland, age fifteen."

"Kelly Barkum, age sixteen."

"Karissa Swenson, age fifteen."

"Steve Swenson, age eighteen."

"Mr. Charland, Please describe for me, what happened at your school."

Seth inhaled deeply. "We had an active shooter situation, sir. Sixteen of our classmates and teachers were killed, and six more were injured, including Kelly, here."

"Miss Barkum, could you please describe your injuries?"

"The shooter had his assault rifle pointed at my girlfriend's head. He was going to kill her. I tried to stop him and he shot me in the stomach instead," Kelly explained. "I would have died if Tara hadn't put pressure on the wound."

"I see." The ranking committee members looked at the others at the table. "Did you have any other injuries?"

They all shook their heads.

"So, explain to me, why you are here."

"We are here to ask for a total ban on all assault weapons, sir," Steve said.

"You do realize that the city of Albany already has a ban on such weapons, don't you?"

Tara leaned into her microphone. "Yes, sir, we are aware of that, but we think the gun came from another city outside of Albany where assault weapons are legal."

"I believe assault weapons are banned throughout the entire state of New York," he said.

"Yes sir, but not the assault weapons that were already owned before the ban went into effect," Tara replied.

The ranking committee member sat back and smiled. "You've done your homework, young lady."

"Two of my classmates had their heads blown off right beside me, sir. Their brains spattered on my face and clothes. Yes, I've done my homework. This is personal for me."

A collective gasp was heard in the chamber.

"May I speak, sir?" Kelly asked.

"Please do."

"Sir, my father is a colonel in the marines. I have had a lot of discussions with him about assault weapons—especially since the shooting at our school. Sir, assault weapons are designed to destroy a human body. Once the bullet enters the body, if you're not lucky enough to have it immediately exit like mine did, it ricochets around and shreds everything it hits. Very few people survive that type of gunshot wound, so when Tara says her classmates' heads exploded, she means that literally."

The committee member cleared his throat. "I see. Does anyone else have any comments to make?"

"I do, sir," Steve said.

"Go ahead, young man."

"Sir, we are not here to ask for *all* guns to be banned. That's unrealistic, and unnecessary. What we *are* here for is to ask for semiautomatic assault weapons to be banned, and for clip limits to be severely limited on other rifles and handguns. Sir, the AR-15 assault rifle has been used in many of the school shootings since Columbine, as well as shootings in churches, night clubs and rock concerts. Using that weapon, a shooter can kill twenty kids in thirty seconds—just like what happened to the first graders at Sandy Hook Elementary School. Sir, did you know some of their funerals had to be closed-casket because of the damage the bullets did to their bodies? Assault rifles are weapons of war…not weapons for hunting. They do not belong in the hands of ordinary citizens."

Karissa raised her hand. "I have something to say."

"Yes, miss?"

"I was not injured during the shooting. Not physically, anyway, but not a day goes by that I don't think about it. I haven't slept through the night since it happened almost eight months ago. None of us will ever be the same. None of us will ever feel safe again as long as weapons of war are on the streets. Our lives have been changed forever. We've had to grow up overnight. Our childhoods are gone. The rules about assault weapons are different all across the country. It didn't matter that they are banned in Albany, because the shooter came from a place where they *are* legal, and he brought his gun to Albany with him."

"Are there any other comments?"

Seth raised his hand. "Sir, I wasn't injured in the shooting either, but nine of my classmates were, and I have all nine of them to thank for my own life. I hid under their lifeless bodies and pretended to be one of them until the shooter left the room. Imagine your own children or grandchildren having to do that. All nine of them were killed in about five seconds. Nine dead in five seconds. Sir, we need you and your committee to take action here. All we are asking is that our lawmakers do what is right to make our schools...our churches...our theaters...our rock concerts...our very existence safe again. Thank you, sir."

Billie stood and slowly clapped her hands. Within seconds everyone in the balcony was on their feet and the clapping was deafening. When the applause finally died down, the ranking committee member stood and declared the hearing closed.

Chapter 28

Finally, nearly eight months after the shooting, the trial date arrived, and with it, the end of a school year that would forever be changed by Ryan Porter when he walked into Nassau High School carrying an assault rifle.

Seth, Steve, Tara, and Karissa were among several key witnesses who would help the jury of twelve decide Ryan's fate.

The first two weeks of the trial were consumed with testimony from firearms experts, forensic pathologists and testimonies from law enforcement agencies, among others.

In the third week of the trial, Billie, Cat, Jen, Fred and all five of their children filed into the courtroom and sat in the spectator seats next to Kelly and her parents, who had arrived moments earlier. Billie had given them all pep talks that morning and told them to be as truthful as possible.

Ryan Porter was seated at the defendant's table, along with his lawyer. Directly behind him sat a middle-aged man and woman. The woman looked very matronly and she wore a cross around her neck. Her hair was pulled back into a severe bun at the nape of her neck. The man wore a white shirt and black trousers, and a poorly tied necktie. Behind them sat an entire row of similarly dressed men and women, all holding bibles.

The bailiff stood in front of the judge's desk. "All rise. The court of the Honorable Gene Bonnett is now in session. On the docket is the State of New York versus Ryan Porter."

The bailiff waited until the judge entered the room and sat behind his desk. He faced the courtroom. "Call to order. You may be seated."

Judge Bonnett looked through the papers on his desk and peered at Ryan over his glasses. "Mr. Porter, do you understand the charges against you?"

Ryan didn't answer.

The defense attorney, John Williams, stood. "Your Honor, I have the authority to speak on Mr. Porter's behalf. We understand the charges against him."

"Will your client be testifying on his own behalf, council?" the judge asked.

"No sir, he waives his right to testify."

"Understood. Gentlemen, please deliver your opening statements."

Justin stood and walked toward the jury box. "Good morning, ladies and gentlemen," he said. "I think I can speak for all of us when I say we are here tragically to decide the fate of a young man who took the lives of sixteen individuals and injured six more, at Nassau High School, nearly eight months ago. The majority of those killed were children, ages fifteen to eighteen, with their entire lives still head of them.

"I will strive to demonstrate that Ryan Porter was indeed in charge of his faculties on the day of the shooting, and carried out his heinous acts in a deliberate and premeditated way. I will also provide a basis for classifying this as a hate crime in which a marginalized group in our society was deliberately targeted.

"As difficult as they are to look at, I have provided photographs of the crime scenes in order to make painfully clear the extent of the chaos and devastation wrought on the victims of this crime, as well as on their families. These victims were children, ladies and gentlemen. Children who will never again see another birthday...never see another Christmas...never get married...never have children or grandchildren.

"By the end of this trial, ladies and gentlemen, you will clearly see that this was a deliberate, planned and cognitive crime and beyond the shadow of a doubt, we will demonstrate full responsibility on the defendant's part for the deliberate execution of this crime.

"Ladies and gentlemen, thank you for your time." Justin walked back to his seat.

Williams rose to his feet and walked to the jury booth. "Ladies and gentlemen," he said. "We are not here to debate whether Ryan Porter took the lives of sixteen students and teachers and injured six others. The evidence is overwhelming.

We are here, however, to determine if Mr. Porter was in control of his faculties at the time of the killings.

"During this trial, I will provide evidence to show Ryan was unaware that what he did was wrong…that he was unaware there would be consequences for his actions. I will provide descriptions of the upbringing Ryan received during his formative years and how Ryan was immersed in an environment for his entire life that stigmatizes certain factions in society. He has been taught that those factions are less worthy, and deserve to be discriminated against, and even eliminated.

"I will bring in a psychological expert that will attest to Ryan's mental state at the time of the shooting. In the end, I will demonstrate that Ryan was, in fact, not in control emotionally and therefore, not responsible for the actions that resulted in the death or injury of twenty-two individuals at the Nassau High School. Thank you for your time."

The judge looked back and forth between the two attorneys. "Thank you, gentlemen for your statements. The prosecution may now call their first witness."

Justin stood. "The prosecution calls Seth Charland to the stand."

Billie squeezed Seth's knee. "Be brave. You've got this."

Seth nodded and approached the bench.

"State your full name."

"Seth Michael Charland."

"Raise your right hand," the bailiff said. "Do you solemnly swear that you will tell the truth, the whole truth and nothing but the truth, under penalty of perjury?"

"I do."

"Please be seated."

Seth sat and waited for the first question. He did his best to ignore Ryan, who sat at the defendant's table with his lawyer. A blank expression masking his face.

Justin stood and approached Seth. "Good morning, Seth," he said.

"Good morning," Seth replied.

"How old are you, Seth?"

"Eighteen, although I was seventeen when the shooting happened."

"And you are a senior at Nassau High School, correct?"

"I was a senior. I just graduated."

"Seth, do you know Ryan Porter?"

"I know who he is, but I don't know him very well."

"Is he in this courtroom right now? And if so, could you point him out, please."

Seth pointed to Ryan. "He is right there."

"Thank you. Seth, how long have you known Ryan Porter?"

"This is his first year at Nassau High School, so I've only known him since the start of our senior year last September."

"What was your first impression of him?"

"He didn't seem much different from any other guy."

"Have you ever hung out with him, either alone or with a group?"

"Not on purpose. I mean…he's not in my group of friends, but we're both on the football team."

"I see. Has there ever been a problem with him on the team?"

"Just once. My friend, Steve was the quarterback for a scrimmage, and Ryan rushed him and slammed him onto the ground harder than he should have."

"Do you have any idea why he did that to your friend, Steve?"

"He did it because Steve decked him at a party the weekend before."

Mr. Williams jumped up. "Objection—heresay!"

"I will allow it. Continue, Mr. Charland," the judge said.

"Thank you, Your Honor," Justin said. "Why did Steve deck him?"

"We went to the party to pick up Steve's sister and we found Ryan assaulting another female classmate. Steve pulled him off and decked him."

"Objection!" Mr. Williams jumped up again. "That testimony cannot be confirmed!"

"Mr. Martin?" the judge said.

"I will withdraw the question, Your Honor. Seth, why is that female classmate not available to testify."

Seth looked shocked. "She's dead," he said softly.

"Please repeat your answer louder, Mr. Charland," the judge instructed.

"She's dead. Ryan shot her, along with eight more of my classmates and my teacher, who also died."

"Objection! Mr. Martin is leading the witness!"

"I will allow it," the judge said.

"Seth, have you ever had a confrontation with Ryan Porter?" Justin asked.

"Once. It was the day he roughed up my friend Steve on the football field. After practice, he tried to intimidate us in the locker room. He called me and Steve faggots and he started quoting bible verses about gays being abominations and deserving to die. Funny thing is, he was all righteous about gay people, but he didn't give sexual assault a second thought."

Once more, Mr. Williams interrupted the proceedings. "Objection—heresay!"

"Your honor, this behavior will be collaborated with further testimony," Justin said.

"I will allow it, Mr. Martin. Please continue."

"A few more questions, Seth. Did you know the shooter was Ryan Porter when he came into your classroom?"

"No, sir. He was wearing a ski mask."

"Did he say anything that might give his identity away?"

"He didn't say a word. He just aimed the rifle and fired."

"Was there anything about his demeanor that was erratic…like maybe he wasn't in control of his own actions?"

"He was in control. He knew exactly what he was doing."

"Objection! This witness is not qualified to make a psychiatric assessment."

"I concur. The witness' statement will be stricken from the record," the judge ruled.

Justin returned to his table. "I have no more questions for this witness, Your Honor."

"Would the defense attorney like to cross examine this witness?" the judge asked.

Mr. Williams stood. "I will be brief, your honor." He approached the witness stand. "Mr. Charland, are you gay?"

Seth looked as though he had been slapped. "Not that it matters, but, no, I am not," he replied.

"Then, can the court assume there has been no inappropriate touching in the locker room between you and any other student?"

Billie nearly came out of her seat, and was restrained only by Cat's hand on her arm.

Seth looked the defense attorney directly in the face and answered in a very clear and firm voice. "I swear on the lives of everyone I love that there has been no inappropriate touching in the locker room...at least not by me or by any of my friends."

Mr. Williams turned his back on Seth and walked away. "No more questions, Your Honor."

"You may take your seat, Mr. Charland," the judge said. "Mr. Martin, please call your next witness."

Justin picked up a piece of paper from the table. "I call Steven Swenson to the stand."

Seth returned to his seat while Steve was being sworn in. He sat stiffly next to his mother and clenched his fists repeatedly. Billie took his hand and smiled at him. "You did really well, love. Relax."

"How dare he accuse me..."

"He did it to discredit you. The fact he did it at all means you were an effective witness. Your response was spot-on. Don't give it another thought. You did really well."

Steve sat in the witness box after being sworn in, and waited for his first question.

"How old are you, Steve?"

"I turned eighteen in May. And I graduated with Seth just a short time ago."

"Am I correct to assume you are not in Ryan Porter's circle of friends?"

"That is correct. I barely know him—except for being on the football team with him."

"Is Seth Charland's account of the encounter you had on the field and in the locker room with Ryan Porter accurate?"

"Yes…and before anyone asks, no, I'm not gay. Steve and I have been best friends since we were seven years old, but we are not gay."

"Thank you for clarifying that, Steve. Let's move to the day of the shooting. You were in your math class that day, correct?"

"That is correct."

"Did you know the shooter was Ryan Porter?"

"Not until after they caught him and removed his ski mask."

"Was anyone injured in your classroom, Steve?"

"One of my classmates was shot in the chest. The shooter didn't actually get into the room because our barricade held."

"Thank you for your testimony, Steve. Your Honor, I have no other questions for this witness."

"Does the defense have any questions for this witness?" the judge asked.

"Only one, Your Honor. Mr. Swenson, you said the shooter never got into your classroom."

"That's right," Steve said.

"If he didn't get in, does that mean you didn't actually *see* him?"

"I admit I didn't actually see *him*, but I saw his rifle. He shoved the barrel in through the broken window and shot one of my classmates."

"I have no more questions for this witness, Your Honor," Mr. Williams said.

"Thank you for your testimony, Mr. Swenson. You may step down," the judge said. "Mr. Martin, one more witness and then we will break for lunch."

"Thank you, Your Honor. "I call Linda Collins to the stand."

Steve returned to his seat while Linda Collins was sworn in.

Justin approached Linda Collins. "Ms. Collins, please tell us your role at the high school."

"I am the principal's secretary."

"Ma'am, I know this is painful, but please tell us the series of events as you know them on that fateful morning when the shooter came into the school."

"I was in the main office, as normal. First period had just begun. I heard a loud crash and when I looked into the lobby, there was a man out there in a ski mask. He had smashed the windows out in the front of the school. I called for Principal Geary. He went into the lobby and the shooter just shot him. He didn't have a chance." Linda sobbed. "I didn't know he had a rifle. I wouldn't have let Principal Geary go out there if I had known he had a rifle."

Justin handed her a tissue. She took a few moments to compose herself. "What happened next, ma'am?"

"The shooter moved toward the science wing, and I called 911. I heard shots coming from the science wing while I was still on the phone with 911. They sent the SWAT team, but by the time they arrived the shooter had already gone upstairs. That's all I know. The SWAT team took me out of the school as soon as they got there."

Justin walked to his table and retrieved a package of papers that he brought to the judge. "I submit this transcript from 911 that collaborates Ms. Collins' testimony."

He turned back to Ms. Collins. "My condolences on the death of Principal Geary, ma'am. I have no further questions for this witness, Your Honor."

The judge looked at the defense attorney.

"No questions for this witness, Your Honor."

The judge picked up his gavel and ended the morning session. "Court will resume at one p.m."

***

The Charland, Barkum, and Swenson families went to the courthouse cafeteria for lunch. While they ate, they talked about the morning hearing.

"I was really angry when they accused me of inappropriate touching," Seth said.

"Like I said, that was an attempt by the defense attorney to discredit you. That means your testimony really damaged his case. It will mean nothing to the jury—especially after your firm answer to his question." Billie looked at Steve. "As for your testimony, his attempt to make the jury think Ryan wasn't the shooter just because you saw only his gun and not him, is ridiculous, especially since he was the only shooter on campus. The defense attorney is grasping. Both of you did an awesome job."

"I'm really nervous about testifying, Mom," Tara admitted.

"Me too," Karissa said.

"All you need to do is tell the truth, girls," Roger said.

"I agree with that," Billie added. "Just listen very carefully to the question, and if you don't understand, ask for clarification. Justin will not try to trip you up, but the defense attorney might. Just have faith in yourselves. *You* know the truth."

Cat looked at her watch. "We need to wrap it up here. Court resumes again in about fifteen minutes."

In the Blink of an Eye

Chapter 29

Tara was the first to testify after lunch. When her name was called, Kelly gave her a quick peck on the cheek and told her to be brave.

Where Ryan had sat stone-faced for the previous three testimonies, he suddenly perked up and stared intently at Tara while she was on the stand.

Questioning began immediately after she was sworn in.

"Hi, Tara. Could you tell us how old you are?" Justin asked.

"I'm fifteen...sixteen in August."

"So, you were a sophomore at the time of the shooting?"

"Yes."

"It says in my notes that you were on crutches during the shooting. Do you mind sharing with us how you were injured?"

"I was camping with my family in Yellowstone National Park this past summer and we were all caught in the wildfires there. Mom and I were kayaking in the middle of it and we had to flip our kayak and hide under it to avoid the fire. By the time we flipped it back, we were really close to a waterfall, and we ended up going over it. I kind of got banged up on the ride."

"Wow! All that, and you were only on crutches," Justin commented.

"Actually, I was in a wheelchair when school started. I was only on the crutches for a few days before the shooting happened."

"I see. So, I assume your friends pushed you around between classes?"

"Sometimes, yes."

"Did Ryan Porter ever push you in your chair?"

"Yes, he did."

"Was Ryan one of your friends?"

"Not really. I met him for the first time when my doctor cleared me to go to school—two weeks after the semester started.

He held a door open for me. I ran into him in the halls every now and then after that. A couple of times, when I was alone, he pushed me to my class."

"Did you want Ryan to be your friend? I mean, were you interested in him as a boyfriend?"

Tara took a deep breath. *Tell the truth.* She looked at Ryan and back at Justin. "No. I never wanted him to be my boyfriend. I like girls, not boys."

An angry murmur rose from the row of people sitting behind Ryan's parents.

The judge picked up his gavel and banged on the desk. "I will have order in this court."

"Thank you for being so honest, Tara. I know it's not easy to share something so personal. So, did you tell Ryan you weren't interested in a relationship with him?"

"No. He never really asked me, but I would have said no if he did. I thought he was a nice guy, so I didn't mind being his friend. Actually, I was trying to find a way to match him up with my friend Karissa."

Ryan snorted.

"Did Karissa like Ryan?"

"Yes, and when she found out he liked me, she was really angry with me, but we're good now."

"So, you rejected him," Justin concluded.

"Not to his face, but, yeah, I guess I did because I wasn't interested."

"Tara, you said you were interested in girls. Is there one girl in particular you like more than others?"

Tara looked at Kelly and smiled. "Kelly."

Ryan looked at Kelly and narrowed his eyes.

"Tara, tell me what happened when the shooter came into your classroom."

"We had the door barricaded, but he kicked it open like it wasn't even there. One of the girls screamed when the door opened, and he shot her right in the face. I was in shock. My teacher had a gun she'd gotten out of her desk and warned him to stop, but he just shot her...three times. He looked around the room until he saw me. I was at the back of the room in the middle of a group of kids. He stopped about three feet from us and he pointed the gun at Michelle on my right and shot her. Then he shot David on my left. He shot them in the head. Their heads exploded and their brains sprayed on the wall and on my face and clothes. I felt like I was no longer in my body. Everything sounded so far away. He took two steps toward me and put the barrel of the gun on my forehead. I was sure I was going to die, but he just said 'bang' and then he lowered the barrel of the gun.

"The next think I knew, Kelly burst into the room and screamed at him to stop. Ryan swung around and shot her in the stomach and watched her fall to the floor. I pushed past him and went to help Kelly. I thought for sure he would kill us both, but he just walked out of the room."

"So, he had the perfect opportunity to kill both you and Kelly, but he didn't do it," Justin said.

"That's right. I didn't understand why at first, but after we learned why he did what he did, it made more sense."

"What do you mean?"

"He hates what we are. He hates gays and he wanted us to feel responsible for the deaths of our classmates. That is something we will both have to live with for the rest of our lives."

"How did Ryan find out you were gay?"

"Karissa told him he didn't have a chance with me because I liked girls."

"And when did Karissa tell him you were gay?"

"The day before the shooting."

"So, when Ryan came into your classroom, he specifically focused in on you, is that correct?"

"Yes. He shot the kids who were screaming just to shut them up, but he made eye contact with me and walked straight toward me without looking away. Even when he stopped in front of me and shot Michelle and David, he did it without breaking eye contact with me. It was really creepy and terrifying," Tara explained.

"So, he didn't go into the room and blindly fire like he was out of control."

"That's right. He focused on me, like I was the reason he came into the room."

Justin walked to his table and pulled a large poster out of a bag. His paralegal set it up on an easel close to where Tara was sitting, but still visible to the judge and jury. He turned to address Tara once more. "Tara, do you recognize this diagram?"

"Yes. I drew it for my mom."

Justin pulled a collapsible pointer out of his pocket and handed it to Tara. "Could I ask you to explain it to the jury?"

Tara walked to the poster and pointed as she spoke. "The shooter came in the front door and shot Mr. Geary in the lobby, then he went to the science wing to Seth's class, then upstairs to Steve's class, then my class, and when he went to Karissa's class. That's when Robert tackled him and the SWAT team caught him. If they hadn't caught him, I think he would have gone to Kelly's class next."

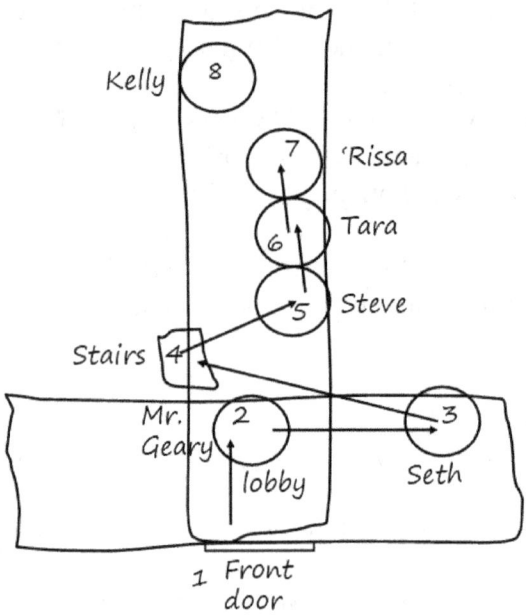

"So what does all of this mean to you, Tara?" Justin asked.

"Don't you see? He only went to *our* classes. There were plenty of other classes he *could* have gone to along the way, but he didn't. It wasn't random. He was targeting *us*!"

"Objection, Your Honor!" Mr. Williams screamed. "This child is speculating!"

The judge addressed Justin. "Do you have any more evidence which collaborates this young lady's testimony?"

"I believe we do, Your Honor," Justin said.

"I will allow it."

"Oh, for crying out loud!" the defense attorney said.

"One more outburst, sir, and you will be held in contempt. Is that clear?" the judge warned.

"Your Honor, I have no further questions for this witness," Justin said.

"Does the defense wish to cross examine this witness?" the judge asked.

"Yes, Your Honor, I do." Mr. Williams approached Tara. "Did you lead Mr. Porter into believing you were romantically interest in him, Miss Charland?"

"No. No, I didn't. I'm in love with Kelly."

Another loud murmur erupted from the spectator seats behind Ryan. Ryan himself, clenched his fists and banged them on the table.

The judge pounded his gavel on his desk. "I will have order in this court immediately. One more outburst and you will be asked to leave."

"I have no more questions for this witness, Your Honor," Mr. Williams said.

"You are excused, Miss Charland. Thank you for your testimony," the judge said.

Even before Tara left the witness stand, Justin called his next witness. "I call Karissa Swenson to the stand."

Tara met Karissa in an embrace halfway across the room. "Be strong. I believe in you," Tara whispered to her friend.

Tara returned to the spectator seats and sat between Cat and Kelly. She slipped her hand into Cat's as Kelly put her arm around Tara. "You're shaking," Kelly whispered.

"That was terrifying, "Tara replied.

Cat leaned in. "You were amazing, Tara. Your testimony really mattered."

"Hi, Karissa. How old are you?" Mr. Martin asked.

"I'll be sixteen next month," she replied.

"Tara testified that you liked Ryan Porter, is that correct?"

"Well I *did*, but not anymore."

"Seth Charland and your brother Steve testified that you went to a party and they had to go get you. Do you remember that?"

"I remember *part* of it."

"What do you mean?"

"I remember going to the party with Robert Johnson, but I don't remember much after I got there."

"I understand the party was at a senior's house and that there were no parents there," Justin said.

"That's right."

"Why did you go to that party?"

"I went because I knew Ryan would be there."

"Ryan Porter?"

"Yes."

"Why do you think you don't remember anything from that party?" Mr. Martin asked.

"I don't know for sure, but I think I was drugged."

"Who do you think drugged you?"

"I don't know. Maybe Robert…maybe Ryan?"

"Objection! Speculation!" Mr. Williams yelled.

"Your Honor, we have further testimony to collaborate this witness."

The judge leaned forward in his seat. "I don't appreciate the theatrics, Mr. Martin. This had better be good!"

"Karissa, let's talk about the shooting. Did the shooter get into your classroom?"

"No. Robert Johnson tackled him before he could open the door, and then the SWAT team handcuffed him."

"Robert tackled him?"

"Yes. He was hiding in the stairwell across from my classroom."

"Why would Robert put his life in danger like that?" Justin asked.

"Robert has liked me since the first day of school," Karissa replied.

"But you liked Ryan instead."

Karissa nodded.

"So, Robert jumped out of the stairwell and tackled Ryan so he couldn't get into your classroom. Is that right?"

"Yes."

"Karissa, did Ryan say anything to you before the SWAT team took him away?"

"Yes, he said something like, Tara and Kelly are an abomination. This is all their fault. They will rot in hell for their heinous crimes against God."

"How did you feel about what he said, Karissa?"

"I felt guilty."

"Why would you feel guilty?"

"When he said it was all Tara and Kelly's fault, he meant it was because they're gay. *I* was the one who told him they were gay. For the longest time, I blamed myself for what he did, but now I realize he made the *choice* to kill all those people. It was his choice—not mine."

Justin walked back to his table. "No more questions for this witness, Your Honor."

"Does the defense want to cross examine?" the judge asked.

"You bet I do, Your Honor. Miss Swenson, you said you think you were drugged at this party you went to. How do you know that to be true?"

"Because I didn't have anything to drink except a glass of water that Ryan got for me. I drank the water and sat down in the basement family room. I don't remember anything after that."

"So let me get this straight. You go to a senior party with one senior, hoping to attract the attention of another senior…all the while, knowing there would be no parents there. You pass out in the basement after drinking some water. Is that accurate, Miss Swenson?"

"Yes. I know it was bad judgment on my part," Karissa said, sadly.

"Bad judgment, indeed. No more questions for this witness, Your Honor."

Karissa dismounted from the witness stand and ran toward the spectator seats, directly into her father's arms, where she sobbed softly.

"It's okay, love. You did well. It's done."

The judge picked up his gavel and brought it down on the strike plate. "Court will adjourn for today and resume at nine a.m. tomorrow morning. The jury will be sequestered and is instructed not to discuss this case among themselves, or with other individuals.

Chapter 30

"Call your next witness, Mr. Martin," the judge said when court resumed the next morning.

Justin stood. "I call Robert Johnson to the stand."

Justin asked his first question as soon as Robert was sworn in. "How old are you, Robert?"

"Nineteen."

"And you were a senior at Nassau High School when the shooting occurred?"

"Yes, but I was suspended when the shooting happened."

"Why is that?"

"I was arrested at a party for aiding and abetting minors. I was suspended from school for alleged assault."

"Alleged assault?" Justin asked.

"Yes sir. I was accused of something based on how it *looked* rather than how it actually *was*."

"Could you explain what you mean by that?"

"Yeah. I took Karissa Swenson to the senior party and we got separated not long after we got there. I asked Ryan if he knew where she was and he said in the basement. He told me he put something in her water to make her more receptive to my advances. I was really worried about her, so I went to the basement to find her. She was passed out on the couch. I knelt on the floor beside her and leaned way over her to see if she was breathing. The next thing I knew, I was on my back and Karissa's brother, Steve was punching me. I would never hurt Karissa. I swear it."

"So if I understand the situation correctly, you were arrested for making alcohol available to minors, and suspended from school for this alleged assault."

"That's right, but the charges were dropped back in November."

"But you were still suspended at the time of the shooting."

"Yes, sir."

"If you were suspended, why did you go back to the school when you heard about the shooter?"

"I was worried about Karissa…and everyone else, of course, but I really wanted to protect Karissa. I knew which class she would be in at that time, so I snuck onto the grounds and hid in the stairway. It didn't take long before I heard gunshots. I had the element of surprise in my favor, so I just jumped out and tackled him."

"How did you get into the school undetected, Mr. Johnson?"

"I came in through a back entrance near the music room. I had to break a window so I could open the door. There was no one around. I assume they were all in the front of the school. "

"Did you know the shooter was Ryan?" Justin asked.

"Not at first, but when I tackled him, he smelled like Ryan. You know, he used the same cologne."

"You were on the football team with Ryan—right?"

"Yes."

"Did you ever have any bad encounters with Ryan? During practices? Games? In the locker room?"

"I didn't have any problem with him, but he used to rant a lot about gays. He said they all needed to die. One time, he even said they should all be put on an island and nuked. I heard he had problems at his last school for the same reason."

Justin made one more trip to his table to pick up a document, which he carried to the judge. "Thank you for your input, Robert. Let the record show that Ryan Porter was expelled in his Junior year from a high school in Syracuse, New York for threatening LGBTQ students there. I have no more questions for this witness, Your Honor."

The judge looked at the defense attorney. He had his head in his hands. "Sir?" he said.

"No questions for this witness, Your Honor," he said.

The judge inhaled deeply. "Mr. Martin, do you have any more witnesses?"

"One more, Your Honor. I call Michael Mott, commander of the SWAT team, to the stand."

"Mr. Mott, first let me commend you on your apprehension of the shooter," Justin said.

"We owe partial credit to Robert Johnson for subduing him first."

"Duly noted. I have just one question for you, sir. What, if anything, did Ryan Porter say when you arrested him?"

Michael Mott pulled a piece of paper from his vest pocket. "That's easy, considering we were wearing body cams. We have a live video and audio record of the arrest. Here is a direct quote from it: *Leviticus, chapter eighteen, verse twenty-two. You shall not lie with a male as a woman; it is an abomination. Chapter twenty, verse thirteen. If a man lies with a male as with a woman, both of them have committed an abomination. They shall surely be put to death*!"

"Thank you, Mr. Mott. Your Honor, the prosecution has no more witnesses."

"Very well. Mr. Williams, does the defense wish to question this witness?"

"No questions, Your Honor," Mr. Williams said.

"The defense may now call their first witness," the judge said.

Mr. Williams stood. "The defense calls Jacob Porter to the stand."

The severe looking man sitting directly behind Ryan stood and walked to the witness booth. The bailiff held a bible out for him to place his hand on.

"No thank you. I swear only on my own bible," the man said.

"You have the option of not swearing on a bible at all," the bailiff said.

"That is my choice."

"Understood. Raise your right hand," the bailiff said. "Do you solemnly swear that you will tell the truth, the whole truth and nothing but the truth, under penalty of perjury?"

"I do."

"Please be seated."

Mr. Williams approached the witness. "Sir, please state your name and your connection to the defendant."

"My name is Jacob Porter, and I am Ryan's father."

"Mr. Porter, your family recently relocated from Syracuse, New York, to the Albany area. Could you explain why that move was made?"

"I had to remove my son from the Syracuse school system."

"Why is that, sir?"

"They were corrupting him and disregarding the teachings of our religion."

"Could you elaborate on that, sir?" Mr. William asked.

"He was being exposed to females who dressed like men, and males who dressed like females. When my son confronted them, and tried to make them see the evil in these practices, they disregarded him. Instead of acknowledging their evil ways, they ridiculed and punished him for his beliefs."

"Just how did they punish him?"

"They ostracized him. They excluded him, and they reported him to the principal," Mr. Porter said.

"So in other words, they did not respect that he had a right to his religious views."

"That is correct."

"Mr. Porter, what it is about these student's wardrobe practices that are offensive to your religion?"

"Homosexual behavior and masturbation are contrary to natural law. It undermines morality and it is condemned by God. Women who play the male role and couple with other women, and men who couple with other men, practice unnatural vices. It is second only to bestiality in the eyes of God."

Billie leaned into Cat. "Can you believe this rubbish? If Ryan was raised with this kinds of belief, no wonder he hates gays."

"What I'm afraid of, is that Mr. Williams is attempting to show the jury that Ryan is mentally unstable for just that reason," Cat pointed out.

Mr. Williams picked up a piece of paper from his table. "Mr. Porter, it says here that Ryan has been quoted as saying gay people must die. Should that be interpreted in the literal sense?"

"Our ancient teachings recommend death as a final solution for those sodomites and sexual traitors who refuse to repent.

250

Upon first offense, men are castrated and women undergo clitoral mutilation. Second offense often involves dismemberment, and finally, a third offense involves burning at the stake."

"Are you seriously recommending these actions in today's society, Mr. Porter?"

"As I said, these are the punishments handed down through ancient teachings. Unfortunately, modern laws do not allow physical punishment for such heinous crimes against nature."

"Regardless of the ability to carry out the recommended punishments, are these lessons and religious morals still passed down to children under your religious practices? In other words, sir, were these specific beliefs taught to your son, Ryan?"

"Yes, sir, they were."

"I have no further questions for this witness, Your Honor."

The judge turned to the prosecution. "Mr. Martin, do you wish to cross examine this witness?"

"I do, sir." Justin approached the witness. "Mr. Porter, what is the current year?"

"Twenty-nineteen"

"Yes. Twenty-nineteen. Sir, is it safe to say that Medieval inquisitions have been past for quite some time now?"

"Unfortunately, yes."

"Unfortunately?"

"Yes," Mr. Porter said. "The inquisitions were a time of lawfulness, compared to today where crime, homosexuality, immorality and religious persecution run rampant. You, yourself are an example of women trying to take the rightful place of men in society."

"I am not on trial here, sir. Your son is. Mr. Porter, is it fair to say your ancient teachings go back at least five hundred years?"

"Yes. That is fair."

"Is it also far to assume your religion uses the Christian bible as a basis for teaching religious morals?"

"Yes," Mr. Porter said.

"And the bible indicates that homosexuality is an abomination. Is that correct?"

"That is correct."

"Mr. Porter, I am going to quote a passage from the modern-day Christian bible. Leviticus 18:22. *Man shall not lie with man, for it is an abomination.* Do you recognize that passage, sir?"

"Yes I do. It is one of the most important passages in the bible. It explicitly states that homosexuality is a sin."

Justin nodded. "I see. Sir, I have done research on bibles dated as far back as 1534. Are you aware that in versions of the bible dating to the fifteen hundreds, that exact passage is translated as *Man shall not lie with young boys as he does with a woman, for it is an abomination* and in fact, that the word homosexual didn't actually appear in the bible until 1983? In short, that passage, as originally written, condemns pedophilia, not homosexuality. Are you aware of that, sir?"

Mr. Potter frowned, but did not answer.

"I have no further questions for this witness, Your Honor," Justin said.

Justin walked back to his table and before turning around to face the judge, he looked at Billie and Cat and mouthed the word, *Wow!*

"Thank you for your testimony, Mr. Porter. You may step down. Mr. Williams, call your next witness, please," the judge said.

"I call Dr. Caroline McDonald to the stand."

Dr. McDonald was sworn in and took her seat in the witness box.

"Dr. McDonald, please state your name and credentials," Mr. Williams said.

"Dr. Caroline McDonald, PhD. I am the head of the Albany Psychiatric Institute."

"Thank you for coming, Dr. McDonald. You have heard the testimony of Mr. Jacob Porter about the religious beliefs he practices, and has raised his son, Ryan Porter under. If you would, please describe the affects, if any, on the psyche of a person raised under such beliefs."

"In general, Christian fundamentalism is like a parasite. When it is inserted into the brain, it creates rigidness in the way the host thinks. They become unwilling to accept—or to even consider—other viewpoints, and they tend to make connections between actions and events that are otherwise unrelated. In short, they create self-fulfilling prophesies. They also seem to make decisions based more on intuition than on rational or analytic thought, and often without fear or acknowledgement of consequences."

"So, rigid thinking, inflexible viewpoints, manufactured situations, and no concept of right and wrong. Is that an accurate summary, Dr. McDonald?" Mr. Williams asked.

"More or less…yes."

"Dr. McDonald, you have had an opportunity to evaluate Ryan Porter. What would your assessment be of his personality?"

"His personality very much fits the mold of someone raised in a Christian fundamentalist household."

"Do you believe he would feel justified for carrying out the school shooting he recently participated in?"

"Based on the tenets of his beliefs, as described by his father, yes, I believe he would feel justified."

"Dr. McDonald, do you believe Ryan Porter suffers from mental illness?" Mr. Williams asked.

"I believe Ryan Porter suffers from strong Christian fundamentalist influences that have indeed had an effect on his mental psyche."

"Thank you, Dr. McDonald. Your Honor, I have no more questions for this witness."

"Mr. Martin?" the judge said.

Justin jumped to his feet. "Thank you, Your Honor." He approached Dr. McDonald. "Ma'am, you included in your list of characteristics attributed to someone raised in Ryan Porter's faith, a lack of fear or acknowledgement of consequences. Is that correct?"

"Yes, sir."

"Is that the same thing as not knowing the difference between right and wrong as suggested by my esteemed colleague, Mr. Williams?"

"No! Not at all. They are two very different concepts. They could quite easily exist separately or simultaneously."

"So, in other words, someone could know the difference between right and wrong, but still not fear or acknowledge the consequences of their actions."

"Yes. That is correct."

"Dr. McDonald, you agreed with Mr. Williams when he implied Ryan Porter had no sense of right or wrong, yet, you just testified that a lack of fear or acknowledgement of consequences is not the same as not knowing the difference between right and wrong. Could you clarify that for the court, please?"

"It is my belief that Ryan Porter knows the difference between right and wrong, but does not acknowledge that he would be judged for carrying out an action that is clearly wrong, specifically because it is justified by his religious beliefs. He has no fear or concern about potential consequences."

"You also testified, Dr. McDonald, that his extreme religious upbringing had an effect on his mental psyche. Is that the same things as saying Ryan Porter is insane?"

"My comments were meant to indicate that his religious upbringing had an impact on his psyche…not his level of sanity."

"I have no more questions for this witness, Your Honor."

"Mr. Williams, please call your next witness," the judge said.

Mr. Williams rose. "I have no other witness, Your Honor."

"Understood." The judge looked at the clock on the wall. "You have until two tomorrow to prepare closing arguments"

"Yes, Your Honor," both men said together.

The judge hit the strike plate with his gavel. "Court adjourned until two p.m. tomorrow. The jury will remain sequestered until then."

***

The following day

The Charland, Barkum, and Swenson families were in their seats well before two. Billie was confident that the ruling would go in their favor, pending some unlikely surprise from Ryan Porter's defense team. Her only worry was Ryan's strange behavior during court. He spent the entire time either staring straight ahead, or staring down at the table. Considering his team would most likely be arguing mental illness, it was a good strategy to sway the jury in his favor.

At exactly two o'clock, The Honorable Judge Gene Bonnett seated himself behind his desk and called his court into session. "Are we ready for closing arguments, gentlemen?" he asked.

"Yes, Your Honor," both men replied.

"The prosecution shall proceed."

Justin stood and walked toward the jury.

"Thank you, Your Honor, honorable colleagues and members of the jury.

"Ladies and gentlemen, I think we can all agree that killing in the name of religion is not an acceptable defense. It was a bad defense in the Dark Ages, a bad defense in the Middle Ages, a bad defense in colonial times and it is a bad defense now. But that is not why we are here. We are here to determine if Ryan Porter intentionally murdered sixteen people, and injured six more. We are here to determine if this was a premeditated act.

"It is clear from the testimony in this trial...and from the testimony of those who expelled him from a Syracuse high school, that Ryan Porter hates our cherished members of the LGBTQ community.

"It is clear that Ryan Porter has no regard for human life other than when it serves his purpose. He shot Amanda Jacobs in her classroom without a second thought after trying to sexually assault her at a party. He intentionally drugged Karissa Swenson so she would be more receptive to amorous advances.

"The defense's expert witness, Dr. McDonald, has testified that Ryan Porter's extreme fundamentalist upbringing could result in him not fearing consequences, but also admitted that it was not the same as knowing the difference between right and wrong. Dr. McDonald also testified that she did not believe Ryan Porter to be insane.

"I submit, ladies and gentlemen, that Ryan indeed knows the difference between right and wrong, but *chose* to do wrong anyway. He *chose* to kill nine students, and a teacher in Seth Charland's classroom. He *chose* to kill the principal of the school and the bodyguard assigned to Karissa Swenson. He *chose* to kill three students and a teacher in Tara Charland's classroom. He *chose* to injure six other students in those same four classrooms.

"As Tara Charland testified, Ryan Porter intentionally sought her out and specifically focused on her when he entered her classroom—even while he was killing the other students around her. He clearly did that with focused intent. He *chose* to let Tara Charland and Kelly Barkum live. Tara is admittedly gay. If his religion dictates that he kills gay people, as our esteemed defense attorney would like us to believe, he would have been compelled to kill Tara and Kelly as well...yet, he let them live. He intentionally *chose* to let them live.

"As clearly demonstrated on the diagram Tara Charland so eloquently explained to us, he planned his kills. He intentionally *only* visited the classrooms of Seth Charland, Steve Swenson, Tara Charland and Karissa Swenson...and clearly, he would have visited the classroom of Kelly Barkum if he hadn't already shot her in Tara Charland's classroom. There were dozens of other classrooms he could have targeted, but he didn't. They weren't in his plan.

"The only question that remains is...why. Why kill at all...and why did he specifically target Seth, Steve, Tara, Karissa and Kelly? Is it because his fragile ego couldn't tolerate being rejected by Tara? Is it because he really does hate gay people?

"Let's assume for a moment that his motivation is his hatred of gays. Per Seth's testimony, Porter accused him and Steve of being a gay couple. He already knew that Tara and Kelly were gay, because Karissa told him as much. Did he assume Karissa was gay as well, simply through her association with Tara and Kelly...or was he angry with her for pointing out that he'd have no chance with Tara?

"We may never know the answers to these questions, but it is clear by his actions that he *planned* and *chose* to carry out these murders. As Tara Charland stated so clearly...these were not random acts of violence. He was intentionally targeting *them*. In the blink of an eye, Ryan Porter forever changed the lives of the young people in this courtroom today, as well as the sense of safety and security of every man, woman and child in Nassau High School.

"With this in mind, it is the duty of this jury to put forth a guilty verdict against Ryan Porter, and to further consider this a hate crime since the intentional focus of these killings were members of the LGBTQ community, or perceived members of the LGBTQ community. Ladies and gentlemen, I thank you for your time."

"The court thanks the prosecution for their statement. We now yield the floor to the defense," the judge said.

Ryan Porter's defense attorney rose from his seat and read from a prepared statement.

"Your Honor, honorable colleagues and members of the jury, we are here today to determine the fate of Ryan Porter.

"Ryan Porter was raised in an environment immersed in strict, orthodox religious doctrines that are woefully out of alignment with today's morals. These beliefs originated in the Dark Ages, and although appropriate for their time, they are no longer accepted in today's more lenient society. He believes his religion has bestowed upon him, certain powers to address lifestyles that, although acceptable now, were not acceptable when the tenets of his religion were first established. Homosexuality is one such practice.

"Most people would recognize that archaic, ancient beliefs cannot be applied to today's society, however, Mr. Porter lacks those filters and that understanding.

"That said, immersion in this archaic, fundamentalist religion since birth has mentally handicapped Mr. Porter, to the point that he does not understand that what he has done is wrong. As Dr. McDonald testified, this is a mental deficiency, and it should not be treated with incarceration, but instead, with confinement to an institution with specialized treatment for his condition.

"Mr. Porter is not denying that he killed and/or injured twenty-two people at Nassau High School nine months ago, but he does not recognize it as something he has done wrong. In his mind, he is carrying out the dictates of his beliefs, by ridding the world of what he sees as abominations. Clearly, this is a mental illness, and the defense asks for a sentence appropriate to his condition. We thank the court for this consideration."

"This concludes the testimony portion of this trial. The jury is instructed to deliberate as soon as possible. If you unanimously conclude that Mr. Porter intentionally planned and carried out targeted victims with cognitive intent, you must return a verdict of guilty. If you unanimously conclude that Mr. Porter actions were based solely on insanity, you must acquit.

"Under no circumstances are you to discuss this case with anyone, including with one another, unless under the process of deliberation. If deliberation extends beyond a reasonable hour this evening, you will be sequestered in a nearby hotel and all access to television, social media and printed news will be restricted. The jury is now dismissed.

"The court officers will return Mr. Porter to his cell until such time as the jury is ready to deliver a verdict." The judge picked up his gavel and slammed it against the strike plate. "This court is recessed until the verdict is returned. Good evening."

Chapter 31

Cat and Billie picked up Chinese takeout on the way home to feed themselves, their three children, and Kelly, who they allowed to spend the night after excessive begging by Tara. After a quick stop at Kelly's house for a change of clothes, they dragged themselves into the house and gathered around the kitchen table, exhausted after spending nearly the entire day in court.

"I am so glad this is almost done," Cat said. "Billie, I don't know how you do that day in and day out."

"It's not this intense *all* the time," Billie replied.

"What do you think are our chances of winning, Mom?" Seth asked.

"I'd say the odds are good."

"I can't believe the other side is trying to blame Ryan's religion for this," Tara said.

"That sounds really cray-cray to me too," Kelly added.

"That's the point," Billie said. "They want him to seem crazy. If they get a cray-cray verdict, as you put it, he's declared innocent by reason of insanity," Billie explained.

"But wouldn't he spend the rest of his life in an insane asylum if he gets that verdict," Cat asked.

"Not necessarily. If he can show improvement during a relatively short amount of time, there's a good chance he'd be moved to a minimum security facility. If he's not truly insane, his *condition* could improve quite dramatically, very quickly."

"Since when is a jury of our peers qualified to judge crazy?" Cat asked.

"They aren't," Billie said. "If they return an innocent by reason of insanity verdict, he would have to undergo some pretty intensive psychological evaluations to verify it. An insanity verdict is not a guaranteed trip to a padded room, but someone who is smart...and a good actor could fool even the most experienced psychologist."

"So much for the justice system being just," Cat quipped. She looked at the clock. "Ugh! It's only eight o'clock? It feels like midnight!"

"I'm hitting the sheets early tonight," Seth said.

"I think that's a good idea for all of us. You kids have school tomorrow," Billie pointed out.

"Do we have to, Mom? We'll miss out on the verdict if we're at school," Tara whined.

Billie's cell phone rang. It was Justin Martin.

"Justin, what's up?" Billie said. "Are you serious? Right now? That was fast! Hold on a sec." Billie put a hand over her phone and looked at her family around the table. "The verdict just came in. The jury will be in the courtroom in about a half hour."

"Are you serious?" Cat exclaimed. "I'm exhausted!"

"I don't mind taking the kids by myself."

"No. I'm tired, but I really don't want to miss it either. All right. I'm in," Cat said.

Billie turned her attention back to her cell phone. "We're on our way, Justin. Okay. Bye."

Billie looked around the table. "Who's going with us?"

Four hands went up.

"We need to get moving, or we'll miss it. We've got about twenty minutes left to get there. Kelly, call your parents and let them know. Cat, I'll drive if you want to call Jen."

Twenty minutes later, the Charland clan, plus Kelly, seated themselves in the spectator seats behind the prosecutor's table. The Swensons and Barkums arrived just as the jury filed in.

"Made it!" Jen exclaimed as she slid into place beside Cat.

"It looks like *they* made it as well." Cat nodded in the direction of the secular figures seated behind Ryan, still clutching their bibles.

The judge addressed the court. "I want to thank all of you for taking the time to return to court this evening. We will now hear the verdict."

The bailiff received a copy of the verdict and handed it to the judge, who looked at it and handed it back to the bailiff. The bailiff returned it to the jury spokesperson and went to stand beside the judge.

"Has the jury reached a verdict?" the judge asked.

"Yes, Your Honor, we have."

"What say you?"

The spokesperson cleared his throat.

Everyone held hands and waited for the verdict.

"We, the jury in the case of The State of New York versus Ryan Porter, find the defendant, Ryan Porter, guilty of sixteen counts of premeditated murder. We further rule that since some of the intended targets are part of the LGBTQ community, and that they were specifically targeted because they are part of the LGBTQ community, this classifies as a hate crime."

The spectators sitting behind the prosecutor's table released a collective sigh of relief.

The spectators sitting behind the defense table erupted in a dark and angry uproar.

Ryan Porter stood and pointed to the jury. "Abominations! He exclaimed. Ye shalt not inherit the earth!" He turned to Tara and Kelly, "You two will rot in hell! Mark my words...you will rot in hell."

"Silence!" the judge shouted.

He stood and pointed to Ryan. "Young man, you should be happy that the State of New York has ruled the death penalty unconstitutional. The sentencing stage of this trial will begin tomorrow. Bailiff, call security and have them escort these people out, and if they refuse to go, have them arrested. Officer of the court, take the defendant back to his cell. Court is adjourned."

***

Justin was placing paperwork into his briefcase when he felt a tap on his shoulder. He turned around to see Billie standing there with her hand extended. He shook it firmly.

"I can't thank you enough for all your hard work, Justin," Billie said.

"You worked just as hard as I did on this one, Billie. It was an honor working with you. You made my job a lot easier."

"So, do you think he'll get the maximum sentence?"

"Considering the number of lives he took and his attitude in court, I think Judge Bonnett will give him consecutive life sentences. My guess is he'll never see parole."

"Look, I think what Porter said to you during your cross-examination was way out of line. I probably wouldn't have dealt with it as well as you did. You're a good man, Justin. I look forward to working with you in the future."

***

The Charland, Barkum, and Swenson families met in the lobby of the courthouse and spontaneously fell into a group hug that lasted for nearly a minute. There was barely a dry eye when they separated.

"I can't believe it's finished," Cat said.

"The fight won't really be finished until we get better gun laws," Seth said."

Billie reached up and pushed Seth's bangs off his forehead. "You're right, scout, but for now, we need to savor this victory."

"I think we need pizza and ice cream – our treat!" Roger said.

A chorus of cheers filled the lobby as the group moved toward the exit.

Kelly took Tara's hand and held her back. "We'll be right there," Kelly called out as their families retreated through the door. She grabbed the front of Tara's shirt and pushed her up against the closest wall. Their lips met for a tender kiss.

"I love you, Tara Charland."

"And I love you, Kelly Barkum...to the moon and back."

"To the moon and back sounds like an awesome trip. "I might take you up on that," Kelly said.

"There happens to be just two seats left on the flight," Tara said.

"When does it leave?"

"Tonight."

"Book it!"

The End

Photo Credit: Song of Myself Photography

See Karen's author page at www.karendbadger.com

About the Author

Karen D. Badger is the author of *On A Wing And A Prayer, Yesterday Once More* (a 2009 Golden Crown Literary Award winner for Speculative Fiction), *In A Family Way, Unchained Memories, Happy Campers, Collective Identity, Sweet Angel, and Relative-ly Speaking, Tailspin* and *Flashpoint* (Books I, II, III, IV, V, VI, VII and VIII of the Commitment Series), *The Blue Feather, All My Tomorrows* (sequel to the 2009 award winning *Yesterday Once More*), *1140 Rue Royale* (a 2017 Golden Crown Literary Award winner for Paranormal Fiction), *Over The Crescent Moon*, and this, her most recent release, *In The Blink Of An Eye – A Young Adult Novel*. All of these works have been released by Badger Bliss Books, which Karen co-owns with her wife Barbara Sawyer (aka Bliss).

Born and raised in Vermont, Karen is the second of five children raised by a fiercely independent mother, who remains one of her best friends. Karen earned her B.A. in 1978 in Theater and in Elementary Education, and in 1994, earned a B.S. in mathematics. In addition to her novels, Karen is the author of more than two dozen technical papers and journal articles on photomask manufacturing, which she has published and has presented at numerous semiconductor industry conferences. She is also the holder of several technical patents. Karen is currently in her 42nd year as a Principle Member of the Technical Staff with a prominent semiconductor manufacturer in Vermont.

Karen and her wife, Barb (a retired Lt. Colonel, U.S. Air Force) live in the beautiful state of Vermont—home of Ben and Jerry's. They spend their spare time with family as well as doing home improvement projects on both their homes in Vermont and New Mexico. They also enjoy camping, kayaking, motorcycling and singing Karaoke.

Please take a moment to visit Karen's author website at www.karendbadger.com, or the Badger Bliss Books website at www.badgerblissbooks.com. Also like us on Facebook!

TITLES BY KAREN D. BADGER
www.badgerblissbooks.com

On A Wing and A Prayer
First edition published by Blue Feather Books, Sept, 2005
Second edition published by Badger Bliss Books, Sept, 2014
Third edition published by Badger Bliss Books, August, 2016
ISBN 13: 978-1-945761-01-0, ISBN 10: 1-945761-01-6

Yesterday Once More
First edition published by Blue Feather Books, July, 2008
Second edition published by Badger Bliss Books, Sept, 2014
Third edition published by Badger Bliss Books, August, 2016
ISBN 13: 978-1-945761-02-7, ISBN 10: 1-945761-02-4
2009 Golden Crown Literary Society Award - Speculative Fiction

In A Family Way – Book One of the Commitment Series
First edition published by Blue Feather Books, March, 2010
Second edition published by Badger Bliss Books, Sept, 2014 Third
edition published by Badger Bliss Books, August, 2016
ISBN 13: 978-1-945761-05-8, ISBN 10: 1-945761-05-9

Unchained Memories – Book Two of the Commitment Series
First edition published by Blue Feather Books, Oct, 2011
Second edition published by Badger Bliss Books, Sept, 2014 Third
edition published by Badger Bliss Books, August, 2016
ISBN 13: 978-1-945761-06-5, ISBN 10: 1-945761-06-7

Happy Campers - Book Three of the Commitment Series
First edition published by Blue Feather Books, Sept, 2013
Second edition published by Badger Bliss Books, Sept, 2014 Third
edition published by Badger Bliss Books, August, 2016
ISBN 13: 978-1-945761-07-2, ISBN 10: 1-945761-07-5

The Blue Feather
First edition published by Blue Feather Books, July, 2014
Second edition published by Badger Bliss Books, Sept, 2014 Third
edition published by Badger Bliss Books, August, 2016
ISBN 13: 978-1-945761-04-1, ISBN 10: 1-945761-04-0

Collective Identity – Book Four of the Commitment Series
First edition published by Badger Bliss Books, January, 2015
Second edition published by Badger Bliss Books, August, 2016
ISBN 13: 978-1-945761-08-9, ISBN 10: 1-945761-08-3

All My Tomorrows – Sequel to Yesterday Once More
First edition published by Badger Bliss Books, May, 2015 Second
edition published by Badger Bliss Books, August, 2016
ISBN 13: 978-1-945761-03-4, ISBN 10: 1-945761-03-2

Sweet Angel – Book Five of the Commitment Series
First edition published by Badger Bliss Books, June, 2015 Second
edition published by Badger Bliss Books, August, 2016
ISBN 13: 978-1-945761-09-6, ISBN 10: 1-945-761-09-1

Relative-ly Speaking – Book Six of the Commitment Series
First edition published by Badger Bliss Books, March, 2016 Second
edition published by Badger Bliss Books, August, 2016
ISBN 13: 978-1-945761-10-2, ISBN 10: 1-945-761-10-5

1140 Rue Royale
First edition published by Badger Bliss Books, Sept, 2016
ISBN 13: 978-1-945761-00-3, ISBN 10: 1-945761-00-8
2017 Golden Crown Literary Society Award – Paranormal Fiction

Tailspin- Book Seven of the Commitment Series
First edition published by Badger Bliss Books, December, 2017
ISBN 13: 978-1-945761-22-5, ISBN 10: 1-945761-22-9

Flashpoint – Book Eight of the Commitment Series
First edition published by Badger Bliss Books, December, 2018
ISBN 13: 978-1-945761-24-9, ISBN 10: 1-945761-24-5

Over The Crescent Moon
First edition published by Badger Bliss Books, June, 2019
ISBN 13: 978-1-945761-26-3, ISBN 10: 1-945761-24-5

In the Blink of an Eye – A Young Adult Novel
First edition published by Badger Bliss Books, December, 2019
ISBN 13: 978-1-945761-28-7, ISBN 10: 1-945761-29-4

COMING SOON FROM KAREN D. BADGER AND BADGER BLISS BOOKS

www.badgerblissbooks.com

Love in the Shadows
- Paranormal
- Tentative release, 3Q-2020

Udder Nonsense - Book IX of the Billie/Cat Commitment Series
- Comedy
- Tentative release, year-end, 2020